Dear Reader,

The ever-surprising Aunt Edie and her secrets take center stage once again. Anne discovers her great-aunt may have been in London in the 1960s and was good friends with a famous playwright! There's also a fun Victorian mystery dinner play being put on at the library.

I love going to plays, and it was fun for me to write about this exciting chapter in Aunt Edie's life and the dinner play that the Blue Hill Community Theater Club is organizing.

There is a restaurant near where I live that hosts a dinner play once a month. It's so popular that you need to make reservations. The food is always excellent. It's a seafood restaurant, so there's always some yummy fish or shellfish dish, and the play is not only entertaining, but the actors get the audience involved too. The results can be hilarious.

The library is the perfect place to host a Victorian-set dinner play since the house is such a beautiful example of Victorian architecture and decor. And as everyone gets involved in the play, Anne and Alex's friendship continues to grow and deepen.

In Christ,
Camy Tang
writing as Emily Thomas

Secrets of the Blue Hill Library

Stagestruck

Secrets of the
BLUE HILL LIBRARY

EMILY THOMAS

Guideposts

New York

CHAPTER ONE

Anne Gibson stepped back from the Victorian mystery novels display she was setting up in the Fiction Room of the Blue Hill Library and viewed the effect. She turned to her helpers, her five-year-old daughter, Liddie, and her nine-year-old son, Ben. "Well? What do you think?"

Ben tilted his head sideways. "I think the lamp is crooked."

Anne straightened the fake oil lamp suspended from the wall. "Anything else?"

Liddie had her arms full of crocheted lace doilies from the attic. "I think it needs more of Aunt Edie's lace."

"It doesn't need more lace," Ben objected.

"How about this one?" Anne held up a doily with several holes where the thread had broken and the crochet unraveled. "If I drape it over the candlesticks, it'll look like spiderwebs."

Ben grinned. "Cool."

Liddie made a face. "Yuck."

After arranging their "cobwebs," Anne turned to Liddie. "Now I need Aunt Edie's hat." She untied the purple ribbons under her daughter's chin and removed the bonnet-style hat with white feathers and silk violets decorating the crown.

As the hat was removed, Liddie blinked her chocolate brown eyes. "Now I can see."

"You always could see," Ben said. "It didn't cover your face."

"But I couldn't see on the sides." Liddie turned her head from side to side.

"Over one hundred years ago, women wore these all the time." Anne perched the bonnet on a small nail in the wall. "I wonder if they ran into lampposts a lot?"

Ben and Liddie giggled.

Ben pulled the black silk top hat from his head. "Can I stop wearing this now?"

"But you look so handsome," Anne teased him.

Ben rolled his eyes. "*Mo-om…*"

Anne hung the hat on another nail. "There. A perfect pair."

Ben scratched his hands through his scalp, ruffling his brown hair. "How did they wear those things? It itches."

"Wasn't it just like when you wear a baseball cap?" Anne asked.

"No. I felt like I had a building on my head."

"I suppose it was heavier than a baseball cap." Anne looked at the display with satisfaction. The decorations drew the eye, and she had displayed cozy mystery novels set in the Victorian era. "It looks like we're done. How about some raspberry spoon bread?"

"Yeah!" Both kids were delighted with that suggestion, and they headed through the doorway to their living quarters on the second floor of the library. In the kitchen, Anne served up the new recipe she'd tried last night, using the spring season's earliest raspberries. The fruit-studded cake melted in her mouth.

"Can I have more yogurt?" Ben asked.

She gave Ben another generous spoonful of raspberry Greek yogurt on top as a healthier alternative to whipped cream.

After their afternoon snack, Anne stood. "I'm going to wash the dishes and then go back downstairs. Ben, did you take your dog out?"

"Yes, I took Hershey out when I came home from school."

Anne was proud of how responsible Ben had become about his chocolate Labrador retriever, but his eyes seemed to slide away from hers, so she asked, "How about your homework?"

Ben groaned. "But school's almost out for the summer."

"And what does that have to do with finishing your homework or not?" Anne hid her smile. She could remember the antsy feeling she'd had in the month before summer break. Homework had been especially onerous.

Ben heaved a dramatic sigh and slid off his seat to head to the living room.

"Finish up quickly," Anne told Liddie, who still had a few bites of spoon bread. "It's almost time for story hour."

"Okay." Liddie shoved a gigantic piece into her mouth.

Anne washed their dishes and then sent Liddie to the Children's Room where kids were gathering. Anne was surprised that her friend Wendy Pyle wasn't yet there to do Story Time. Wendy had a flair for it, with lots of fun props and crafts.

At the checkout desk on the first floor, fraternal twins Remi and Bella Miller were checking books and stacking them in a cart to return to the shelves. As Anne reached the desk, the front door to the library opened and Wendy breezed in, bringing the unusually crisp air and the scent of new leaves from outside.

"Sorry I'm late." Wendy shucked off her cardigan. "I was at the community center. Looks like that spring storm last week was the last straw — the roof over the theater caved in."

"Oh no!" Anne said.

"Oh no!" Remi and Bella echoed. The twins belonged to the community theater club. "What happened? Was anyone hurt?"

"No, thank goodness, but the hole is right over center stage."

"You were planning your next production, weren't you," Anne asked.

Wendy was on the planning committee, and she'd told Ben and Liddie she'd help them get small parts in the next play.

Wendy nodded mournfully. "We'd almost decided on the play too, but now we'll have to postpone and figure out how much it'll cost to repair the roof. The director was calling Alex just as I left."

"I'm sure he'll give a fair estimate." When Anne's aunt Edie had left her lovely Victorian home to Anne, she had stipulated that it be renovated into a library for Anne to run, and Alex Ochs, Anne's old high school sweetheart, had done a wonderful job on the renovations.

"I'm sure he will," Wendy said, "but the community theater group simply doesn't have a lot of money. We'll need to figure out some type of fund-raiser we could do."

"I suppose a bake sale wouldn't bring in quite enough," Remi asked.

Wendy laughed. "That might pay for a few shingles. We need something really big that a lot of people would be interested in."

"We'll put our heads together and come up with ideas," Remi said.

"I'd better run to do Story Time." Wendy grabbed her bag to head upstairs. "The kids must be climbing up the walls by now."

As Wendy left, the front door opened again and Reverend Tom Sloan entered. Anne smiled. "Reverend Tom, you're just in time to see your Victorian mystery novels display upstairs."

His hand smoothed the graying hair at the top of his head that had been blown about by the spring breeze. "Surely it's not *my* display. I only gave the suggestion to you after reading that Sir Arthur Conan Doyle biography."

"It's definitely your display." Anne pulled him upstairs to the Fiction Room. "Your idea was great."

Reverend Tom's eyebrows rose as he saw the display. "That's wonderful. I recognize that purple bonnet too. Edie wore it one Easter."

"All the decorations are from the attic or Aunt Edie's closet."

"I had no idea there were so many Victorian mystery authors." He bent over the stacks of books on the table.

"There were Victorian writers such as Sir Arthur Conan Doyle, Wilkie Collins, and Charles Dickens, but in the past decades there have been more contemporary mystery authors who set their books in that time period, like Emily Brightwell's Mrs. Jeffries series and Elizabeth Peters's Amelia Peabody series."

Reverend Tom had picked up the first book in the Mrs. Jeffries series. "Now, this looks interesting…"

Anne left him happily perusing the books as she went to peek into the Children's Room. The kids were doing some sort of twirling dance, led by an enthusiastic Wendy, which made Anne dizzy just watching it. She wondered which book Wendy was reading to them as she went downstairs.

Bella's mouth drooped as she and Anne shelved books in the Nonfiction Room. "I can't believe the roof to the theater caved in. I was looking forward to the next production."

"How often does the community theater club put on shows?"

"Usually once a year, or once every eighteen months, because of the cost."

Anne was surprised, but maybe she was spoiled because there had always been plenty of new shows when she lived in New York City.

"Maybe for the fund-raiser, we could do a play here in the library," Bella said as they moved to the History Room next door. Her blue eyes sparkled. Couldn't you see this room as perfect for some play like *The Maltese Falcon*?" She gestured to the dark cherry wood furniture and upholstered chairs in rich tapestry colors.

"It's nowhere near as large as the theater," Anne said.

"If we did a small play, we could fit in more people for the audience."

"Do you know any plays for only a few people?"

Bella grimaced. "No. But do you know who probably would? Ms. Sanchez."

The name was familiar to Anne. "Do you mean Flores Sanchez? The nurse at the elementary school?" She had called Anne about Liddie or Ben a few times for minor things like rashes and coughs.

"Yeah. When she's not working, she writes plays. She's got an agent and everything. She's hoping one of her plays gets produced off Broadway or in London."

"Wow, she's really serious about it."

"Remi and I acted in at least one of her plays a few years ago." Bella shelved a book on railroad history. "It was a family drama, sort of like *The Glass Menagerie* but with more people."

Anne shelved a book on Lewis and Clark. "I'm still not sure the library has the space for a large enough audience."

"Maybe Remi and I can come up with a really great fund-raiser idea."

When they returned to the checkout desk, a woman was speaking to Remi. "I'm looking for Anne Summers."

"I'm Anne Summers Gibson," Anne said.

The woman looked at her from beneath a very fashionable turquoise-green velvet toque hat, which Anne wouldn't have been surprised to have found in Aunt Edie's hat collection. She had soft green eyes and straight, fine, ash-blonde hair with subtle lowlights pulled back from her round face into a smooth chignon. She smiled when she saw Anne, and then Anne recognized her.

"Tami?" Anne said in amazement. In high school, Tami Bates had been quiet and shy, dressing in loose clothes and drab colors that seemed to enable her to fade into the background—a completely different style from the fitted tweed jacket with turquoise-green velvet trim to match her hat, her turquoise silk blouse, and cleverly tailored tweed slacks that she wore now. "Tami Bates, is that really you?"

Tami laughed. "In the flesh! Although it's Tami Bates O'Brien, now."

Anne gave her a hug. "I haven't seen you since high school. You look amazing!" Anne felt distinctly underdressed in her slacks and pullover.

"You don't look like you've aged a day." Tami grinned.

The years fell away and Anne was sixteen again, roller skating with Tami and Jennifer at the park, laughing and teasing each other. "I heard you were living in London now."

"Yes, I'm a theater producer's assistant, and my husband is an actor. I'm back in Blue Hill to visit my folks since it's in between our spring and summer productions."

"You work in the theater?" Bella's eyes were the size of saucers. "That's so cool!"

A faint blush appeared on Tami's cheeks, reminding Anne of the shy Tami she'd known in high school. "It's not very glamorous being a producer's assistant, believe me."

"But your husband's an *actor*." Remi's expression was as awed as her sister's.

"And he's quite good, if I do say so myself." Tami winked. "He'll be arriving in two weeks, as soon as the play he's in finishes its run, so you'll probably get to meet him."

Bella and Remi grinned at each other in excitement.

Tami leaned closer to Anne and touched her sleeve. "Anne, do you have time to talk privately?"

Anne looked at her in confusion. "Of course. Let's go upstairs."

As Anne led Tami through the connecting door into their family's living quarters on the second floor, Tami started in surprise. "You live here in the library? I didn't know that."

"When Aunt Edie left her house to me to turn into a library, we renovated the third floor and half the second into our home." Anne peeked into the living room, where Ben was doing his homework, the tip of his tongue poking out of his mouth. "How are you doing, Ben?"

"I'm almost done."

"This is my friend Mrs. O'Brien. Tami, my son, Ben."

"Hi, Mrs. O'Brien," he said.

"Hi, Ben." Tami tilted her head toward Anne. "He looks just like you."

"I also have a five-year-old, Liddie, who's in the Children's Room for Story Time. She looks more like my late husband." Anne waited for that same pang to hit when she mentioned Eric, but she realized that it wasn't there. She wasn't sure if she was relieved that she no longer felt the rawness of her grief, or if she was sad that his memory was fading ever so slightly.

"I'm sorry about your husband," Tami said.

"Thank you. It's been three years, and our family has been blessed to have this opportunity to move here to Blue Hill." Anne put a kettle on for tea. "Tell me, how did you meet your husband?"

"Aiden was chosen for a play produced by my boss." Tami sat at the kitchen table. "We immediately hit it off. By the time the play ended, we had fallen in love."

"How romantic."

"My husband is the romantic one. I'm actually rather practical. It makes me a good assistant for my producer."

Anne put the serving container of raspberry spoon bread on the table in front of Tami. "I have to admit, Tami, I had never thought you would work in the theater."

"No one is more surprised than I am. But in college, my roommate was a theater nut. I didn't want to act, but the logistics of putting together a production were really fun. It appealed to the organizational side of me, but it was still creative."

"I can see how that would be." Anne took out cups and tea bags, as well as plates and utensils for the raspberry spoon bread.

"I applied for a prestigious study-abroad program, and no one was more surprised than I was when I was accepted. I loved Great Britain, and I met my future boss, Gideon Rossiter, during my year there. When I graduated, I went back and applied for a job, and he hired me right away."

The water boiled, and Anne filled the cups and brought them to the table, sitting across from Tami. "I've got lots of different tea bags to choose from."

"I'm English now." Tami laughed. "Do you have any Earl Grey?"

After tasting—and praising—the raspberry spoon bread, Tami put her fork down. "Actually, that study-abroad program relates to why I need to talk to you. The program was created by Roy Underwood. Have you heard of him?"

Anne shook her head.

"He grew up nearby in Deshler, but he was a well-known theater director in London. I met him when I won his study-abroad program, and over the years our paths crossed in London. He always remembered who I was and had a smile for me. I've always been grateful to him for the opportunity that allowed me to do what I love."

"He sounds like he's a nice man."

"He was wonderful, but he died only a month or two before your aunt Edie did."

"Oh, I'm sorry, Tami."

"He had wanted his things auctioned off and the money set up to support his study-abroad program for western Pennsylvania students, and so I attended the auction. Oh, Anne, some of the things that were auctioned off were amazing. Antiques you wouldn't believe, famous costumes and props. I couldn't afford most of it, but I did manage to win a couple costumes from a lesser-known production of *Henry IV* that he did shortly before his passing."

"That's terrific you were able to get a memento of a man who did so much for you."

"Actually…" Tami reached into her purse, a classic leather handbag that looked Parisian, and withdrew a small white envelope. "I've had the costumes since the auction, but I was storing them until I could figure out how to display them. A couple of months ago, we moved to a bigger house, so I unpacked the costumes. That's when I found this hidden in an inner lining pocket of the man's costume."

Anne took the envelope from Tami and was surprised to recognize Aunt Edie's flowing handwriting addressing the letter to Roy Underwood in London, with her return address here in Blue Hill. There was a card inside with a lilac design that was exactly like the cards Anne had seen in one of Aunt Edie's desk drawers:

Dear Roy,

Thank you so much for calling me last week. It made the anniversary of my mother's death a little easier to bear.

I know you always tell me that what you did for my mother all those years ago was something anyone would have done, but if anyone else found my mother after she fell in that Deshler parking lot, they would have simply taken her to the hospital and left her there. I will forever be grateful to you for taking care of her when I was not able to because of my work overseas.

But now I think I can finally repay your kindness. I was in the attic the other day, cleaning up some water damage from a leak in the roof, when I found a play I had tucked away for safekeeping. It is the famous "missing" script by Hugh Bettridge. I'm afraid I can't tell you how I managed to get this script, but I want to lend you the play to produce.

The next time you come to Deshler to visit your family, come visit me and I will hand it to you. I would prefer not to send something so valuable to you through the mail.

I look forward to seeing you again, dear friend.

Edie

Anne looked up in astonishment at Tami. "A missing script?"

Tami's green eyes sparkled like emeralds. "I recognized the name Hugh Bettridge as soon as I read Edie's note. He was a famous playwright who died about twenty years ago. I did more research on him and found that in the months after his death, there were rumors that he had an unproduced script, but no one ever found it. Tami reached over to grasp Anne's hands in an excited grip. "If this is really the 'missing' script, Anne, it could be worth thousands of dollars today."

CHAPTER TWO

A nne blinked in astonishment. She choked out, "Thousands of dollars? And Aunt Edie had it?"

"It might still be here, in this house." Tami pointed to the card. "Look at the date."

Anne squinted at Aunt Edie's handwriting. "She wrote this only a few months before Roy Underwood died."

"I did a little research, looking through some theater magazines and some gossip columns, but it's not clear if Roy Underwood was in London the entire time between receiving this note and his death, or if he got a chance to return to Deshler."

Anne sat back in her chair. "I don't know anything about Roy Underwood or Hugh Bettridge. Aunt Edie never mentioned either of them to me. So, Roy's family still lives in Deshler?"

"His parents live there. I don't know much about them. Roy has one sister, Krista Underwood Bennett, who's a playwright living in New York City. Her career hit a high point about fifteen or twenty years ago with one very successful play, *Time's Fool*."

Anne shrugged. "I've never heard of it."

"Unfortunately, none of her plays since then have been very well received. According to some friends of mine, her plays have gotten some very bad reviews from the critics."

"That's too bad."

"Sadly, that's the theater for you. It's a tough business."

"Did Roy have any other family?"

"He has one cousin, Collin Avery, who's a theater director in New York City. It's almost a joke in the industry that anything Collin Avery touches is doomed to fail. It's very sad, because I went to a few of his plays and they weren't bad. Not brilliant," Tami admitted, "but not as horrible as people said."

"He must really love the theater."

"Loves it. I've spoken to him a few times, and he's very…intense. Very passionate about theater."

"It seems the entire family loves theater. Roy was a producer, his sister, Krista, is a playwright, and his cousin Collin is a director. Next you'll tell me his parents were actors."

"Actually, they met at a college theater group and were very involved in their local community theater, but they never were professional actors."

"Aunt Edie liked plays, but she never spoke to me about being involved in any theater work. I wonder how she could have gotten hold of a famous script?"

"When I found the note, I didn't know anything about the 'missing' script, so I spoke to some people I know in the theater, and I also posted on a few online forum boards I belong to," Tami said. "There was a rumor that Roy had uncovered the famous unproduced play written by Bettridge. But after Roy's death, there was no news about it."

"It wasn't in Roy's possessions that were auctioned?"

"If they were auctioning Bettridge's missing script, everyone would have heard about it. It definitely wasn't there."

"And it's been over a year since Roy died. If he had received the script from Aunt Edie, and if someone had found it, I'm assuming they would have produced it by now?"

"Unless they had a reason to keep it hidden away. When I was looking into it, there was a lot of online chatter about the script after Roy died. Maybe someone stole the script, but they can't do anything with it until the rumors die down. That's assuming Roy had it. He may not have traveled back to Pennsylvania before he died."

"This just seems so far-fetched." Anne laughed. "A famous missing script, hidden in Aunt Edie's attic?"

"I know it sounds crazy."

Anne looked at the note again. "I hate to even suggest it, but is this really Aunt Edie? It could possibly be someone posing as Edie Summers, or maybe someone else who happens to be named Edie Summers, who wrote the note to fool Roy or get money from him."

"I didn't think of that." Tami's brows knit. "Is that Aunt Edie's handwriting?"

"It looks like it, but it could be a forgery."

"Something like the missing Bettridge script would be worthwhile for a con man."

"How could we know if this note is real or not?"

"Find the script, I suppose. It's not as if there's anyone we can ask about it."

Anne suddenly straightened. "Actually, maybe there is someone I can ask about it."

* * *

The next morning at the library was busier than normal because the Tea and Book Club was meeting. Anne bustled about in the library kitchen, filling the kettle and putting it on to boil and arranging cups and dessert plates. Usually at least one or more of the club members brought goodies to eat. Anne had a hard time resisting the decadent treats, especially if they involved chocolate.

Mildred Farley, Aunt Edie's best friend, was the first book club member to arrive. Anne was delighted, for more reasons than one. "Hello, Mildred."

"I'm looking forward to less spring showers and more summer sun." Mildred unwound her knitted blue scarf. She placed a container of peanut brittle on the kitchen table. "I received this from a nephew a few days ago. The box was so big I knew I should bring some to book club or else I'll eat it all."

"Oh, we'll definitely help you eat it," Anne said with a wink.

"Hello!" Wendy Pyle bustled in, her arms laden with not just one, but two containers of cookies. "Hannah and I made cookies for a fund-raiser bake sale at her school, so I figured, why not make some extra for book club?"

Anne helped her place the containers on the table. "It looks like an entire bakery's worth of extra."

"I guess I went a little overboard. We made lots of different kinds—chocolate chip, chocolate chip and walnut, toffee and caramel, chocolate peppermint…"

"Stop!" Anne laughed. "I'm gaining weight just listening to you list them all. How am I going to choose one?"

"Why not one of each?"

Several other book club members came, and the meeting started quickly. As usual, they spent the first few minutes chatting and catching up on each others' lives. Then they dove into discussion questions about the book they'd chosen last week, which was a departure from their normal fare—a young adult book set in a future postapocalyptic society.

"I can understand why this book was a *New York Times* best seller," Anne said. "It was very gripping and interesting, even though it's not the normal genre I read."

Wendy nodded. "Even though all the protagonists were teenagers, I could empathize with the hard choices they had to make in such a difficult society."

"It makes me wonder what kinds of hard choices our own children and grandchildren will need to make," Mildred said.

Anne briefly thought of Ben and Liddie, who were both at school. *Lord, please help them grow up to be a man and woman of God who will love You and obey You with all their hearts.*

At the end of the meeting, Wendy cleared the kitchen table. Mildred washed the cups and plates, and Anne helped her.

"Mildred, I have a question about Aunt Edie." Anne rinsed a teacup. "Did she ever mention having a 'missing' script written by playwright Hugh Bettridge?"

"No, not that I recall."

Wendy wiped a plate. "What do you mean, a 'missing' script?"

Anne explained about the note Tami had found.

"That sounds mysterious," Mildred said.

Wendy's eyes shone. "It's like a treasure hunt."

"I'm afraid I don't recall Edie mentioning anything about owning an unproduced play," Mildred said. "But she did love the theater."

"I know she was a patron for the community theater club, but I don't remember her acting in any plays," Anne said.

"She did a few times when she was younger. Edie and I would sometimes go to New York City for a weekend to watch a special production by one of her friends."

"She had friends in the theater?" This was the first Anne had heard of this.

"Oh yes," Mildred exclaimed. "Many years ago, when she was still traveling extensively, she worked as a director's assistant in London for a couple of months."

"I didn't know that." Anne shook her head at the thought of yet another surprise revelation about her aunt Edie.

"She didn't want to have a career working in the theater, but she enjoyed that brief stint. She said it was fun to meet new people and see the inner workings of a play. She sent me a copy of the playbill for the production she worked on. I think I still have it somewhere."

"I'd love to see it. When was this?" Anne asked.

"I think it was before her parents passed away."

"I wonder if she met Hugh Bettridge then," Anne pondered out loud. " He lived in London, and from what Tami said, he was only a few years years younger than Aunt Edie."

The three of them sat at the kitchen table. "How did Aunt Edie know Roy Underwood?" Anne asked Mildred.

" Edie's mother had fallen in a grocery parking lot, and Roy happened to be there—you know his family lives in Deshler?"

Anne nodded.

"Well, Roy found Edie's mother and took her to the hospital. This was after Edie's father had passed away. Edie was still working as a travel writer, and she was in Switzerland at the time. Bad weather made the airport shut down and she couldn't fly home for several days. So Roy stayed with Edie's mother at the hospital and took care of her. He helped make arrangements for her care and called Edie to update her every day until she came home. Roy was such a nice young man."

Anne smiled, since that "young man" was about Anne's father's age and had already passed away.

"I was out of town when Edie's mother was injured, but I met Roy a few times when Edie and I went to New York. He was the sort of man who would give his jacket to a homeless man on the street."

"He and Aunt Edie were close friends?"

"As close as they could be, considering he lived in England. He visited his parents in Deshler every two or three years, but he'd always come to Blue Hill to see Edie for coffee or lunch."

"I think I met him once, three or four years ago," Wendy said. "In Coffee Joe's, I saw Edie with a man with salt-and-pepper hair and a mustache. I waved and didn't stop to chat, but I could hear them talking about the theater."

"Yes, that sounds like Roy. He had a mustache," Mildred said.

"And that explains what Aunt Edie wrote about repaying him," Anne said. "But I don't know how she got Hugh Bettridge's script."

"What type of a play was it?" Mildred asked.

"I only know what Tami told me about it. I haven't had time yet to do research on it."

"Edie produced a Victorian mystery dinner play once, many years ago, with the Blue Hill Community Theater Club," Mildred said. "I wonder if that was the play in the note?"

"A mystery dinner play?" Wendy said.

"I love those," Anne said. "You buy tickets for dinner, and while the guests are eating, the servers act out a mystery play. The actors usually involve the guests too. Eric and I had a favorite restaurant in New York that put those on once a month."

"The theater club had the dinner play here, in her home," Mildred said.

"The library would be a perfect setting for a Victorian mystery play." Wendy's face lit up. "That would be a great fund-raiser for money to repair the theater roof."

"You could charge a higher-priced ticket per person, since only a small number of people can fit in the library. But what about the dinner part?"

"I could do something fancy enough," Wendy said. "I took classes in culinary school before Chad and I married, but with seven kids, I haven't had occasion to do anything restaurant quality. This would be really fun."

"Would the food be expensive?" Mildred asked.

"The owner of the local grocery store has a daughter in theater club. He might be willing to donate produce for dinner. I'll have to think up a menu."

"I have a few of the costumes from Edie's play still in my attic," Mildred said.

"Some of the theater club members also have Victorian costumes," Wendy said. "Would it be all right to do this in the library?"

"Of course," Anne said. "I want to help any way I can. After all, Remi and Bella are in the club, and Liddie and Ben had been looking forward to being in the next production."

"I'm sure we can find a play where they can have small parts," Wendy said. "We should talk to Flores Sanchez."

"That's a good idea," Anne said. "Bella mentioned she was in the theater club."

"The dinner play will match your Victorian mysteries display in the Fiction Room," Mildred said.

"I can put fliers for the mystery dinner play on the display," Anne said. "It might garner more interest for the play, as well as the books."

"Well, I need to get home," Mildred said.

"Me too," Wendy said. "You'll let us know if you find the missing play?"

"I was going to look in the attic tomorrow morning, since Remi and Bella are coming in to work."

"I can come help," Wendy offered.

"That would be great. That attic is huge."

Anne said good-bye to her friends and went back to work. How had Aunt Edie gotten hold of a famous missing script? Anne had a feeling that was going to be a mystery in itself.

Chapter Three

The next morning, Anne led Wendy up into the attic and turned on the light. The weather was still crisp, despite the fact summer was around the corner, so the attic wasn't too hot.

"I've been through this attic, repacking and labeling some boxes," Anne said. "However, there's still a lot I haven't gone through very thoroughly."

"Let's skip anything with clothes in them, for now," Wendy suggested.

"Yes, I doubt the script would be in a suitcase," Anne said.

They looked through drawers of tables and desks. Anne found office supplies and equipment, such as an older computer printer. There were several boxes with papers and books; they didn't find anything, but they did end up with a few paper cuts.

"Ouch!" Wendy sucked on her fingertip. "Who knew a thank-you card could be so dangerous?" She tossed the card back into a box. "These are all letters and cards Edie kept but no manuscripts or anything like a script."

"Here's the sympathy cards I received when Aunt Edie died." Anne handed her a second large box. "I might as well keep them together in case we need to find them later."

Wendy stacked the two boxes near the door.

Anne opened a trunk and was greeted with a swath of purple silk. Something about the soft, liquidy silk made her lift the dress from the trunk. "*Ooh.*" It was a Victorian style gown with black lace trimming the neckline, sleeves, and hem.

Wendy peered inside the gown's square neck. "It's a reproduction." The nylon tag sewn into the neckline seam was a costumer company. "We could use this for the Victorian mystery play."

"I wonder if Aunt Edie wore this for the Victorian mystery dinner play she produced? It looks to be about her size."

"I can take it with me to the theater this afternoon. That reminds me, Anne, I ought to introduce you to the theater director, Stephan Ullrick. You can tell him how you want to set up the library."

"Have you found a script for the dinner play?"

"Not yet, but Stephan will want to know how much space he has to work with. We'll also need to figure out how many people we could seat for the dinner."

"You won't need much for sets, since the History Room has great ambiance."

"You know what? You should be in the play too, Anne."

"Me? No way." Anne laughed. "My Sunday school plays were the extent of my theatrical career, thank you very much."

"But wouldn't it be fun to be a Victorian lady from one of those Sherlock Holmes novels?"

Anne tilted her head. "I suppose that would be interesting..."

"I'll talk to Stephan—"

Anne interrupted her. "But not interesting enough to want to get up in front of a bunch of people. Sorry, Wendy."

Her friend grinned. "Well, you can't fault me for trying. Ugh." Wendy's face transformed into disgust. "There's tons of mold damage in this box."

Anne looked over at the box. It was filled with a variety of things—a jar of seashells, a tarnished silver monogramed box of drawing charcoal pencils, a stiff pair of old-fashioned dancing shoes with filigree buckles, an ivory fan, some old journals that looked like they may have belonged to Edie's grandmother or even great-grandmother, but the writing was terribly faded on the aged yellow pages.

"There are water stains on one side of the box. Luckily, these journals didn't get damaged." Anne lifted them out. "Let's put all this stuff in another box and throw this one away."

They found two more water-damaged boxes but very little was damaged—only a few paperback books with pages hopelessly wavy and spotted with mold, and some cotton men's shirts with moth holes as well as mold stains.

"Where did the water come from?" Anne studied the wall and ceiling. "These boxes weren't near a wall, but they all have damage on only one side of the box, as if they were leaning against something wet."

"Maybe Edie had a leak in the roof repaired but didn't realize these boxes were wet, and over time the damp cardboard got mold."

They searched but still didn't find a sheaf of papers or booklet or even a bound book that could be Bettridge's missing play.

"I'm ready for lunch." Anne closed a box full of sweaters. "Want to join me?"

"Sorry, I can't." Wendy dusted off her jeans. "I have to meet Alex at the theater. He's going to look over the roof damage and give us an estimate. I'll see you tomorrow, though. I'm scheduled to volunteer. I'll ask Stephan Ullrick to come see you."

"I'm free all morning tomorrow. Oh, don't forget the dress." She handed Wendy the Victorian dress they had found.

After gulping down a quick lunch of vegetable soup and some bread, Anne headed downstairs to the checkout desk just as Remi and Bella's shift was about to end. That afternoon, Anne had a few moments free, so she went online to look up Hugh Bettridge.

The British playwright had had a long career with many successful plays, a few badly received ones, and several awards for his writing. His wife died when his two children, a boy and a girl, were still young. He died when Anne was only nine or ten years old. She couldn't remember if Aunt Edie had gone to a funeral in England when she was a child.

Anne discovered a biography written of Hugh Bettridge's life, and immediately ordered it through interlibrary loan. It would take about a week to get to her.

Anne also looked up Roy Underwood on the Internet but didn't find much more than what Tami told her. On several rumor-filled message boards, Anne didn't know what she could believe and what was false. She found a list of the plays he had directed, several he had produced, and even a few early in his career which he had acted in. He had won many awards for his directing. When he died last year of a heart attack, he had actually been ten years younger than Anne's father. She sighed.

How sad. She thanked God for her parents' good health as they enjoyed their semiretirement in Florida.

There wasn't much information about Roy's family except a brief mention that he hailed from Deshler, which was a few miles away from Blue Hill. Tami had mentioned that Roy's parents still lived there. Perhaps Anne could visit them to talk about their son. Anne always felt that speaking to people gave more information than reading about them, because people said as much with nonverbal cues as they did in conversation.

Tami had been friends with Roy. Had she met Roy's parents? Maybe she could introduce Anne to them.

Anne looked up Roy's cousin, Collin Avery. Tami was right when she said his career hadn't been very successful. Some theater critics were very derisive of his directing ability. However, several fan Web sites assessed his plays with fairness, describing both the bad and good aspects of his directing. Collin hadn't won any awards, but some plays had been relatively successful, enough to balance the ones that weren't as lucrative.

Would Collin have stolen the Bettrige play from Roy in order to use it to boost his sagging career? Because of the fervor about the script right after Roy died, Collin could be keeping it hidden for a while to prevent suspicion from falling upon him. Then later, he might say he had "discovered" it. Thousands would flock to see a previously unproduced play by Bettridge. Or perhaps he wanted to sell it—since his plays weren't doing well, he might need the influx of cash.

Roy's sister, Krista Underwood Bennett, was a playwright living in New York City. Krista's play, *Time's Fool*, had been a huge hit off Broadway twenty years ago, with an impressive three-year run. However, since then, Krista's plays had only had mediocre responses from the critics and theatergoers. Her cousin Collin had directed a few of her plays, but the plays had done badly.

✗ Would Krista have stolen the Bettridge play from her brother in order to pass it off as her own work? Her career didn't appear to be doing very well, and no one would know it was Bettridge's writing since the play had never been produced. Or would she have wanted the script to sell it? Or would she produce the Bettridge play herself and make money that way? She could be simply waiting for the rumors about Roy discovering the missing Bettridge play to die down.

Anne was excited to see that *Time's Fool* had been videotaped for airing on public television, and she could order a copy through interlibrary loan. She did so, since she had a VHS player in the library so patrons could view other old videotape resources.

But what if Roy had never received the play? Anne recalled the letter, written in what looked like Aunt Edie's handwriting and posted from Blue Hill to London. The incident mentioned about Aunt Edie's mother and Roy's help couldn't have been known by many people, and that seemed to point to the fact that Aunt Edie had indeed written the note and not some con man trying to get money out of Roy. That meant the script was somewhere in the house, but where in the world could it be?

At that moment, Tami entered the library, and Anne could immediately see that something was wrong. There was tension around her green eyes, and her shoulders were stiff. As the front door closed behind her, she glanced back through the glass panes.

"Tami, what's wrong?" Anne asked, alarmed.

"I decided to walk to the library and I thought…" Tami swallowed. "I thought maybe there was a man following me."

"What? Are you all right?" Anne reached out to touch Tami's hand.

"I'm fine. He didn't get very close."

What did he look like?"

"Short, stocky. Dark hair. I didn't get a good look at him."

"We should call the police, Tami."

"But you know how Blue Hill is. I don't want to get a guy in trouble just because he happened to take my same route across town. He probably lives near here."

"That description doesn't sound like any of my neighbors," Anne said.

"I was probably being paranoid. It wasn't as if he dramatically stared at me with some cold killer look." She laughed, and she sounded more like her normal self.

"If you're sure…"

"I am. Now, please tell me you found the script?"

Anne shook her head. "Sorry, Tami. Wendy and I looked all morning, but there's still a few boxes to go through."

"I can help you the day after tomorrow in the morning. I hope you find it. I wouldn't want you to go through your attic for nothing."

"We always knew there was that possibility. We don't know if Roy got the script from Aunt Edie or not."

"Maybe Aunt Edie hid the script somewhere to keep it safe?"

"If it was something precious to her, I can't see her hiding it away," Anne said slowly. "She'd put it somewhere safe but not necessarily squirreled away so no one else could find it." Anne rather thought Aunt Edie would have put something so precious in her secret room upstairs, but she'd searched the drawers and hadn't found it.

However, maybe Aunt Edie had put it in her safe deposit box. Anne decided to check it tomorrow. She didn't recall seeing a manuscript there the last time she looked in it, but maybe she'd simply overlooked it.

"I've got to get home," Tami said. "Mom and I are going to visit one of my cousins this afternoon."

"Where did you park your car?"

"In front of the pharmacy. I was picking up Dad's prescription for him."

"I'm heading out too. Do you want me to walk you to your car?"

Tami gave Anne a grateful smile. "I think I'm just being silly about that guy following me, but I appreciate it."

"Nothing silly about it," Anne said. She spoke to Mrs. Bultman, who was manning the checkout desk, and after grabbing a cardigan, headed out the front door with Tami.

The spring day was sunny but with a breeze that had a little bit of bite to it. The air smelled of blossoming flowers, signaling that summer would be here soon.

Tami looked around as soon as they turned onto the street, then her shoulders relaxed.

"Do you see the man from before?" Anne asked.

Tami shook her head. "It was probably nothing. Maybe I spooked him, poor guy."

The two of them laughed, and they chatted as they walked to Thrifty Drugstore. Tami got into her parents' car, and Anne waved as she drove away.

Anne walked to the elementary school. She'd deliberately come early to pick up Ben and Liddie in order to talk to the school nurse, Flores Sanchez.

She knocked on the nurse's door. "Hello?"

The young woman with olive-toned skin looked up from the desk, where it looked like she was reviewing a medical file. "Hello! How can I help you?"

"I'm Anne Gibson, Ben and Liddie's mom."

"Yes, I thought I recognized you. I'm Flores Sanchez. Is there anything the matter with your kids, Mrs. Gibson?"

"Please call me Anne. And no, I wanted to pick your brain about playwriting."

Flores's chocolate brown eyes lit up. "Are you a writer too?"

"No, but I heard you know everything about plays."

Flores blushed. "Not everything, but I have read and seen a lot of plays."

Anne sank into the chair in front of her desk. "My friend Tami is in town. She attended the estate auction of Roy Underwood, who grew up in Deshler."

Flores nodded. "I know of him, although I haven't seen his plays because he worked in London."

"Tami was telling me about some 'missing' Bettridge script that Roy had. Do you know anything about that?"

Flores gave a disgusted sound. "That old rumor. All my online friends were talking about it in the weeks after Roy died last year. People were saying that Roy Underwood claimed he had a play Bettridge supposedly wrote and that Roy was going to produce it posthumously."

"So it doesn't exist?"

Flores paused to think a moment. "I remember reading somewhere about it. There's a chance that Bettridge did write a script during a certain time period of his life, maybe in between writing two of his other plays. But just because he had that time to write another script doesn't mean he actually did."

"But how did the story about the 'missing' script start?"

"I don't know." Flores made a face. "I'm not a huge fan of Bettridge's plays. I tend to like comedies, and his plays are always really sad."

Anne laughed. "It's like books. Not every author is going to appeal to every reader."

"I do remember hearing something about Bettridge's daughter, though," Flores suddenly said.

"Lynne Bettridge Sallman? I read about her online. She's a theatrical literary agent, right?"

Flores nodded. "She's been an agent for a long time and is well respected in the business. I would love to have her as my agent." She sighed. "But anyway, the rumor about the missing script has been circulating ever since Bettridge died years ago. Recently, a writer for a theatrical journal asked Lynne about the missing script, and she responded rather acidly. Something about how the 'missing' play was stolen from her father and rightfully belongs to the family."

"I can see how she would think that," Anne said slowly. How in the world had Aunt Edie acquired the missing script, if she had indeed had it? Anne didn't want to think her aunt had gotten it through suspicious channels, but didn't the note tell Roy not to ask her how she'd gotten the script? Anne shivered. Maybe the note writer was indeed a con man posing as her aunt, trying to get money out of Roy. But if that were the case, why would the note writer tell Roy to visit her when he was next in the states and how would he have known about the incident with Aunt Edie's mother and Roy?

"Lynne seemed to think the missing script really did exist," Flores said, "so maybe it does. But no one knows where it is and why it was never produced during Bettridge's lifetime."

At that moment, the school bell rang. Anne rose to her feet. "Thank you so much."

"No problem. It's fun talking about plays and historical theater rumors."

"I almost forgot, did you hear about the Victorian mystery dinner play the theater club is doing in the library?"

Flores grinned. "I heard about it last night. I'm already looking through plays to find one for us."

"I don't know if it's possible, but Ben and Liddie were hoping for small parts…"

"No problem. A few other cast members have kids who want to be involved, so I'm looking for a play with some children parts."

"Thanks, Flores. And thanks for your help."

Anne usually waited in the car for the kids, but since she was in the school halls already, she headed to their classrooms. She arrived at Liddie's classroom and caught sight of her little girl giggling outrageously over something with another girl in her class. The pure, enthusiastic joy on her daughter's face made

Anne smile too. Eric would be so proud of how beautiful and joyful his daughter was.

The thought of Eric only caused a sad, soft weight on her breastbone rather than a painful pang. Maybe she really was starting to move on with her life rather than clinging too hard to the past.

"Mommy!" Liddie had seen her. "Now I can tell you about the purple cow too!"

"But there's no such thing as a purple cow," Anne teased her daughter.

"Yes, there is. On Mars!" And Liddie and her friend erupted into giggles again for no reason that Anne could fathom.

Liddie's teacher, Miss Reed, came up to Anne. "They've been laughing nonstop for the past fifteen minutes. I haven't a clue what about."

Anne and Miss Reed laughed, which somehow made Liddie and her friend giggle even harder.

On their way to Ben's classroom, Liddie explained how the purple cow flew to the moon, but she didn't like eating cheese, so she decided to move to Mars.

"So do purple cows on Mars give purple milk?" Anne asked as they arrived at the fourth grade classroom. Ben, who was talking with his friend Ryan, saw her and quickly grabbed his backpack.

Liddie answered her, "No, Mommy, they give orange juice!"

"What gives orange juice?" Ben asked.

"Purple cows on Mars," Liddie said with a straight face.

Anne could tell Ben wanted to argue about the existence of purple cows and their residence on Mars, but instead he sighed.

Anne smiled and patted his shoulder at his forbearance for his little sister.

"Hey, Mom, can Ryan come back home with us?" Ben asked as Ryan joined them.

"Is it okay with your uncle?" Anne asked Ryan. Alex Ochs had been raising Ryan, his sister's son, for the past four years, since Ryan's parents had died.

"I…think so," Ryan said.

"Why don't we give him a call and see?" Anne pulled out her cell phone and called Alex.

"Hi, Anne," Alex answered.

Anne could hear a hammer pounding in the background. "Is it all right if Ryan comes back to the library with us this afternoon?"

"Actually, you'd be doing me a favor. I'm still at the job site and it would help if I could pick him up at the library later."

"Great. Don't worry, I'll make sure the boys do their homework."

"Thanks a bunch, Anne." Alex hung up.

Anne headed home with the kids. The information she'd received from Flores seemed to only bring up more questions.

She hoped she could find the script and shed some light on her own modern day mystery.

Chapter Four

The next morning dawned gray and drizzly, which was likely why Ben and Liddie were slow to get up for school.

"Come on, slugabed." Anne shook Liddie for the second time that morning.

"Ew," Liddie moaned into her pillow. "I'm not a slug."

"Well, in this house, you're a slug if you're the last one to the breakfast table." Anne tickled Liddie under the ribs.

She squirmed and turned over. "Mommy, you're mean." Liddie pouted.

"Weren't you supposed to do something special in class today?"

In an instant, Liddie opened her brown eyes wide and sat up. "We're doing warm and cold colors today. I can't miss that."

It still amazed Anne sometimes how Liddie had only two modes—sleep and full steam ahead. She helped her daughter dress, steering her away from yellow and orange leggings that clashed with her pink and purple top.

Ben brushed his teeth, zombie-like, with his brown hair sticking up in all directions.

Anne smoothed a hand over it and kissed the top of his head. "Don't forget to brush your hair, Ben."

"*Mm-hmm*," he mumbled, making his toothpaste bubble around his mouth.

"I'll let Hershey out this morning," Anne offered, feeling sympathy for Ben's sleepy eyes.

Ben rinsed his mouth. "Thanks, Mom."

Anne let the dog outside while she made toast and poured orange juice and milk for the kids. She spread peanut butter on each toast slice and then used the squeezable bottle of strawberry jam to draw smiley faces on the toast for the kids.

Liddie sat down and grinned at her smiling toast. "Good morning, Mr. Toast."

Ben sighed like the long-suffering older brother he was, but he smiled at the sight of the toast too.

"Ben, can you say grace for us?" Anne folded her hands and bowed her head.

"Dear Jesus, thank You for this day…" He paused to give a gigantic yawn. "…and for school today and for peanut butter toast. Please help us all have good days today. In Jesus' name, Amen."

"Amen," Anne and Liddie chorused.

Liddie promptly bit the left eye off of Mr. Toast. She showed her one-eyed breakfast to her brother. "I see you."

"He's a pirate," Ben said.

"No, he's a bunny," Liddie said.

Ben looked perplexed for a long moment, then he shrugged. "Okay."

Anne gave him an encouraging smile. Since the loss of their father, they'd been doing their best to be strong and to cope, and Ben had matured, increasing in generosity and his love for his sister. She was so proud of him.

While they were finishing up, Anne's phone rang. She was surprised, since it was still early. "Hello?"

"Hello, Anne Gibson? This is Blanche Underwood. You called and left us a message yesterday afternoon?"

"Hello, Mrs. Underwood. Thank you for calling me back."

"I'm sorry we couldn't return your call sooner. We were out yesterday until late. It was so nice to hear from you. I didn't know your aunt Edie very well, but I knew that she and Roy were good friends."

"I hope it's not an imposition, but I was wondering if I could come over to visit you sometime? I recently discovered a note my aunt wrote to your son before he died, and I have a few questions about it."

Ben had finished his breakfast and dutifully took his dishes to the sink. Anne mimed to Liddie to hurry up and finish eating.

"That would be fine. Are you free tomorrow afternoon? Three o'clock?" Mrs. Underwood asked.

Anne looked at her calendar and the volunteer schedule. She would need to make arrangements for someone to pick up the kids from school and take care of them. "Let's schedule it for now, and I'll call you later if I need to reschedule." Anne said good-bye and hung up the phone.

Liddie had finished her juice and milk and now had only one small piece of toast left. She'd nibbled around Mr. Toast's remaining eye. "Look, Mommy, Mr. Toast is winking at you." She held up the toast eye and folded it in half like an eyelid closing.

Anne laughed, then winked back. "And now, finish your toast."

Liddie popped the last bite in her mouth.

Since the sky looked cloudy and might turn into a drizzle, Anne made sure the kids had their rain jackets as she drove them to school. When she dropped them off, Liddie raced out of the car to her classroom with a backward wild wave and a quick, "Bye, Mommy!"

"Bye, Mom." Ben ran after his sister.

Anne paused a moment to watch them. They were growing up so fast, and it seemed they were starting to enjoy life here in Blue Hill as opposed to New York. She was again thankful to Aunt Edie and to the Lord for this opportunity to move here and run the Blue Hill Library.

Anne returned home with a few minutes to spare before she had to open the library, so she threw together chicken soup in the Crock-Pot to simmer all day. She'd become good at planning meals ahead for Thursdays since the library remained open until eight o'clock that night.

Anne called Wendy Pyle. "Hi, Wendy. I have a favor to ask."

"Sure," she said quickly.

Anne laughed. "You haven't even heard my request yet." She was reminded again of how generous Wendy was with her time and was thankful she had made such a good friend here in Blue Hill. "Tomorrow afternoon, could you pick Ben and Liddie up from school and take them to your house for the afternoon? I have an appointment with Roy Underwood's parents."

"No problem. They can help me make thumbprint cookies. It's my turn to take cookies to church on Sunday for coffee after service."

"Liddie will love that. Thanks, Wendy." Anne hung up.

By the time Donna Slade came by in the early afternoon for her volunteer shift, there wasn't much else to do.

"Donna, would you mind holding the fort while I go to the bank?" Anne asked. "I'll swing by the school to pick up the kids and be back here before your shift ends."

"Sure." Donna removed her jacket and put her purse away behind the checkout desk. "How many people are in the library right now?"

"A few kids and their parents in the Children's Room, and one person each in the Nonfiction and History Room."

"No problem. I'll see if they need any help." Donna bustled off. As a member of the Library Guild, she took great pride in the library and was an enthusiastic volunteer.

Anne found Aunt Edie's safe deposit box key and drove to the bank. The young woman at the teller desk gave her a friendly smile when she requested to see her safe deposit box.

"Sure thing, Mrs. Gibson." The teller double-checked Anne's driver's license and then led her to a back room where the boxes were stored. After using her key and Anne's to open Aunt Edie's box, the teller left Anne alone in the room.

Anne set the safe deposit box down on the table and sat in one of two chairs. She opened the metal cover and peered inside.

Nothing looked different from the last time she'd checked Aunt Edie's box, which was right after she'd arrived in Blue Hill. There were family birth certificates, many of them for people long dead, a copy of the deed to the property, a stack of savings bond certificates which were for Ben and Liddie, and some old family photographs, several of them wavy from extensive water damage sometime in the past. There were also passports for Aunt Edie's parents, which were also wavy with water damage, and a key chain with extra keys for the house.

At least, Anne had assumed they were extra house keys, since they looked like the keys she'd been given when she took possession of Aunt Edie's house. Anne looked more closely. Maybe they were for something else? There were four keys, each a different brand of maker, along with a circular key fob printed with the logo of the Blue Hill bank.

Anne pocketed the key ring. At the very least, she could verify the keys were to the house.

Anne rifled through the papers, but there was nothing even remotely like a play script. She closed the lid to the box with a feeling of disappointment. She had held out hope that maybe she had overlooked something.

As Anne left the bank, she squinted up at the gray sky. She drove to the elementary school and just as she pulled up to the curb the first drops of rain splattered on the sidewalk. Liddie was standing under the eaves. When she ran to the car, she gave a squeal as rain dropped onto her head.

Ben ran faster than his sister, and the two of them reached the car at the same time. Liddie climbed into her booster seat, and Anne reached back to help her buckle herself in as rain pattered a rhythm against the roof of her Impala.

"Good timing, Mom." Ben buckled himself in, dropping his backpack onto the floor.

"I'll say." Anne put the car in gear and headed out of the parking lot.

"Mommy, my head is cold." Liddie patted the top of her head.

"That's because it's damp from the sprinkling you got. What did you do today in school?"

"Cool colors are cold and hot colors are hot." Liddie nodded as if she had imparted some great words of wisdom.

"So what's a cool color?"

"Blue."

"And what's a hot color?"

"Red." Liddie patted her head again. "Maybe if I had red hair, my head wouldn't be cold."

"I'll warm it up for you." Ben ruffled his sister's hair. She shrieked, giggling at the same time, and the two of them began messing each other's hair until they both had strands sticking straight up out of their heads.

Anne looked in the rearview mirror. "You look like two wild beasts."

"Ben's a beast," Liddie said. "I'm a princess."

"You don't look like any princess I've ever seen." Ben grinned as he mussed her hair again.

Liddie laughed and reached for his head. Her arms weren't long enough to reach him, but Ben good-naturedly bent his head close.

When they walked into the library, Donna froze at the sight of Ben's and Liddie's new hairdos. She laughed. "Rockin', dudes," she said, sounding like a skateboarding teenager.

As they entered their living quarters on the second floor, the delicious smell of chicken soup from the Crock-Pot welcomed them. Then Hershey bounded forward and greeted Ben and Liddie with enthusiastic licking as if they'd been gone a week rather than just a few hours. Ben took the dog outside while Anne got their after-school snacks — apple slices and cookies. Liddie put napkins on the table.

Ben described the battle in the Revolutionary War that he'd learned about in school that day. Liddie asked an occasional question, which made Ben excited to explain the answers to her. Anne didn't rush him but delighted in listening to him talk about something that interested him so much. Discovering her son's enthusiasm for some of the same things she enjoyed, such as history, continued to surprise her.

After their snack, Ben settled into the living room to do his homework. Liddie lay on the floor next to him with her coloring books, practicing her "warm" and "cool" colors.

There was a rush of patrons in the library since school had let out, but later that afternoon, it slowed down. Anne took the opportunity to check the keys on the keychain she'd taken from Aunt Edie's safe deposit box. The largest key fit in the front door—although she'd replaced the door itself during the renovations, Alex had used the old antique-style handle and deadbolt from the old door in the new one. Another key fit into the side door to the unattached garage. A third key fit into the door to the basement.

Try as she might, Anne couldn't think of where the fourth key could go. She stood in the middle of the front foyer of the library, tapping the key against her palm and aimlessly circling as she looked around. Then a patron came up to check out books, and she slipped the key ring back into her pocket as she went to the checkout desk.

When Mildred arrived promptly at five o'clock to volunteer, the library had grown busy again.

"It's pouring out there." She removed her raincoat and unwound a soft angora scarf.

"Then it's good weather for the chicken soup I have upstairs."

"I'll man the desk while you feed your kiddos."

Anne slipped upstairs to serve chicken soup and ham sandwiches to Ben and Liddie for dinner, gulping down her own food quickly so she could return to help Mildred. She felt faintly guilty at leaving Mildred to handle the large number of patrons on her own.

However, Liddie was feeling disgruntled at being cooped up all afternoon, despite Ben's attempts to entertain her. She picked at her sandwich and stirred her soup messily, splashing a little on the table.

"Eat your soup," Anne said.

"I want hamburgers." She pouted.

"We can have hamburgers another night."

Ben tried to tease Liddie out of her doldrums. "How about I race you to finish?"

"No," Liddie said, clearly in a bad mood.

Anne smiled at Ben to thank him for trying. The rest of the meal passed with Anne and Ben chatting and Liddie reluctantly eating with a permanent scowl on her face. When Ben had finished, Liddie had eaten little more than half her food.

"Liddie, if you're done eating, why don't you go with Ben into the living room? We'll put on a movie."

Liddie looked as if she was going to protest, but then Ben said, "Come on, Liddie. I'll let you watch *The Little Mermaid*."

"Okay." She slid from her seat.

Anne rushed through cleaning up while Ben put on the movie. When Anne headed downstairs again, her two kids were settled in front of the television. Liddie's eyes were already drooping.

As she entered the foyer, Mildred came to meet her. "I was about to go up to look for you. Stephan Ullrick is here."

Anne had completely forgotten that the community theater club director was coming by to talk to her about the dinner theater. "Has he been waiting long?"

"Not at all. He's in the History Room right now."

Anne hurried to meet Stephan and found him in the center of the room, which only had two patrons browsing the bookcases. At least, she assumed it was Stephan Ullrick, because he was looking at the walls and ceiling as opposed to the books.

"Stephan?"

He immediately smiled and came forward, his hand outstretched.

"I'm Anne."

"Pleased to meet you." He was a little older than Anne, and he had a rich, deep voice with rolling consonants.

"I'm so sorry I wasn't here when you arrived. I was giving dinner to my children."

"No need for apologies." He gestured to the History Room. "I wanted some time to 'scope out the place,' so to speak."

"So will this work for the Victorian mystery dinner play?"

"It will be perfect. One of our members, Flores Sanchez, has already found us a play which will fit the number of cast members we have, and she asked me to tell you that there will be small parts for your children, as well."

"That's wonderful. Ben and Liddie will be so excited."

Stephan nodded toward the tables. "You will not mind if we move aside the furniture for the dinner guests?"

"Of course not. But I'm afraid you'll be limited in how many people will fit in here."

"A small intimate gathering will work best, because we can have more interaction with the audience." Stephan's blue eyes twinkled. "I think the guests will have fun."

"How much room will you need to rehearse?"

Stephan sketched out an area at the far end. "About this size, if you move this chair and lamp."

"That won't be a problem."

Stephan stepped up to her and clasped her hand in both of his. "Thank you for allowing us to use the library for our fund-raiser. I don't know what we would have done if you hadn't."

With Stephan this close to her, his charisma was like a thick cloud of sweetly scented cologne. Anne smiled. "I'm more than happy to help out the community theater club. And thank you for allowing Ben and Liddie to be a part of it."

"You should act in our production, as well."

"Oh no, I couldn't—"

A lock of gray-streaked black hair fell over his wide forehead, making him look boyish. "Nonsense, you would be a wonderful addition to our cast. I believe one of the female parts is a librarian. It's perfect for you."

"I'm flattered you'd ask me, but I can't act at all. And I'm too busy with the library." And with figuring out the truth about her aunt Edie's note and the missing Bettridge script.

Stephan sighed, and a dimple appeared in one cheek. "Well, you can't say I didn't try."

Anne laughed. "No, there's nothing you could say to induce me to act in a play."

Stephan grinned, his teeth white and even against his skin. "I never pass up a challenge."

CHAPTER FIVE

"Oh, come on, Anne, you should act in the play," Tami said the next morning as they searched through the last boxes in the attic.

"I couldn't possibly act in a serious theater production." Anne sneezed as she opened a box filled with dusty sweaters.

"But we acted in the Christmas plays at church every year. Even me, and I was so shy and quiet that you could barely hear me, even from the front row."

"But the only people who attended the Christmas plays were parents and Sunday school teachers, and none of them minded how awful we were. Remember when little Lori Deets threw up in the middle of singing 'Silent Night'?"

Tami giggled. "I shouldn't laugh, because Lori was mortified, but it was pretty funny, if a little gross."

"*I'll* probably throw up if I get up in front of an audience that actually paid to see the play."

"But it's a fund-raiser. It'll be people who want to support the community theater club, not theater critics."

"All the more reason for them to get a quality performance." Anne set aside another box of clothes, this one filled with seventies-era dresses.

"But don't you remember how fun it was just to pretend to be someone else?" Tami said.

Yes, Anne had to admit it had been fun to transform herself into another personality, not just in words but with clothes and hair and makeup. Then she shook her head. "The community theater club has plenty of cast members. I wouldn't want to take a part away from someone."

She and Tami searched through the rest of the boxes in the attic, but there was still no sign of the script. They retreated in defeat to Anne's kitchen, where she made them some tea and served a few cookies leftover from the kids' snack yesterday.

"I suppose we could go through the clothes boxes more thoroughly," Anne said. "I did a quick search through each one, but nothing more than that, because I can't see Aunt Edie hiding a valuable script in the middle of a stack of old men's suits or her old bridesmaids' dresses."

Tami munched on a chocolate chip cookie. "Do you think Roy got the script from your aunt before he died?"

"If he did, then he gave it to someone else, or someone might have taken it from him."

"I don't think he'd have given it to anyone else. And he wouldn't have shown the script to just anyone. He would understand how valuable it was and precious to Edie. If someone did take it from him, who would know he had the script?"

"Someone with easy access to his house. I'm visiting Roy's parents this afternoon. I wanted to know more about Roy's relationship with his cousin and his sister."

Tami frowned thoughtfully. "It would be a boost to both their careers, in different ways."

Anne shrugged. "I don't know anything about Roy's family. Maybe he was very close to his cousin and his sister and he gave it to one of them, or maybe neither of them would even think to steal the script from him." Anne paused. "Speaking of steal...You haven't told anyone about the note, have you?

"No, just you."

"I've only told Mildred, since I asked her about Aunt Edie, and Wendy, since she was helping me to search for the script, but I don't think I'll tell anyone else unless absolutely necessary."

"Because of Roy's cousin and sister?" Tami asked.

"No, but...I want to be careful. Lynne Bettridge Sallman said that the missing play was stolen from her father. If I do find it, Lynne might try to insist that it belonged to her father and not to Aunt Edie. She may even accuse Aunt Edie of stealing the script from her father, and I know Aunt Edie would never do something like that. If Aunt Edie had the script, it must have been because it was given to her, maybe by Bettridge himself. I need to discover how Aunt Edie got it in the first place."

Tami had to leave just before lunch because she was driving her parents to her grandparents' house, which was about two hours away from Blue Hill. "I come home once every two years or so, but it's like this every time. I have a ton of relatives and they all want to see me. And I'll have to do this all again when Aiden comes, because they'll all want to see him too!"

"Enjoy it. You won't know how long you'll have your family around."

Tami's eyes softened. "You're right, and I'm very grateful for my family. Aiden doesn't have many relatives at all."

As Anne waved good-bye to Tami, she sent up a prayer to ask God to bless all her own family, including her grandparents and cousins, her parents in Florida, and Eric's parents up in Ithaca, New York.

Remi and Bella Miller's shift ended at lunchtime, but Anne had asked them to stay for the afternoon to man the library while Anne went to visit Roy Underwood's parents.

Anne had made a batch of cranberry oatmeal cookies last night, and she took them with her as she drove out to Deshler, a slightly larger town than Blue Hill and only twenty minutes away.

The Underwoods lived in a quaint Colonial style house with green trim and flower boxes at the windows. Multiple colors of tulips lined the brick walkway up to the front door, and the brass door knocker that Anne used was also in the shape of a tulip.

Blanche Underwood answered the door with a bright smile on her face. "How lovely for you to come." She was somewhere in between Anne's parents' ages and Aunt Edie's age, with blonde hair and a neat, slender figure.

"Thank you for inviting me to visit." Anne handed her the container of cookies and stepped into the wide, airy foyer. "I made cranberry oatmeal cookies for you."

"Wilfred loves oatmeal cookies." Blanche led the way through the first doorway to the right, which opened into a bright living room.

Wilfred sat in a comfortable recliner, his leg propped up on a stool. "I apologize for not standing." He tapped his leg. "I twisted my knee while gardening the other day."

Blanche rolled her eyes. "Gardening? Anne, he climbed a ladder to trim the tree branches. At his age."

"So? Trees equal gardening, in my book." Wilfred's blue eyes twinkled at his wife beneath his thick head of snow-white curly hair.

"Did you want some coffee?" Blanche asked Anne.

"I'd love some."

"Cream or sugar?"

"Black, please." Aunt Edie had introduced Anne to black coffee at the age of thirteen, and she'd taken it the same way as her aunt ever since.

"You are my kind of girl," Wilfred said.

Blanche brought the coffee in a beautiful blue porcelain coffeepot. After serving everyone, she settled back in her chintz overstuffed armchair. "How is your aunt?"

"I'm afraid she passed away several months ago. Only a couple months after your son, actually."

"I'm so sorry. We didn't know her well, but she was a good friend to Roy."

"It wasn't until recently that I found out Aunt Edie was friends with Roy. They apparently met through my great-grandmother Summers?"

Blanche told Anne about how Roy had happened upon Edie's mother in a parking lot after she'd had a bad fall, and how he had taken care of Edie's mother until Edie could fly back to Blue Hill.

"That was so kind of him," Anne said. "I wish I could have met him."

"You would have liked him," Blanche said. "We were so shocked when he died."

"He was bad about going to the doctor," Wilfred said with a grunt. "He had a heart attack. They said his arteries were completely blocked."

"That's why I've been so strict about Wilfred's health." Blanche gave her husband a fond look.

"Do you have any other children?" Anne asked.

"Yes, our daughter Krista is married and living in New York City."

"I used to live in New York City. Does she like it there?"

"She loves it. She's a playwright, so she's close to where all the theaters are."

"What plays has she written? I don't recall if I've seen any of them."

Blanche rambled on about several of Krista's plays, all of which she had seen, and going into great detail about aspects of each.

"Did Roy ever direct any of her plays?" Anne asked.

"No," Blanche said, with a bit of hesitation. "Roy's directing style wasn't…a good fit for Krista's plays."

Blanche's hesitation was curious. Had Krista and Roy gotten along with each other? Had Roy refused to direct his sister's plays because of his "directing style" or because he didn't care for them? Had it caused tension between the siblings?

"You're very knowledgeable about plays," Anne said. "Is it from what you picked up from your children, or did you two do some theater work?"

"Nothing professional," Wilfred said, "but Blanche and I met through the theater at our college."

"We've been involved in the local community theater for years," Blanche added.

"I'd love to see the two of you perform," Anne said.

"Oh, we're nothing special." Faint red tinged his weathered cheeks.

"I prefer comedy," Blanche said, "but Wilfred is wonderful at Shakespeare. He played a magnificent King Lear a few years ago."

With his snow-white hair and deep voice, Anne could believe it. "Theater seems to run in your family. Do any of your relations perform?"

"No one else performs, although all our cousins and their children enjoy going to plays," Blanche said.

"And Collin's a director in New York City," Wilfred added. "Collin Avery, Roy's cousin."

"Oh." Blanche's face seemed pinched. "Yes, I had forgotten about Collin."

There were several seconds of silence. It seemed obvious that Blanche didn't care much for Collin.

Anne asked, "What plays has he directed? Perhaps I've been to one or two."

They listed titles, but Anne shook her head. "I don't think I've seen any of them."

"We went to a couple," Wilfred said.

"So, Collin and Roy were both directors? They must have enjoyed talking shop with each other."

Blanche hesitated, then said a trifle reluctantly, "They didn't always agree on certain things."

"Like what?"

"Collin tends to be very impulsive and a little flighty in his directing style. Some actors like that, but others find it frustrating."

"What was Roy like?"

"Roy was always a careful planner, and he never made changes unless he had thoughtfully considered all the consequences. It's what made him such a good director."

Anne could guess that Roy's directing style contributed to his successes as a director in London, while Collin's style may be why his plays hadn't done as well. "I'm so sorry I haven't seen any of Krista's or Collin's plays. I thought I might have, but my husband and I didn't go to plays as often as we wanted to. He was always busy."

"What did he do?" Blanche asked.

Anne spoke for a few minutes about Eric and her children. Then she finally said, "There's another reason I wanted to visit with you today. My friend Tami went to Roy's estate auction a year ago and bought a couple costumes. Tami happened to find a note from my aunt Edie to Roy in the pocket of one of the costumes she bought. That's how I found out Aunt Edie knew your son."

"His auction was so successful," Blanche said. "All the proceeds went to Roy's favorite charities."

"After what you've told me about him, that sounds exactly like something he'd want," Anne said.

"What did the note say?" Wilfred asked.

"Aunt Edie mentioned how grateful she was to Roy for what he'd done for her mother, and she wanted to show him a script the next time he came to visit her. The letter was dated only a few months before Roy died."

"Why, I never knew Edie was a playwright," Blanche said.

"It was a play written by a friend of hers. But I haven't found it. I wondered if maybe Roy had gotten it from Aunt Edie and then shown it to someone close to him. He didn't show it to you or to his other family?"

Blanche shook her head. "Roy didn't show us any script. He had been in the middle of a production, and he hadn't yet decided on his next project."

"Do you think Roy might have told Krista or Collin about the play? Maybe he wanted Krista to critique it, or perhaps he thought Collin may want to direct it."

Blanche shook her head vigorously. "He wouldn't have shown the script to Collin."

Anne wondered, from Blanche's reaction, if Collin and Roy were fierce rivals. "Perhaps he showed it to Krista?"

"I doubt it," Wilfred said. "Krista's always so busy with her own plays that she wouldn't have time to look at a different one."

"I wondered if I could ask a favor from you," Anne said. "Could you ask Krista and Collin to call me? I'm curious about the script, and I'm also a little worried if it belonged to someone else and Aunt Edie gave it to Roy."

"We'll just give you their telephone numbers," Blanche said. "Krista won't mind, and I doubt Collin would."

Anne had a suspicion that Blanche didn't want to call Collin or speak to him. "Are you sure? I wouldn't want to impose."

"Oh, they won't be upset," Wilfred said.

"I'll get those numbers for you." Blanche rose and left the room, and Wilfred chatted with Anne about gardening. He had apparently done all the landscaping around the house on his own, and Anne praised the tulips bordering the front walkway.

Blanche returned with a piece of paper and handed it to Anne. "Here you go."

"Thank you so much." Anne rose. "It was wonderful to meet you and talk about Roy and Aunt Edie."

"The pleasure was ours, dear." Blanche walked Anne to their front door.

As Anne drove away, she realized she had learned more about the relationship between Collin and Roy through what Blanche hadn't said as opposed to what she had said. Apparently, Collin and Roy hadn't gotten along very well and may have been in competition with each other. Anne couldn't imagine that Roy would have shown the missing Bettridge script to Collin.

But would he have shown it to his busy sister, the playwright? Krista may have been excited for Roy's good fortune in acquiring the Bettridge script. Or had the two siblings not had a good relationship with each other, and Roy wouldn't have thought to share something like that with Krista?

But if Roy hadn't shown the script to Krista or Collin, then where could the script be? Either it was extremely well hidden somewhere in Aunt Edie's house, or perhaps someone stole it from Roy.

Would Krista or Collin have done something like that?

CHAPTER SIX

On Saturday morning, Anne woke up at seven o'clock to the sound of Ben and Liddie talking in the living room. She padded downstairs to see them both in front of the television, watching cartoons.

"Good morning." She yawned. "Why are you two up so early?"

"It was Liddie," Ben said. "She came into my room."

"I had a dream," Liddie said. "Ben and I were riding pink horses."

Ben made a face but didn't say anything to his sister about the color of his dream-horse.

Liddie continued, "And we had lots of adventures. So I went to his room to tell him about them."

"Did you slay any dragons?" Anne asked.

"No," Liddie said seriously, "but we petted some purple kittens."

"What's for breakfast?" Ben asked.

Anne didn't feel like cooking this early. "How about we get dressed and go to the diner for waffles?"

"Yay!" Liddie jumped to her feet.

Ben and Liddie dressed in record time, and they went to the diner. It was early enough that they got a seat quickly, and the waitress gave Anne a steaming cup of coffee. She sniffed deeply of the aroma before taking her first sip.

They all ordered waffles, and Liddie wanted berries and whipped cream with hers. The waitress gave Ben and Liddie small boxes of crayons, and the two of them started coloring on the paper children's place mats in front of them.

"Hi, Anne!" Tami and her parents had apparently just entered the restaurant and were following the waitress to their table.

Anne greeted them. She didn't often see Mr. Bates at the library, but Tami's mother came in regularly to check out books, mostly novels.

"Looks like you had the same idea we did," Mrs. Bates said. "What did you order?"

"Waffles," Anne said.

"Mine has berries and whipped cream," Liddie spoke up.

"Now, that sounds good," Mr. Bates said, smacking his lips.

"Dad, you need to watch your blood sugar," Tami said.

"What do you mean? There's no sugar in waffles and berries." He had an innocent expression on his face.

"Of course there is," Mrs. Bates said to him.

"No, there isn't," he replied, but there was a lively twinkle in his eye as he turned to his wife. Mr. Bates had always loved to tease his wife and daughters. Once during high school, when Anne had been over at Tami's house, Mr. Bates had insisted that her hair was red that day. Tami had given up in exasperation while Anne had been giggling.

"We'll argue about this at the table." Mrs. Bates rolled her eyes.

"See you," Mr. Bates said as they followed the waitress to a table near the back of the diner.

Tami held back to speak to Anne. "What happened yesterday when you went to the Underwoods' house?"

In a low voice, Anne told her about how Mrs. Underwood's reaction made her think Collin and Roy hadn't been very close to each other, and that there may have been an unknown reason Roy never directed any of his sister's scripts.

"That's great you got their phone numbers," Tami said. "Did you call them?"

"I called them both yesterday afternoon, but I only got Collin's answering machine. I left a message asking him to call me back. And when I called Krista, a woman answered and at first I thought I was speaking to her, but then the woman said that Krista was away at a writing retreat, working on her latest script, and she had no idea when she'd return. I left a message."

"Maybe they'll call you back soon."

"I hope so. After all, I'm a complete stranger to them. I wonder if I ought to have mentioned the note...?"

Tami shook her head. "Like you told me yesterday, you still don't know how your aunt got the script in the first place."

"I know Aunt Edie wouldn't have done anything wrong to get the script, but until I can prove that, I can't even know if the note is really from Aunt Edie or if it's a forgery."

"Let me know if you find anything," Tami said, then went to her table.

"Mommy, look!" Liddie showed her the picture she'd colored, a rabbit with a shock of pink hair on its head and a green tail.

"He's a very handsome rabbit. Why don't you tell me a story about him?"

Breakfast with her children that morning was full of laughter and waffles dripping with gooey maple syrup. They got back to the library in plenty of time for Anne to open at ten o'clock. Anne left Ben and Liddie watching cartoons when she went downstairs.

The library was busy since it was a Saturday and parents liked bringing their children in to look at books. She was still open at fifteen minutes past closing time, checking out a huge stack of books to a harried looking parent with three children milling around her, when Mildred Farley entered the library.

"I'm not here for books." Mildred waved an envelope. "I have something for you, Anne. Go ahead and finish."

Anne checked out the last book and locked the library after the family. Upstairs, she called out, "I'm back."

Mildred poked her head into the living room to say, "Hello, there."

"Hi, Mrs. Farley," Ben and Liddie chorused.

"Come have a cup of coffee." Anne led the way to the kitchen and began preparing a fresh pot.

"How are things going with the Victorian mystery dinner play?" Mildred asked.

"The community theater club is coming to the library in about an hour to start setting things up. They'll be practicing at the library after hours too, since they can't use their theater stage."

"I'm so glad no one was hurt when that roof fell in."

"Me too." If it had fallen a few weeks later, when people would have been on the stage rehearsing, they might have gotten serious injuries. In fact, Ben and Liddie might have been onstage at that point since they had been hoping for small roles in the play. Anne shuddered. "God was watching over everyone, that's for sure."

"He always does," Mildred said. She slid the envelope she was carrying onto the table. "I found that playbill that Edie sent to me."

The envelope had been mailed from England to Mildred in March of 1962. Anne recognized Aunt Edie's handwriting. "Hang on a second." Anne went to get the note Tami had brought to her.

Tami's note was still in the envelope, and Anne set it beside the envelope Mildred brought. Aunt Edie's return address had been written in the top left corner on both envelopes, and the handwriting seemed to match, with slight imperfections. "It looks the same, but a good forger might have gotten a different envelope Aunt Edie had sent to someone else to copy her handwriting. It's hard to believe someone would go through so much work to pretend to be Aunt Edie."

"If the note wasn't forged, then you're still left with the question of how Edie acquired that script. There's a letter in the envelope that Edie wrote to me, but I'm afraid it doesn't give much information."

Anne pulled out a letter and a playbill for a play titled, *Practice to Deceive*. The director was Quentin Chandler. At the time the letter was written, Roy would have been too young to have met Edie in London. The scriptwriter was someone named Montgomery Penn, not Hugh Bettridge. The playbill listed all the theater staff on the back, and there as director's assistant was Edie Summers.

"How did Aunt Edie get a job as a director's assistant?" Anne asked.

"I think she told me in another letter she sent a few weeks before this one. I looked for it, but I'm afraid I couldn't find it. If I remember correctly, Edie was visiting a travel writer friend living in England. That travel writer was friends with the original director's assistant, who had some emergency. Since Edie was free for a few weeks, her travel writer friend introduced her to the director and she was hired to fill in."

"It sounds exactly like something interesting that would appeal to Aunt Edie."

"She loved it and hated it. Read the letter and see what I mean."

Anne unfolded the letter and read:

Dear Mildred,

The play is in full swing and they tell me they expect it to have a run of about six weeks. Being a director's assistant is certainly different from what I had imagined it to be. While it's exciting to see what goes on behind the scenes, it can also be difficult dealing with people as tempers rise and things get emotional. And actors can be very intense, let me assure you! Quentin has had to juggle the demands from his producers with some forceful suggestions from the actors and rather acidic comments from Montgomery, the playwright.

But there is something wonderful that happens when the curtain goes up. There is an emotional energy on stage and in the audience that is mesmerizing. I wish you could be here to experience it. Or maybe it feels more exciting to me since I've been here as all parts of the play have come together, and it's amazing and satisfying to see the final production.

I've met so many new people here in London. Quentin often takes me to parties he's invited to. I mentioned in my last letter about meeting Billy. He has been so nice about introducing me to people he thinks I would like. That's how I met Prudence MacTavish a couple weeks ago. You would love her—she's feisty and always says what she thinks.

I saw Raymond McConnell again two nights ago. He attended the performance and came to the Green Room afterward. He looks more and more like a pirate every time I see him. I half expect him to brandish a sword and declare liberty for all Scotland or something like that. His accent is really very charming, but he continues to shamelessly flirt with me. Billy rescued me from Raymond, which I think made Raymond jealous. He doesn't know that Billy's grief over his wife, Miriam, is still too fresh for him to think of any woman, and you know I could never give my heart again. But I don't think I will enlighten Raymond, because otherwise he might be more persistent.

Well, that is all the gossip from London. Be sure to write more about what is happening in Blue Hill.

Love, Edie

Aunt Edie's breezy tone in the letter made Anne feel a pang as she missed her aunt afresh. How Aunt Edie would have loved being a part of the Victorian mystery dinner play here at the library.

"There's nothing about Hugh Bettridge," Anne said, "but she might have met him at these parties she wrote about."

"I don't know very much about him."

"I ordered a biography of Bettridge through interlibrary loan, and it should be here this coming week."

"I had better go." Mildred rose to her feet. "I only stopped by to give that to you. I promised Helen Smith I'd bake two cakes for the next women's sewing group, which meets tomorrow morning. I'll see you later, Anne."

Anne went to check on Ben and Liddie only to find them both asleep on the couch in front of the television. She turned it off and snuck out, content to let them rest. They'd be full of energy when the community theater club arrived in half an hour.

While Anne was waiting for that Bettridge biography to arrive, she could do a little more Internet research on the family. Anne had been meaning to look online for Bettridge's daughter but had forgotten.

She went downstairs to use the computer, and a quick search showed the Web site for the Bettridge Sallman theatrical literary agency. The Web site had information about Lynne's agency, submission instructions, and some writing resources for aspiring playwrights. It also listed the plays that Lynne had sold for her clients, and Anne recognized the title of one of them, *The Mandarin of Mayfair*, because it was such an unusual title. Where had she seen that before?

In an instant, she knew. She opened a new browser window and found a Web site she'd looked at before when researching Roy Underwood which listed all the plays he had directed, and *The Mandarin of Mayfair* was one of them.

So Lynne Sallman had sold a play that was directed by Roy. Anne realized she shouldn't be surprised, because Lynne was a literary agent and Roy was a director. Decisions such as which play to buy and which director to hire were probably determined by producers. A quick scan of Lynne's list against Roy's list showed that there were at least two other plays that Lynne had sold for her clients which Roy had directed.

Anne read Lynne's biography carefully, but there was nothing about Hugh Bettridge except for a brief mention that the famous playwright was her father. She had worked in the theater as a production assistant, then production manager for a few years before becoming a theatrical literary agent, which she had done ever since. It listed the agencies she had worked for before she started her own literary agency.

Anne found a phone number, which she called. It went immediately to an answering service, and Anne guessed it was screened so that only the most important calls were forwarded to Lynne. At the beep, Anne left a message. "Hello, my name is Anne Gibson, and I'm the librarian at Blue Hill Library. I was hoping I could speak to you about your father. He might have known my aunt Edie." Anne paused, at a loss as to what she could say. She didn't want to mention the missing script because of what Flores had said about Lynne's insistence that it had been stolen from her father. "If you could please give me a call back, I would love to chat with you. I won't take up too much of your time. Thanks." Anne gave the number of the library and hung up.

She had the sinking feeling that the message she had left sounded a bit idiotic, but she didn't want to call back and leave another one.

She looked around Lynne's Web site and found a list of clients, with links to their Web sites if they had one. Anne clicked through and studied each client's Web site. She found that most of them mentioned in their bios that they lived in England, which made sense since Lynne's agency was based there. However, Anne clicked through to the Web site of Phoebe Ramsey, and in reading the bio, she was surprised to find the writer lived near Harrisburg, which was only about ninety minutes away from Blue Hill.

The writer had a contact page, and Anne clicked on it to leave her a message.

Dear Ms. Ramsey,

My name is Anne Gibson, and I am the librarian at Blue Hill Library, which is not far from Harrisburg. I was wondering if you had time to meet with me for coffee. I hoped to speak with you and ask a few questions about your agent, Lynne Sallman.

Anne left the contact information at the library and her e-mail address, and hit the Send button. She wasn't entirely sure what information she could glean from one of Lynne's clients, but unless Lynne called her back, Anne thought there was no harm in it. Being Lynne's client and a playwright in the theatrical world, Phoebe might know something about Lynne's father and the missing play that she felt comfortable sharing with Anne.

At that moment, there was a knock at the front door to the library. Anne glanced at the clock and realized it was a little before two o'clock. That must be the community theater club.

She hurried to open the door and saw Alex Ochs standing there with his toolbox.

"Hi, Anne." Alex stepped inside. "I'm here to measure the History Room for the sets for the play."

"I should have known you'd be building the sets. Will there be many of them?"

"The play they chose was written so that it's only got a set for each act. So three sets, I guess?"

"Stephan measured out this area." Anne sketched it vaguely. "But I'm not entirely sure what he wants, so I suppose you should wait for him to get here."

"It shouldn't be long. He texted me to tell me he might be a little late."

"Is Ryan going to be in the play too? Stephan said that Ben and Liddie have small parts."

"Yes, there's apparently a scene involving a few children, so Ryan's one of them." Alex grinned. "He pretends it's not a big deal, but I can tell he's excited about it."

"Ben isn't even trying to pretend it's not something he's looking forward to."

"Are you going to be in the play?" Alex asked.

"Are you kidding? I'm about as likely to act in the play as you are."

However, she was surprised to see a rosy flush rise to Alex's cheeks.

"Don't tell me you're in the play," she said.

He shrugged. "Okay, if you want me to lie to you." He had a mischievous twinkle in his eye.

"I can't believe it. You complained *every* year when the youth group had to do a skit for the Christmas and Easter programs at church."

Alex scratched the back of his head. "Well, I didn't intend to, but when I went to the theater to put a tarp over the hole in the roof, Stephan was there and he...well...I'm not sure exactly how it happened, but suddenly I was agreeing to take the part of the gypsy suspect."

Anne burst into laughter. "That man could sell ice to Eskimos. He tried to get me to take a part too, and I had a hard time saying no, even though I know I'm too busy here at the library."

"Are you really that busy? And after all, Ben and Liddie are in the play so you'll need to be around for at least part of the time."

"Well, I have something of Aunt Edie's that I'm looking for."

"Oh?"

"An old script. I just found out from Mildred that Aunt Edie worked as a theater director's assistant in London for a few weeks many years ago."

At that moment, the front door opened and the sound of several feet echoed through the doorway. "Hello?" It was Wendy's cheerful voice.

"In here," Anne called. She gave Alex a teasing look, then added, "With your mysterious gypsy suspect."

Alex only grinned. "You just wait, Anne. Stephan will get you to take a part in the play yet."

CHAPTER SEVEN

S unday morning dawned cool and wet, so Anne bundled the kids up warmly before driving to church.

Reverend Tom greeted them as they entered the church. "Good morning."

Anne returned his greeting warmly as she noticed that even with the gray clouds outside, the light shone through the narrow stained glass windows on both sides of the sanctuary, casting cheerful colors on the rows of pews.

"Hi, Reverend Tom," Ben and Liddie said at the same time. Liddie's voice was a little muffled because she had burrowed her mouth down into her rain coat.

"By the way, Anne, I'm enjoying the Victorian cozy mystery novel I checked out on Monday. The characters are very entertaining." He chuckled. "It's been a long time since I've laughed so much while reading a book."

"I'm so glad you enjoy that series."

"I heard about the Victorian mystery dinner play. It sounds as though it'll be fun for all involved."

Anne nodded to Ben and Liddie. "These two even have small parts in it."

"We're puppies begging for treats!" Liddie said.

Reverend Tom looked confused. Anne laughed, but it was Ben who said, "Paupers, not puppies. Poor, homeless kids, Liddie."

"Oh." Liddie's face fell. "I wanted to be a puppy."

"You can be my puppy," Ben offered. "You'll be a pauper's puppy." That made the two of them giggle.

"We'll see you later, Reverend." Anne ushered her family down the aisle. She spotted Alex and Ryan already seated in a pew. "Hi there."

"Hi. Have a seat," Alex said as he and and Ryan scooted down.

"Look, Ben." Ryan flourished the newsboy-style cap he was wearing. "Uncle Alex found this in his closet for me. He says I can wear it for the play."

"Hey, Mom, can I wear that black hat?" Ben asked Anne.

"The top hat on the library display? I thought you said it itches."

Ben tilted his head. "I guess it doesn't itch *that* much."

Anne and Alex exchanged amused glances over the tops of the kids' heads.

"I'll find you a great pauper's hat," Anne promised. "There are lots of things in the attic."

Then the music started, signaling the service would begin, and they all fell silent.

For the service, they sang the hymn "Trust and Obey." Liddie especially loved this hymn. She didn't always sing the verses correctly, but she never failed to belt out the chorus with enthusiasm.

Reverend Tom called the children up to the front for the children's message. This morning's message was about trusting God.

Reverend Tom asked the children, "You trust your parents to take care of you, right?"

Little heads nodded solemnly.

"Well, when difficult things happen, and you get scared or worried, Jesus wants you to trust Him to take care of you just like you trust your parents to take care of you. How many of you worry about things?"

Several hands shot up into the air.

"It doesn't matter if you're worried about something little or silly or embarrassing. Jesus doesn't want you to worry. He wants you to trust Him to take care of things for you. You believe Jesus can take care of you, right?"

"Uh-huh," several of the children said.

"So when you start to get worried or scared, stop and pray to Jesus: 'Jesus, please help me to remember that You're taking care of me, no matter what.'"

Reverend Tom dismissed the children to junior church, and they hurried to their Sunday school rooms for an activity and Bible lesson during the rest of the service.

The theme of Reverend Tom's message was also trusting in God in all circumstances. Anne could remember how helpless she had felt after Eric died, and how some days, the only thing she could trust in was God's love for her. She was so grateful for how God had given her a new start here in Blue Hill and the many new friends she'd made.

After the service, they all stayed for cookies and coffee in the fellowship hall. Anne was excited to see that Wendy had made Oreo truffles. While Wendy had given her the recipe, the chocolaty truffles were so delicious that Anne couldn't limit herself to only one or two when she made them. She helped Liddie choose her cookies from the heavily laden table, then snagged an Oreo truffle onto a napkin for herself.

Even though her kids had just come from junior church, they went off to talk and eat with their friends from their classes as if they hadn't seen them in a year. Anne wandered to where her old schoolmates, Jennifer and Michael Banks, were chatting with another schoolmate, Heather Stafford and her husband, Mark.

"Have you said hi to Tami yet?" Anne asked them.

"For all of two seconds," Jennifer said with a grin. She nodded toward where Tami was surrounded by people chatting with her. "Everyone's eager to talk to her now that she's back in town for a few weeks. It's been almost two years since she last came back to Blue Hill."

"Well, tickets from London are expensive," Heather said. "I'd like to travel to London sometime to visit her, though. Musicals in the West End and operas at the Royal Opera House!"

Anne smiled. She could have predicted that Heather would be enthralled most by the prospect of shows and concerts, since she was a high school music teacher.

"And Charles Dickens's house, and the Jack the Ripper walking tour, and Sherlock Holmes's 221b Baker Street house," Jennifer added.

"Speaking of which, when are tickets going on sale for the Victorian mystery dinner play?" Michael asked. "Jen and I want to go."

"Us too," Mark said, putting an arm around Heather.

"Soon," Anne said. "The theater club is in charge of ticket sales."

A cry from across the fellowship hall by Jennifer's youngest, Mia, sent the concerned parents off to make sure she was okay.

"I'd better get my two and head home," Anne said. "We still have some cleaning up to do before the theater club comes this afternoon for rehearsal."

As Anne headed toward the door, she passed Mildred, who was talking to Mr. Willet, a church deacon. He reached a hand out to Anne, causing her to stop.

"That new fiction display you have has been great," he told her. "I haven't read Wilkie Collins in years. It was such a nice surprise to see *The Woman in White* and to read it again."

"I'm glad you like the display," Anne said. "It was a joy to find books for it. Many of them were like old friends I hadn't seen in a while, and I also found a few new authors who write in the genre."

"I saw that," Mr. Willet said. "I'm hoping to go back to the library this week when I'm done with *The Woman in White* so that I can look at some of the others on the table."

The rain had stopped, although the sky was still dark with low-hanging clouds and the air felt cool and heavy. As Anne got to their car, she saw that Tami's parents had parked next to her and Tami herself was rummaging around on the backseat. She emerged with her cell phone. "Found it! Oh, hi, Anne."

"Left your phone in the car?"

Tami nodded. "Which might have been a good thing, because I forgot to put the ringer to silent. Did Krista or Collin call you back?"

Anne shook her head. "I also called Bettridge's daughter yesterday and left a message, but I don't know if she'll call me back. I still don't know if my aunt knew her father or not."

"Mom?" Ben had already buckled himself into his seat and helped Liddie with her seat belt.

"I'm sorry, I didn't mean to keep you," Tami said. "I'll see you this afternoon."

"I should have guessed you'd be helping with the dinner play."

Tami rolled her eyes and gave a mock groan. "Blame Stephan. I can never say no to the guy. If he'd been in charge of the community theater club when we were in high school, I'd have been roped into it and known right away that I loved theater."

Tami waved to them as Anne drove away. But as she pulled out of the church parking lot, she happened to look at a gray car parked near the driveway. There was a man sitting in the car, but it wasn't a church member Anne recognized. He was dark haired, and he sat low in the driver's seat of his car, as if he were slouching or perhaps because he was a bit short. It seemed to Anne that he had just turned his head away from looking at her.

A chill passed through Anne as she saw him. Had he been looking at her? Why? He also matched the description of the man Tami had said might have been following her. Why was he sitting in a parked car in the church parking lot?

Anne shook her head. Surely her imagination was just going overboard. After all, why would anyone be interested in her?

* * *

Anne and Wendy stood at the back of the History Room with Ben, Liddie, Ryan, and two of Wendy's children, Emily and Justin, as the theater club director, Stephan Ullrick, stood at the other end of the room and said grandly, "My friends, for the next few weeks, this will be your theater." He gestured around the History Room, with its dark furniture and elegant rug.

A spattering of applause erupted from the sixteen adults in the room.

"We have Anne Gibson to thank for offering this wonderful setting." Stephan swept a hand in Anne's direction. "Let's be sure to be respectful of the building."

"At least this roof won't fall in on us," said a young woman with a saucy smile. A few people laughed at her joke. Anne saw that it was Shelby Truman, who was the secretary at Blue Hill High School. Anne had gone to school with her sister Nancy.

"Let's hope this dinner play will raise enough funds for us to repair our poor theater," Stephan said. "Alex Ochs has generously offered to fix the roof without charging us for his time and strenuous labor."

There was another round of applause. Alex, who was standing near Ryan, smiled at the faces around the room, but his cheeks flushed pink with embarrassment.

Stephan then introduced Tami, who started talking about ticket sales. Anne leaned closer to Alex and whispered, "How much will it cost for materials for the roof?"

Alex sighed and gave an amount Anne had not expected. He said, "The materials are going to cost more than I originally thought."

Anne calculated how many people would fit into the History Room for the dinner play and how much the theater club was going to charge per person. "I don't know if the dinner play will make enough money," she said.

"What?" Wendy whispered to her, and Anne repeated her exchange with Alex.

Wendy frowned thoughtfully as she looked around the History Room just as Anne had done, but then she craned her neck and peered through the doorway into the Nonfiction Room next door. The doorway wasn't very wide.

"I don't think we could put dinner guests in the Nonfiction Room," Anne whispered to Wendy. "They wouldn't be able to see the play."

"I wasn't thinking about dinner guests," Wendy said. "I was thinking that we could use this space for something else to help raise money for the theater club."

"Like what?"

"I'm not sure." Wendy suddenly grinned. "My first thought was a bake sale so that dinner guests could buy some treats before they went home that night, but I doubt a few cakes would raise enough money."

Stephan now started talking about the sets that were planned and how the play would work out on the area designated as the stage. His descriptions and the way he moved around the area made Anne start to see what the sets would be like, and the haunting atmosphere of the mystery dinner play. She had a feeling it would be like being in a Sherlock Holmes mystery, and the idea excited her.

She remembered what Aunt Edie had written about the energy and excitement of a play, and now Anne could understand what she meant. This play would be different from any of the Christmas plays she'd participated in while growing up, which were usually humorous or a solemn retelling of the Christmas story. In contrast, this play would involve the elaborate backdrop and costumes to make the setting seem real, to create the mysterious, fog-shrouded streets of London where the game was afoot. Anne was looking forward to seeing the finished production.

Wendy had caught the excitement too. "This is going to be so much fun!" she whispered to Anne.

Liddie had been having a hard time standing quietly because the "grown-up talk" was obviously rather boring for her, but she was making a valiant effort. She turned to Anne and said in a voice a little louder than a whisper, "I wish you were in the play too, Mommy. Then you and me can be in the play together."

Wendy gave Anne a pointed look. "Yes, why aren't you in the play?"

"I can't act—"

"Oh, we're just a community theater club. We're not professionals," Wendy said. "I think you'd have fun."

Tami now took center stage to address the issue of costumes. "Because Victorian dresses were very elaborate, we're limited in what costumes we have available. Some have been donated for the production by community members, and a handful of the rest of you have some squirreled away. We have just enough for all our women actors, but you may not have a choice on dresses. Extensive alterations on Victorian style dresses would be as expensive as alterations on a wedding gown—many of you ladies remember the cost of altering your own wedding gowns, right?" Tami grinned as several woman nodded vigorously. "So we'll have to give you whatever dress we have that fits you best."

Stephan ended the meeting with information on auditions. "I've worked with pretty much all of you before, so auditions will be casual. If you want a part, let me know. If more than one of you want a part, we'll have a reading and I'll make the final decision. Flores Sanchez did a great job picking the play." Stephan nodded to Flores, who smiled back. "Besides the pauper children, there are only twelve adult parts, which fits the size of the stage perfectly."

Stephan then passed out copies of the play to everyone to look over. Rehearsals were to start tomorrow night, with the exception of the pauper children, since their roles were small.

The five pauper children—Ben, Liddie, Ryan, Emily, and Justin—had gotten antsy by the end of the meeting, and the five of them went upstairs to the living quarters to entertain themselves. The adults mingled, chatting about the play and what parts they might want to play. Alex went to talk to Stephan about the sets, while Anne and Wendy headed over to Tami.

"Having fun?" Anne asked.

Tami shrugged, but there was also a smile on her face. "It's a little different from my other job, since there are usually people already in charge of costumes and tickets and things. But I've never done a dinner play, so this'll be interesting."

"I've never done a dinner like this either," Wendy said. "I've been talking to local farmers and grocers about donating the ingredients, and I'm planning the menu so I can do the majority of the prep and cooking in the day or two before the dinner."

"I can't imagine coordinating something like that," Anne said to her.

"I love it," Wendy said. "Besides, with seven kids, I have to be organized or the house would explode. Organizing this dinner isn't too different from planning Thanksgiving or Christmas dinner for our extended family."

Stephan came up to the three of them and smiled warmly at Anne. "Thank you again for allowing us to use your library this way."

"It's not a problem, I assure you. It looks like it's going to be a lot of fun, not just for the diners, but also for the actors and crew."

Stephan gave Anne a winning smile. "Are you certain you don't want to take a small part? It seems wrong for us to be using your home and for you not to have a small part in the production. I would truly enjoy having you join us."

After seeing the excitement of the theater club and the picture painted by Stephan's description of the production, Anne could see the allure of being part of the play. "I thought you already have enough actors."

"Flores has told me several times that she prefers working backstage rather than acting. She's in this production only because of the number of female roles required by the script."

Anne wasn't an extrovert, but the idea of dressing up, playing a part, and interacting with friends in her community — she knew many of the theater club members already — appealed to a sociable side of her. But... her library duties and the mystery of Aunt Edie's script were taking up a lot of her time. "No, I'm afraid I don't have time."

"Not even a small part?" Tami said. "I've read the script, and it's a really cute play."

Anne hesitated, but then shook her head. "Sorry."

"Well, if you change your mind, don't hesitate to call me." Stephan saw Alex waving to him from where he was with a few other crew members. "I think Alex needs to ask a question about sets. I'll see you ladies later." He wandered toward the group.

Tami eyed Alex. "He still looks as handsome as when he was in high school."

"Stephan?" Anne said, deliberately misunderstanding her.

Tami elbowed her friend. "You know who I'm talking about."

"Don't let your husband hear you saying that about Alex," Anne said with a smile.

"Oh, I wasn't thinking of Alex for *myself*…" Tami winked at Wendy, and the two of them gave little giggles as if they were both in high school again.

At that moment, Anne was rescued from further teasing by Shelby Truman hurrying up to them. "Tami, Stephan asked me to tell you that Mildred Farley found an extra dress, so you don't need to have your husband bring over your dress when he comes to Blue Hill."

"Good." Tami grinned. "He's got the job of bringing over presents for my family, so he's already pretty weighed down."

Wendy explained to Anne, "We thought we were short one costume, and Tami has an extra costume she was going to lend to us, but then Mildred found a second dress in her attic."

"I'm actually wearing the dress you donated, Anne," Shelby said to her.

"In fact, it should fit without needing alterations," Tami said.

"Well, I'll see you all later," Shelby said.

"You're leaving already?" Anne asked.

"I belong to a women's soccer recreational league, and we have a game this afternoon. Most of the rehearsals are at night, so it's only today that I had a conflict." After calling out a general good-bye to the room at large, Shelby left the library.

"Your own costume? Did you act in a Victorian play?" Anne asked Tami.

"No, I bought this one from another estate auction," Tami said. "The auction was similar to the one Roy Underwood had for his estate, but the items weren't as expensive as Roy's collection."

"That's it!" Wendy suddenly said. Her blue eyes blazed like twin gas flames. "That's how we can raise enough money for the roof repairs. It was right in front of me the entire time."

"What do you mean?" Anne asked.

"We'll hold a silent auction in the Nonfiction Room." Wendy pointed through the open doorway into the other room. "We can put the items up a few days before the dinner play, and anyone can bid, including the people who come for the dinner play. We'll close the auction the day after the play, to give people a chance for last-minute bidding."

"Do you think people will donate items?" Anne asked.

"I'll ask around. Lots of businesses like offering stuff for silent auctions because it doesn't usually cost them too much and it's good advertising for their businesses. Plus, there are items for all price ranges, including some more expensive packages."

"That's a great idea," Tami said. "I wonder if I have anything that people would want to bid on?"

"You don't have any Shakespeare folios lying around, do you?" Anne winked.

Wendy leaned in to ask in a low voice, "Speaking of plays, did you find your aunt's script?"

Anne shook her head. "I'm not sure where it could be. It wasn't with Aunt Edie's papers or in her desk, and even though I'm looking through boxes in the attic when I have time, I have a hard time believing she'd hide the script at the bottom of a clothes box."

"Maybe she would," Tami said. "We keep our important papers in an envelope taped under the dresser in the bedroom, since we were renting our other apartment and in our new house, we haven't gotten a safe yet. Would your aunt put her important papers somewhere out of the way?"

"She might, but I'm not convinced she'd put the script somewhere like that." Anne dug in her pocket. "I went to her safe deposit box but didn't find anything that might point to the script except these keys." She showed them the key ring. "I figured out where three of the keys go, but I searched the entire house and can't find the lock for the fourth key."

"This looks like the key to a door, as opposed to a lockbox or something like that," Wendy said. "It might not have anything to do with the missing script."

"The more I search, the more I worry that Roy managed to fly back here to pick up the script sometime before he died," Anne said.

"But then who would have it?" Wendy said. "That note said the script was special to your aunt. Roy wouldn't just give it to someone, would he?"

Tami shook her head. "Because he knew how important the script was to Edie, I don't think he would. I got to know him a little through the overseas study program he sponsored and also the theater world. If someone else has the script, I think they took it from him. Did you hear back from anyone, yet?" she asked Anne.

"I called Roy's cousin, Collin, who's a director in New York City, and also Roy's sister, Krista, who's a playwright," Anne explained to Wendy. "I left messages, but neither of them have contacted me. They might never call me back—they don't know who I am."

"Do you think one of them stole Edie's script from Roy?" Wendy said.

"I don't know anything about either of them, but the script might be a boost to their careers. I want to find out more about them, to see if they would have a reason to steal the script."

"After talking to you yesterday, I remembered something about Collin that Roy had mentioned to me once," Tami said. "I had forgotten about it since it wasn't very important. Roy said that he and Collin attended the same high school. They were in drama club together."

"I didn't know that," Anne said. "I don't remember reading anything about Collin's high school in the bios I've read about him online." Some of Anne's high school friends remained in Blue Hill, so perhaps some of Collin's friends still lived in Deshler and might be willing to chat about him. It could be that Collin didn't care for the style of Bettridge's plays at all and would never want to direct one of them, or maybe he was a huge fan of the playwright and would have even greater motive for wanting to possess a play that Roy had gotten his hands on.

And the easiest way to look into Collin's old school friends would be his high school yearbooks. The Deshler High School would have copies she could look through.

Tami said, "Yes, Collin's not as famous a director as Roy was, so I would expect his biographies to be a little sparse. But he's been in the theater industry for decades."

"I've only looked at his online biographies, but I wonder about old newspaper articles and reviews that aren't available online?" Anne mused. "I could go to Deshler to look at their newspaper archives and maybe find out more about the early years of his career. I could look up Krista's career too, since her most famous play was twenty years ago."

From what Blanche Underwood had said and not said about Collin, Anne suspected some rivalry between the two directors. Was Collin jealous of his more successful cousin? Would Krista, whose career seemed to be currently flagging, also be jealous of her brother's success? Was it possible family rivalry was behind Aunt Edie's missing script?

CHAPTER EIGHT

Monday dawned just as cloudy as the day before, but there was no rain forecasted so Anne gave in to Liddie's pleas to wear a pink hoodie rather than a heavier jacket to school. Ben had just finished taking Hershey out and was starting on his breakfast when the phone rang.

"Hello?" Anne answered the phone.

"Hi, Anne, it's Alex. I'm sorry this is so last minute, but could you pick up Ryan from school today and keep him at the library with Ben?"

"Sure, no problem."

"Thanks." Alex blew out a breath of relief. "I got a call from the job site, and there's a problem. It'll take me longer than expected."

"Ryan is always welcome at our house."

At hearing his friend's name, Ben looked up from his oatmeal.

"I'll pick him up after I get off work," Alex said, then added, "But it may be a little later than usual."

"Why don't you stay for dinner? I was going to roast a chicken."

"Are you sure?"

"Of course. If you're working late today, you probably won't have time to cook."

"Thanks. I'll bring over dessert."

"That's an offer I can't refuse."

After they had hung up, Ben asked, "Ryan's coming over?" At Anne's nod, he gave a quick "Woo-hoo!" then went back to his breakfast.

"I wish Ryan could come over all the time," Liddie said through a mouthful of oatmeal.

"Don't talk with your mouth full," Anne reminded her gently.

Liddie swallowed. "Mommy, you should marry Mr. Ochs."

Anne choked on her oatmeal. She managed to say in a calm voice, "What makes you say that, sweetie?"

"Then Ryan could be here all the time," Liddie said. "I like Ryan."

"There's more to marriage than living together."

"Yeah, Liddie," Ben said. Anne could tell that he wasn't sure how he felt about the thought of Anne marrying anyone else, let alone Alex.

It seemed like it was only a short while ago when the thought would have horrified Anne. However, now, while the idea was awkward and strange, it didn't cause grief to well up in her.

Still, it wasn't something she wanted to think about. "Hurry up, or you'll be late for school."

She dropped the kids off at school and when she got back to the library, she sat at the kitchen table with her Bible and a cup of coffee.

The passage she read was Matthew 6:28–34: *"And why do you worry about clothes? See how the lilies of the field grow. They do not labor or spin. Yet I tell you that not even Solomon in all his splendor was dressed like one of these. If that is how God clothes the grass of the field, which is here today and tomorrow is thrown into the fire, will he not much more clothe you — you of little faith? So do not worry, saying, 'What shall we eat?' or 'What shall we drink?' or 'What shall we wear?' For the pagans run after all these things, and your heavenly Father knows that you need them. But seek first his kingdom and his righteousness, and all these things will be given to you as well. Therefore do not worry about tomorrow, for tomorrow will worry about itself. Each day has enough trouble of its own."*

There had been a gnawing worry in the pit of her stomach ever since she read that note that Tami found. Did Aunt Edie write it or was it a forgery? How did Aunt Edie acquire this famous script? Did Roy get the script from Aunt Edie before he died? If he did, who had it now? Would Collin or Krista try to profit from it? Would Lynne insist Aunt Edie had stolen it?

She wanted answers, but she hadn't prayed about the things worrying her. So she bowed her head.

Lord, thank You for reminding me that if You want me to know these answers, You will help me to find them. Help me not to worry about this script business, but to seek You first in everything I do. In Jesus' name, Amen.

Remi and Bella Miller arrived just before the library opened, breezing in with the scent of grass still damp from the rain yesterday. "Hi, girls," Anne said as she let them inside. "I'm glad you're here early. I need to head to Deshler this morning for a couple hours."

"No problem, Mrs. Gibson," Remi said.

Anne left them some tasks to get done, then drove to the Deshler Public Library. As she turned off Main Street, she immediately saw the two-story gray building. She had no problems finding a spot in the half-full parking lot.

When she entered the glass door to the library, she immediately looked to the checkout counter but didn't see the library director, Kim Olivett. Instead, one of the other librarian staff was there checking in books.

Anne knew where the newspaper archives were, thanks to the tour Kim had given to her when she visited the Deshler library after first arriving in Blue Hill. Hopefully, she could find Kim later and ask if the library had copies of the Deshler High School yearbooks.

The Deshler Public Library had microfiche archive copies of the major New York newspapers in their reference area, which was a room near the front counter. Anne headed inside and straight to the shelves with the microfiche reels stored in binders.

She pulled from her purse a printout of a list of Krista's plays. She started with the *New York Times* and pulled out the binder for the year Krista's most famous play was released.

It wasn't hard to find the review of the play after opening night. The newspaper critic was effusive in his praise, describing *Time's Fool* as "a clever farce that uses melodrama like a top restaurant chef wields his knife, cutting deep into the heart and evoking a wide range of emotions."

Anne found some articles about *Time's Fool* a few months after it opened, with news about awards it was nominated for or tidbits about the production. The information wasn't particularly useful, so she pulled out the microfiche to grab another one.

She found the reel for the month of Krista's next play on the list. The reviewer opened with backstory on how good Krista's previous play had been, but said her next play failed to live up to expectations. He seemed to almost take delight in shredding the play to pieces. Anne winced as she read and thought of how Krista must have felt as she read such a horrible review. It was only one person's opinion, but the play hadn't had a long run, so apparently it hadn't appealed to audiences as much as her previous one.

Anne continued down her list, reading the newspaper reviews for each of Krista's plays. Some plays received slightly better reviews than others, but none of the reviews were as enthusiastic as for *Time's Fool,* and the other plays had significantly shorter runs. The critics repeatedly mentioned how the humor in her later plays failed to entertain because the characters were unsympathetic, selfish, or bitter.

The reviewer for the third play that Krista wrote after *Time's Fool* said, "After the disappointing reception of Ms. Bennett's last three plays, it might be supposed that perhaps a career change is imminent. Rumor has it that in the next episode of the TV program *Behind the Curtain,* which will air two weeks from now, Ms. Bennett will be interviewed and will discuss her thoughts on producing plays as opposed to writing them."

Hopefully the interview would reveal more about Krista than these reviews did. Had Krista been planning to produce plays? Would she want to produce the Bettridge play as a boost to her career? Did she produce any plays in the past several years? Anne hadn't thought to search for that information online. She wrote down the title and the approximate date the TV episode might have aired.

Anne didn't need to search the microfiche for the reviews in the past few years because she had been able to find the articles online. She put the microfiche binder back on the shelf.

Anne went out to the front counter again and saw the library director, Kim Olivett, behind the desk and speaking to a patron. Anne waited patiently until Kim was done and the patron had left the library.

Kim smiled at Anne. "Hi, Anne, how's the Blue Hill Library doing?" Today, she wore her salt-and-pepper ringlets swept back from her face and secured in a brown horn clip.

"We're doing great. I just put up a Victorian mystery novels display this month that seems to be a big hit."

"We did something similar a few years ago. It was fun looking up Victorian authors and novels set in Victorian times."

"I was surprised at how many modern authors write Victorian mysteries."

They discussed authors for a few minutes and then Kim asked, "So what brings you into the Deshler library today?"

"I was looking at the newspaper microfiche archives. I wanted to read some reviews of a play that ran in New York City about twenty years ago. *Time's Fool* by Krista Underwood Bennett. I believe she grew up in Deshler."

"Yes, I've met her. She was in town visiting her parents one summer when the library hosted a playwriting class, and she agreed to come and speak for one session. It was very popular."

"How about her cousin Collin? Has he ever spoken here?"

"Yes, we've asked Collin Avery to come and speak, but he's always been too busy. His mother's a regular here at the library, and she said that whenever he visits, it's always a quick trip because he has to get back to New York for work. Krista's brother, Roy, was also a director in London, but he died a year ago."

"Do you happen to have the old Deshler High School yearbooks? I'd love to look up the three of them."

"Sure." Kim came out from behind the desk. "Some of our copies are the only ones left because of a basement leak at the high school that damaged their copies, so I moved the yearbooks to our archive room."

Kim headed upstairs to a small, temperature-controlled room that held some of their oldest books and even some original town documents from the founding of Deshler. She opened the door with her key and headed straight to the far wall, where a bookshelf held rows of yearbooks stacked neatly by year.

"Here you go," Kim said. "When you're done, just head out the door — it should lock behind you."

"Thanks."

After Kim had left, Anne looked at her notes. She was able to guess at the years that Roy, Krista, and Collin had been in high school and pick out the yearbooks for their senior years. She knew, from working on her own high school yearbooks, that more of the pages were given to the seniors and showing their hobbies and interests. There was a small table in the center of the room, and she set the yearbooks down and sat in a wooden chair.

She picked up the oldest yearbook, which was for Roy's senior year, and flipped through the pages. She found Roy in various photos in the clubs he had participated in—drama, naturally, as well as the speech team, where he'd done dramatic interpretation as opposed to debate. He had also been in the National Honor Society and on the track team. Anne noted the names of his fellow classmates in each of these clubs, and she also took the time to look up the people in candid photos of Roy with other schoolmates, although she couldn't always figure out people's faces in the candids. She was a bit overwhelmed at how many people Roy knew. He never seemed to be in a photo with the same person twice.

She saw Collin's freshman photo and also one candid photo of Collin and two classmates at a drama team event. She looked them up, and they turned out to be Gwendolyn Ross and Auggie Falcon. Anne wrote their names down also.

Next was Collin's senior yearbook, and she again saw Gwendolyn and Auggie in the photo of Collin with the drama team. What's more, she saw a photo of Collin at homecoming standing next to Auggie, and a photo of the spring drama production with Gwendolyn. Collin only participated in drama team, so he didn't have as many photos in the yearbook as Roy.

In Collin's yearbook, Anne spotted Krista as a sophomore in the drama team photo. Krista had also been in the young writers club and on the golf team. Anne jotted down the names of her teammates and friends in the photos in the yearbook.

In Krista's senior yearbook, Krista was in the same three clubs, as well as the art and photography club and the French club. Krista seemed rather popular, although not quite as popular as Roy.

Anne noted most of the names of the people in the candid photos she found of Krista, as well as her classmates in her clubs.

When Anne finished, she sat back and rubbed her eyes. She felt as if she had been squinting at grainy black-and-white photos for hours. Then she checked her watch. Apparently she had. She needed to get back to pick up Ben and Liddie from school.

She put the yearbooks back in their proper places and then left the archive room. She stopped by the checkout desk to thank Kim and say good-bye.

The librarian looked up from her computer. "Did you find what you needed?"

"Yes, thanks."

"Let me know how your Victorian mysteries display turns out."

"Sure thing." Anne waved good-bye and left through the front door.

She got back into her car and swept her eye over her notepad before putting it away. Anne was a bit dismayed by the size of the lists she had compiled, but she hoped a few of these people still lived in the area and wouldn't mind chatting about Collin and Krista. It would make it easier for her if both of them hated Bettridge's writing and would never even consider touching a Bettridge script. Then she'd know Roy wouldn't have told either of them about the missing script, and neither of them would have a motive for wanting to take it from Roy.

After all, what were the chances that both Collin and Krista loved Bettridge?

* * *

That afternoon, Ben and Ryan did their homework and walked Hershey, and then Alex arrived to have dinner with them and pick up Ryan. After they had left, Anne was surprised to see Ben sprawled out on the living room couch with the script for the Victorian mystery dinner play, which he'd gotten from Wendy. Liddie lay on the floor with her crayons and drawing paper and listened as her brother read the play out loud to her. He had to ask Anne for a few words, but on the whole, he read rather well. Anne was proud of him, but carefully avoided the "mushy stuff" as she praised him.

"I like reading this. It's a challenge."

Anne felt the familiar wave of sadness that Eric wasn't here to see how his son was growing up so fast, but with the sadness was the happy conviction that Eric could see them all from heaven.

Ben hadn't gotten very far through the script before the library closed and they had dinner. He and Liddie were bouncing with excitement. Tonight would be the first read-through of the script. Anne had been apprehensive about Liddie's ability to remain quiet if there were long stretches where she and Ben had no speaking parts, but apparently the "pauper children" had small speaking lines scattered here and there throughout the play. Anne was hopeful Liddie, especially, wouldn't get too bored. Her little girl was always so full of energy that it was hard for her to sit still.

The theater club arrived a little before seven o'clock, and everyone seemed excited and anxious to start rehearsals for the play. Anne sat in the back of the History Room with Liddie, Ben, Ryan, Alex, Wendy, Emily, and Justin. Anne was glad she had thought to bring folding chairs so that everyone could sit down.

Stephan stood up. "Welcome. Before we begin, I have some upsetting news. Shelby Truman injured her knee yesterday during her soccer game."

"Oh no," Anne murmured along with several other people.

"She's fine, otherwise. She's hobbling around on crutches and saw the doctor today. She has an MRI scheduled for tomorrow."

"Will she be able to perform?" someone asked.

"We're not sure at this point. Shelby will have more information when she goes to the doctor again after her MRI scan." He held up his hands to quiet the murmurs. "Until we know more, we won't be recasting her part just yet. However, for the read-through during the next few days, we'll need someone to fill in."

Anne saw a suspicious twinkle in his eye as he looked directly at her across the room. "Anne, would you be willing to read Shelby's part? Since you'll be here anyway."

"Cool, Mom!" Ben said.

"Mommy, will you be a puppy like me?" Liddie asked. Those closest to her erupted into soft laughter.

"Not a puppy, sweetie." Anne couldn't refuse when they only needed her to read Shelby's lines. She would be sitting in on rehearsals anyway because of Liddie and Ben. She said, "I'd be happy to."

He nodded. "Thank you. Now, shall we begin?"

The read-through was more than simply everyone reading their parts. Stephan would stop every so often to describe the setting, to pull actors up to the "stage" to demonstrate how he envisioned them to be standing during certain lines of dialogue, and to give suggestions for emotions and expressions as people spoke their lines. Most of the actors took notes in their scripts, and some good-naturedly argued with him. Sometimes they even won.

Anne had to admit the read-through was fun. Many of the theater club actors were complete hams and read their parts in a way that was over-the-top. She tried simply reading her lines, but it sounded dispirited in comparison, which encouraged her to bring more life to her reading.

They didn't get through much of the script. Liddie had already yawned several times in the past twenty minutes, and Anne was about to excuse herself to put her to bed when Stephan called an end to rehearsal. "We'll continue tomorrow night."

After everyone had left, Anne hustled Ben and Liddie to their living quarters.

"It's a good thing I read the script today," Ben said. "I knew ahead of time when we had to talk, and I could help Ryan."

"You both did a great job," Anne said.

When Liddie crawled into bed, Anne sat next to her. "Time for prayers, sweetie."

Liddie gave another huge yawn and folded her hands. "Dear Jesus," she said in a sleepy voice, "thank You for the re...re..."

"Rehearsal," Anne supplied for her.

"*Re-ershal* today. I had fun. Please be with Miss Shelby. I hope she feels better. Amen."

"Amen," Anne said with a thick throat. She gave Liddie a hug. "That was nice of you to pray for Miss Shelby."

But Liddie was halfway asleep and only nodded in Anne's embrace.

Anne held her sweet little girl a moment longer. *Dear Jesus, thank You for giving Liddie such a caring heart. I pray You will help her to always think of others. Amen.*

She went to Ben's room to hear his prayers. He prayed for the play too, and with a gentle prod from Anne, he prayed for Shelby Truman and her injury. He snuggled down under the covers. "I had fun, Mom."

"It looked like you did."

"You sounded good too. You should take Miss Shelby's part if she can't do it."

"I'm sure the theater club already has some members who are much better than I am."

She kissed him good night and headed to her own room. She said a quick prayer for Shelby also. She hoped the young woman wasn't in too much pain. Would Shelby be able to perform her part after all? After Ben's innocent suggestion, Anne admitted she was tempted to want the part she had read tonight—the character sounded very much like her own quiet personality.

But she didn't really want to act in the play... did she?

CHAPTER NINE

A t breakfast the next morning, Ben said, "Mom, I think I need new shoes."

One of his sneakers had a rip between the rubber sole and the cloth upper. Ben wiggled his toes and Anne saw the flash of his white socks through the hole. "Oh no. You're right." These sneakers were only a month old.

"I think it happened yesterday at school. During recess, Ryan and I were trying to see how far we could kick the soccer ball."

"Well, we'll go shopping after school today."

Ben made a face since he hated shopping, but Liddie crowed with delight. "Can I get new shoes too, Mommy?"

"No, but if you're good, maybe you can get a new hair clip."

"Goodie!" Liddie went back to munching her cereal with relish.

Anne had a spasm of doubt at the thought of bribing her young daughter, and she wished Eric were here to help her. But Eric would probably say something like, "If a pink hair clip will make Liddie behave in the boys' shoes department, why not?"

How she missed Eric, his calm, soothing manner, the way he would transform a shopping trip into a cool guys-only expedition with Ben. It was especially hard being a single parent the first year after he died, but after moving to Blue Hill, things had finally fallen into a comfortable rhythm.

And how thankful she was that she had a relationship with the Lord and that she could trust He was watching over her and her children.

Since the day was a bit sunnier than the day before, she walked the kids to school. She returned to the library and checked the schedule. Sherri Deveraeux was scheduled to work this afternoon while she took Ben and Liddie shopping, and they might even have time for an ice cream before returning to the library.

She checked her e-mail, and was elated to see a message from Phoebe Ramsey, the playwright who was a client of Lynne Bettridge Sallman.

> *Dear Anne,*
>
> *Thanks for your note. How wonderful to meet another playwright so nearby! I would love to meet for coffee to talk about Lynne. She's a fabulous agent. Do you have time on Friday? How about two o'clock? I'm sorry I can't drive to Blue Hill, but if you're willing to drive to Harrisburg, there's a great coffee shop here called Fiona's Brew. Let me know if you can make it!*
>
> *Phoebe*

Anne felt a pang. She had not meant to mislead Phoebe into thinking she was a playwright too, but she could clear that up when she met her. She sent an e-mail back to Phoebe confirming their Friday meeting, then checked the library schedule. Donna was scheduled to work on Friday afternoon.

Anne called Wendy.

"Hi, Anne." A child wailed in the background, but Wendy seemed blissfully unaware of it.

"Did I call at a bad time?"

"No, Ethan is throwing a tantrum because I wouldn't let him play with a pizza cutter that fell out of the drawer."

Anne winced. "Is he all right?"

"He's fine. I snatched up the pizza cutter before he could touch it, but now he's upset I took his 'toy' away from him."

"Ah. Once I dropped a pair of kitchen shears, and Ben got hold of one handle before I could take it away. He cried for the next hour as if I'd spanked him."

Suddenly, a second voice rose in the background to add to the crying. "Sounds like the other twin has joined in. He probably doesn't even know what his brother is crying about."

"Well, I won't keep you long. Could you pick up Ben and Liddie from school on Friday and watch them for a few hours?"

"Sure. What's up?"

"I have an appointment to chat with Phoebe Ramsey, who's a client of Lynne Bettridge Sallman. Since Phoebe's from this area, maybe Lynne mentioned about her father knowing my aunt. It's a bit of a stretch, but since Phoebe is so nearby, I thought it wouldn't hurt to talk to her."

"True." The twins' wails suddenly both ceased. "Uh-oh. I better see what's going on. Bye!"

The morning at the library was very quiet, so Anne had time to do some Internet research. First, she checked for the TV program where Krista had been interviewed, *Behind the Curtain*. She was disappointed to find that it had ended about fifteen years ago.

Anne wondered if it were even possible to get a copy of the interview now.

It was tedious, but she went through the list of high school friends for Roy Underwood, Collin Avery, and Krista Underwood Bennett, to try to find these people. She managed to find a few who still lived in the Deshler area.

Out of the three, Krista was the most tech-savvy. She had a Facebook page, and she participated on a couple of playwriting online forum boards. She posted pictures that she had taken of posed photographs with fans, and even more with her friends. However, none of the people were her high school friends from any of her clubs, and Anne wondered if Krista had kept in touch with them.

Collin had only participated in drama team, so Anne focused on Gwendolyn Ross and Auggie Falcon, who had appeared with Collin in most of his yearbook photos.

She was saddened to see that Auggie Falcon had died in a drunk driving accident ten years ago. He had been driving home from a bar and crashed his car into a lamppost.

However, Gwendolyn still lived in Deshler. What's more, she had posted online about seeing Collin's latest production in New York City and having dinner with him. It sounded like it wasn't the first time she'd done something like that. Apparently, they still kept in touch.

Gwendolyn had married soon after graduating high school but divorced her husband about seven years later and reverted back to her maiden name. She worked as a nurse at the Deshler hospital.

She was also still active in drama. The Deshler community theater Web site listed Gwendolyn among its members.

Online newspaper articles from the local Deshler paper mentioned various productions put on by the Deshler community theater, and Gwendolyn was often listed among the actors in different roles. Anne was surprised to stumble upon Stephan Ullrick's name in the newspaper articles as a consulting director for a couple of the productions. Perhaps he knew Gwendolyn and could introduce them.

She was interrupted in her online search by the arrival of the postman, and she was excited to find that the Hugh Bettridge biography that she'd ordered through interlibrary loan had arrived. She immediately went upstairs to set it beside her bed so she could dive into it tonight.

When she returned to the front desk, several people were filing into the library. She became busy helping Coraline Watson find a book on combatting garden pests, then she was needed by sisters Betty Warring and Nellie Brown to order a biography on Cleopatra that had just been published a few weeks ago. She checked out books to Claire Daniels and Mary Zumfelde, speaking to both of them about the last Tea and Book Club meeting and confirming the next meeting date.

And so her day went, helping patrons find just the right book, tidying the shelves in the Children's Room, checking books in and out. She snatched a quick lunch, then Sherri Deveraeux arrived at one o'clock.

"How's it going?" Sherri stowed her bag behind the checkout desk.

"It was as quiet as a tomb earlier this morning, then suddenly people rushed the library like linebackers."

Sherri grinned. "Well, I'm here to help now."

"I need to take Ben shoe shopping after I pick the kids up this afternoon."

"No problem."

"How's your studying going?" Anne asked. Sherri was studying for her GED, since illness had made her miss much of her senior year in high school.

"Not bad. I'm also looking into what colleges I want to apply to next year."

The two of them discussed New York colleges in between helping patrons until Anne was called away to recommend a Victorian mystery for a mother who wanted to get a book for her teenaged daughter.

Later, Anne drove to pick up Ben and Liddie from school and got into the carpool line to wait for her turn to drive up to the curb. She was idly waiting when she happened to glance over and see a car parked down a side street.

The car was a nondescript gray, but what caught Anne's eye was the driver. It was the same dark-haired man she'd seen in the church parking lot on Sunday. As before, he sat low in the driver's seat as if he were short or slouching, and it seemed he had just turned his head away from looking at her.

Anne's hands tightened on her steering wheel, but then she took a deep breath. She was just being jumpy after Tami had mentioned how she thought a short, dark-haired man had been following her. The man was probably waiting for his own child to get out of school.

The cars in front moved forward, and she pulled up slowly. Ben and Liddie climbed in. "Buckle up," she said, making an effort to be extra cheerful.

Ben looked at her strangely. "Are you okay, Mom?"

"I'm fine." This was obviously proof she was a horrible actress, when she couldn't even convince her own son that nothing was wrong.

The shoe store off of Main Street was busy, but a salesman who was already helping a young woman spotted them and told them to snag him whenever they knew what they wanted. Ben picked out two or three styles of shoes, and Anne showed them to the salesman and gave him Ben's foot size when he had finished waiting on the woman. Liddie entertained herself by looking at all the shoes — mostly the pink ones — and trying them on, regardless of whether they were her size or not.

"Be sure to put the shoes back, Liddie." Anne kept a sharp eye on her daughter in case she forgot.

The salesman returned with Ben's shoes and helped him into each one. Ben screwed his mouth into different shapes as he thought about it, then pointed to some blue ones. "I think I like those."

Anne paid for the shoes, glad the shopping trip had been relatively painless.

As they exited the store, Ben swinging the bag containing his shoes, Liddie said, "Do I get my hair clip now?"

Anne had been about to say yes when her eye fell on the Victorian building housing the *Blue Hill Gazette.* "Can we go in there first? Then we can go to the drugstore for your hair clip and ice cream. How does that sound?"

Ben and Liddie both brightened at the suggestion.

"Can I have a banana split?" Ben asked.

"You can have whatever you want, honey."

"Can I have strawberry with extra whipped cream?" Liddie asked.

"Is there any other way to have strawberry ice cream?" Anne asked, and Liddie and Ben giggled.

They headed to the two-story newspaper building. Ducking under the red-painted, covered porch, they entered the front door.

Anne was pleased to see Grace Hawkins, the editor of the newspaper, manning the front desk. She brightened as she saw Anne and her family. "Hi there."

"We're going for ice cream," Liddie said.

Grace smiled at her. "*Mmm,* that sounds good. My favorite is strawberry."

"Me too! With extra whipped cream."

"And peanuts on top."

"*Ooh,* Mommy, can I have peanuts on top too?"

"Of course," Anne said, "because you're my little peanut."

Liddie giggled. "I'm a peanut. Peanut, p'nut, p'nut."

"What are you going to get?" Grace asked Ben.

He tilted his head. "I'm not sure yet."

"I thought you wanted a banana split," Anne said.

"But your talking about nuts is making me want chocolate almond."

Anne stifled her laughter.

Grace turned to Anne. "What can I help you with today?"

"I'm not sure you can help me, but I can't think of anyone else to ask. I'm looking for the episode of a particular TV program that ended fifteen years ago, and I'm not sure where to start."

"I'm not too familiar with the TV industry, but I can tell you that the studio which produced the show would own it and have the rights to it. They may even have copies of their old programs, but you'd have to contact that studio, if it's still in business. Even if they don't have copies of the program, they might know who does."

"Thanks, Grace, that's exactly what I needed." Anne gave her friend a warm smile. "You're the best."

Grace looked out the window at the sunshine filtering through the clouds. "Enjoy your ice cream. That sounds good to me right now too."

"Did you want me to bring you something?"

"Thanks for the offer, but I'll stop by the soda fountain after work and take home a pint of strawberry ice cream to eat while I read that Victorian mystery I picked up at the library the other day. Thanks for recommending it, by the way."

"I hope you enjoy it. See you." Anne herded her children out of the newspaper office.

They entered the drugstore, which had been on Main Street since she was a child and had come in with her parents and Aunt Edie. They headed to the old chrome-trimmed soda fountain with its bright red Coca-Cola signs and red-and-white-checked tile floors.

Ben ended up choosing a banana split after all, while Liddie got her strawberry ice cream with extra whipped cream and a sprinkling of peanuts. Since she was getting her mountain of extras, Anne convinced her to get a bowl instead of a cone.

"Look, Mommy, now I'm really your peanut." Liddie held her bowl of ice cream.

Anne selected a scoop of vanilla with hot fudge drizzled on top, and the three of them settled on stools at the Formica countertop with its classic gray-and-red boomerang design. The creamy dessert contrasted with the warm fudge and hit the spot for Anne. Ben attacked his banana split with gusto, and Liddie slowly ate all her whipped cream and peanuts without yet touching her ice cream.

"How was school?" Anne asked, and Liddie went into great detail about the smelling activity they had done today, smelling several scents and matching the identical pairs. She chattered on long enough for Ben to finish inhaling his ice cream, and then he talked about the vocabulary Bingo game they'd played in class.

"I tried really hard to win, but I didn't." His shoulders sagged.

"That's all right, sweetie. We can't win all the time."

"But Ryan won. He got Tootsie Rolls, and he shared one with me."

"That was nice of him. Did you say thank you?"

"Yes, Mom." Ben rolled his eyes a bit, but he was smiling as he did it.

When they returned home, Anne left Ben doing his homework and Liddie playing with her dolls while she went to help Sherri with the patrons downstairs. The steady stream of people apparently hadn't slowed much while Anne was gone, and she felt a bit guilty leaving Sherri alone for longer than usual.

After the library closed, Anne hastily threw dinner together—sandwiches and leftover chicken soup. Ben and Liddie didn't mind too much, but Anne made a mental note to do more Crock-Pot recipes in the next few weeks. That way she could have a nutritious meal that wouldn't take too long to put on the table in the evening in the time between the library closing and the theater club arriving for rehearsal.

Anne again sat in the back with her kids, next to Alex and Ryan and Wendy and two of her kids. And again, Anne was asked to read Shelby's part.

"I haven't heard anything else about her," Stephan said to the room in general. "She's resting at home. She has a doctor's appointment tomorrow, I think."

The reading went even slower than the night before because Stephan stopped often to coach actors on how to build more suspicion for their characters. "Remember, we want *all* of you to seem like suspects." He even coached Anne because it would help the other actors get into their characters more easily.

As they wrapped up for the night, Alex leaned close to Anne. "You should take Shelby's part if she can't do it. You really made me wonder if you're the villain."

"Probably because I keep hesitating over the lines. This is such a different type of play than any we did for the church youth group when we were teenagers."

"It's fun being able to ham it up. I think I like playing my character because I'm naturally not as extroverted as he is."

"Your character is certainly a flirt. He's been dishing out compliments to all the female characters so far."

"Maybe I can learn a thing or two from him, then." Alex winked at her, and Anne laughed.

Anne left Liddie and Ben talking to Ryan while she went up to the director.

"Anne, are you enjoying our rehearsals so far?"

"They're a lot of fun, not just for my kids, but for me too."

"Didn't I tell you? Are you sure you don't want a part in the play? It's not too late. Shelby might not be able to do the play…"

"I do hope she'll be all right. I would hate for her to have done something serious to her knee."

"She had her MRI scan today and the doctor will look at her results tomorrow."

"That's good. I came over not to talk about the play, but to ask you a favor."

"Anything. We already owe you so much for letting us use the library for our fund-raiser."

"I wondered if you know Gwendolyn Ross from the Deshler community theater?"

He nodded. "I've known her for years. Gwendolyn is a very good actress."

"Would you be willing to introduce me to her? I wanted to ask her about a former classmate, Collin Avery."

"The director? She talks about him all the time. They're apparently quite close."

"Then there's a good chance she'll know the answers to my questions. I found out recently that my aunt Edie had a script written by a friend, and she might have given the script to Collin's cousin, Roy Underwood, just before Roy died. I don't know where the script is, and I wondered if Roy showed the script to Collin. Collin might have talked to Gwendolyn about it."

"Maybe." Stephan looked thoughtful. "I've never seen one of Collin's plays, but I was fortunate enough to see one of Roy Underwood's productions in London. He was a truly gifted director, but he might have passed the script to his cousin if it wasn't to his taste."

"I don't know what types of plays Collin likes, so I don't know if Roy would have even bothered to show it to Collin or not."

"Gwendolyn would probably know. I'll give her a call tomorrow and ask if she'd be open to meeting you."

"Thank you so much."

"Stephan?" One of the other actors came up to him. "I have a question about this one section..."

Anne excused herself so she could corral her children upstairs. She waved good-bye to Alex and Ryan and Wendy and her two kids, who were also leaving.

"Get ready for bed," she told Ben and Liddie. "I'm going downstairs, and when I get back, both of you should be in bed."

After the theater club left, Anne locked the door behind them, checked the other doors to make sure they were locked, and then headed upstairs to the bedrooms. Ben was in bed, reading the play, so Anne went to Liddie to hear her prayers.

She snuggled on the bed with her daughter. "Are you enjoying the play?"

Liddie nodded. "I like being in it with you."

"I'm only filling in temporarily until Miss Shelby gets better."

"I want you *and* Miss Shelby to be in the play."

"Let's pray that Miss Shelby gets better soon." Anne and Liddie prayed, and then Liddie curled up and almost immediately went to sleep.

Anne went to Ben's room. "How are you liking the play?"

He gave a shrug. Anne reflected that she really couldn't have expected more from her nine-year-old son, but she suspected he enjoyed it more than he wanted to admit. "I'm proud of you. This isn't very easy reading."

He shrugged again, but there was a smile on the edges of his mouth. He put the script aside, and Anne heard Ben's prayers. He didn't fall asleep as quickly as Liddie, but he seemed tired.

Anne prepared for bed, and as she slipped between the covers she reached for the biography on Hugh Bettridge that had arrived this morning. She eagerly opened it to read a little.

What she read was intriguing. He had come from a family of actors, but he himself hadn't been very good as an actor. The book talked about his childhood and a little about his family members, and the tension present because he had no inclination for acting. Instead, he began writing plays as young as eight years old — only a year younger than Ben, Anne realized. One of his plays, titled *Sheep and Frogs,* was performed at his church for an Easter program when he was twelve years old. Rather than following in his family's footsteps and enrolling in a drama school, he won a scholarship to a small university and majored in English.

Anne yawned and closed the book. She'd already stayed up way past her bedtime because the book was so interesting. She turned out the light, but before falling asleep, she sent a silent prayer to the Lord: *Lord, I really don't know where Aunt Edie's script could be. Please help me to find it.*

CHAPTER TEN

Anne was shelving books in the Nonfiction Room when Remi came to the open doorway. "Anne, there's a phone call for you."

"Who is it?"

"He didn't say."

Anne went to the front desk and picked up the telephone. "Hello, this is Anne Gibson."

"This is Collin Avery." The man's voice was high pitched and irritable. "You called me." It sounded almost like an accusation.

"Thank you for calling me back, Mr. Avery—"

"Come on, get to the point," he snapped. "I'm preparing for my summer production."

Anne was a little shocked at his rude tone and impatience. However, she'd been a librarian in New York and had encountered lots of different types of people, including some even ruder. She came straight to the point. "Just before he died, your cousin, Roy Underwood, may have had a script—"

"He had plenty of scripts. Want to be more specific?"

"By Hugh Bettridge."

She was about to explain about Aunt Edie, but didn't get a chance because Collin exploded, "What are you getting at? Are you some reporter posing as a librarian? I don't believe this."

"No, I assure you—"

"I wish you people would stop talking about the missing Bettridge script. It's been a year already, why can't people just forget about it?"

"I'm not—" Anne tried to explain, but then Collin hung up the phone. She was so surprised that she stood there for a moment before replacing the receiver.

"Whoa." Remi's deep brown eyes were wide. "He was talking so loud that I could hear him."

"He seemed to be in a hurry. Now I'm sorry I asked him to call me. He probably had a lot to do."

Remi scratched her head. "I wonder why he was so angry when you mentioned that script?"

Now that she thought about it, Collin had reacted rather violently. "I think there was something else going on. Other people may have asked him about the script, and he's tired of answering questions. He probably assumed I wanted to talk about the same things."

"Still, I think he was kind of rude." Remi sniffed.

Rather than raging about how people kept asking him about the script, instead he'd been upset that people wouldn't stop talking about the script. There was a subtle difference. Did it mean something significant?

She could understand if Collin was tired of being asked about the script, especially if he didn't know anything about it. But why was he upset that people kept talking about something so mysterious as a missing script from a famous playwright? People loved a mystery.

Anne thought to herself that if she had stolen the script, she'd certainly want people to stop talking about it. If someone mentioned the script, she might even respond angrily because of a guilty conscience. Or was she simply being overly suspicious of Collin? She didn't want to think that he would do something like steal from his cousin.

"Stephan Ullrick likes Bettridge's plays," Remi said. "We did one a few years ago, and Stephan went on and on about how Bettridge was one of his favorite playwrights and this was one of his best plays. He was *so* excited about it. Which was kind of funny, because the play was a downer."

Anne chuckled. "Did you like the play?"

"It was okay, but I wasn't nuts about it, so I didn't try out for any of the parts. But Bella loves all that angsty stuff. She had a really great death scene at the end."

Anne smiled. "I can see how that would be fun to do."

"In our freshman year, our drama club in high school did *Romeo and Juliet*, and Bella and I both tried out for Juliet. Bella wanted the part because of the death scene at the end, but I wanted it because I'd get to kiss the guy playing Romeo." Remi grinned. "He was dreamy."

Anne could see how a stage kiss could be fun, but she wasn't sure she would be able to do that. "Who got the part?"

"It went to a senior girl who was four inches taller than the guy who played Romeo. Bella and I were assigned to stage crew, and we spent the entire semester grumbling about it."

At that moment, the door opened and Stephan Ullrick entered the library. "Hello, my lovely ladies."

"Were your ears burning?" Anne asked.

"Were you talking about me? Good things, I hope."

"We were talking about Hugh Bettridge plays."

Stephan's blue eyes lit up. "A truly marvelous playwright. The way he can wring emotion from the audience with a turn of phrase..."

Remi looked sideways at Anne with a smile.

"Oh, stop rolling your eyes, missy," Stephan said to Remi. "I know you've heard me wax poetic about Bettridge before. Mrs. Gibson is a brand-new audience for me."

"I actually would be interested in hearing about Bettridge," Anne said.

"Then I'm going to shelve some books," Remi said.

"Speaking of books," Stephan said, "the reason I popped in is because my wife asked me to return this novel and get the next in the series." He handed them the second book in a Victorian mystery series written by a contemporary author. "She absolutely loves these books."

"Oh, I love Meredith Carruthers too," Remi said. "I'll go up to the Fiction Room and get the next one for you." She hurried away.

"I hear you're somewhat knowledgeable about Hugh Bettridge," Anne said.

"The man was a genius." Stephan spoke at length on Bettridge's writing style, his distinct play on words, and the underlying issues in his plays. At this point, Remi returned with the book his wife wanted, good-naturedly rolled her eyes and left, taking some books to be shelved.

"He wrote on some very heavy topics," Anne remarked.

"He lived during turbulent political time periods, and he felt the need to express his concerns in his writing."

"I'm almost ashamed to admit that I hadn't heard of him before."

"Bettridge had great critical acclaim, but his plays weren't as popular as other playwrights of his time. They did well off Broadway and in London, but they weren't the type of blockbusters of other shows running concurrently."

"I wonder why?"

"Perhaps because his subject matter cut too close to the heart? But he did well enough to have two movies made from his plays."

"He did? Which ones?" Anne wondered if she could order them through interlibrary loan.

"His most famous play was *Nanette*, and so that naturally was made into a movie, and relatively recently too. I think fifteen years ago? The second was *Lanterns*, which I didn't think was as great a script as some of his other ones, such as *Ask Me No Questions*. But then again, I'm not a movie producer."

Anne searched her memory. "I seem to recall hearing about a movie called *Lanterns* a few years ago..."

"If you heard about it, that was a feat in itself. It was very poorly publicized. The only reason I knew it was playing was because one of my friends' literary agents is in the Bettridge Sallman literary agency. He told my friend only a week before opening weekend. The closest theater playing *Lanterns* was a two-hour drive away, so we all took off work and went. It was a good movie, although not as powerfully done as when I'd seen *Lanterns* in an off-Broadway theater."

"I wish I'd gone to see it."

"It wasn't in theaters for long. Only a few weeks before it was pulled."

"That's too bad. Perhaps I can see it on DVD?"

Stephan brightened. "That's a good idea. I wouldn't be surprised if *Lanterns* and *Nanette* were both available. *Nanette* was his most famous play."

"I'll see if I can order the movies through interlibrary loan."

"I'd love to check them out when you're done with them. Luckily, I married a woman as fond of Bettridge as I am."

As he was checking out his wife's novel, he said, "I nearly forgot. I called Gwendolyn Ross this morning, and I told her that you had an interest in Collin's plays. She was more than happy to speak to you. She said she'd look at her schedule and then call you today. I gave her the number here at the library."

"Thanks, I appreciate your doing this for me."

"I had to call Gwendolyn anyway. She's the property manager for the Deshler community theater, and she had some hats I loaned to them a few months ago for their production. I hope you don't mind, I told her she could bring them to her meeting with you and that you'd return them to me."

"Of course."

"Thanks." Stephan then left the library with his wife's book tucked under his arm.

Anne went on her computer and found the two Bettridge movies available on DVD and ordered them through interlibrary loan. Their descriptions indicated they were both serious, dramatic plays. The story lines contrasted dramatically with Krista's plays, which had seemed humorous.

Would Krista really try to pass off a Bettridge play as her own? Their writing styles seemed like they were incredibly different.

But even if not, Krista still might want to produce the missing play. After all, she had a director for a brother. And hadn't those articles in the New York papers mentioned her interest in producing? Anne had to find that TV interview where Krista spoke about her interest in producing.

Following Grace's suggestion, she went online to look up the studio that had produced the program that had interviewed Krista, *Behind the Curtain*. It was a small studio in New Jersey, Sanguinet Broadcasting, and they were still in business. Their most popular show at the moment was *A Night at Alabaster Royal*, a reality show about a group of actors competing for a spot in a play being produced at the Alabaster Royal Theater.

Anne found their phone number on their Web site and called them.

"Sanguinet Broadcasting, Consuela speaking. How may I help you?" answered a pleasant young woman.

"Hello, Consuela, my name is Anne Gibson, and I'm the librarian at the Blue Hill Library. I'm calling about a TV program your studio produced fifteen years ago called *Behind the Curtain*. Does your studio still have copies of the episodes?"

"I'm afraid I couldn't say for certain. I do know there are a lot of old programs still in storage in our archive room."

"There's an interview with Krista Bennett that I'd really like to see. Would it be possible to have a copy of the episode? It was episode number one-one-two." Anne looked down at her notes to double-check the episode number.

"Could I please have your phone number, Ms. Gibson? I'll speak to someone about getting a copy of the episode for you."

"Thanks." Anne gave her information and hung up the phone, feeling hopeful.

Strangely, the phone rang almost immediately, startling her. "Hello, this is Blue Hill Library. Anne Gibson speaking."

"Hi, this is Gwendolyn Ross." The woman had a deep, husky voice with an energetic tone that reminded Anne of Joan Rivers. "You wanted to know more about Collin Avery's plays?"

"Yes, thanks for calling me. Are you free for coffee sometime?"

"Oh, sure. I'm busy this week because I'm on double shifts at the hospital, but how about next week? Are you free at ten on Monday morning?"

Bella and Remi were coming in on Monday morning and could hold down the library. Anne agreed on their meeting place and hung up the phone feeling a bit as if she'd been in a whirlwind. Gwendolyn certainly had a strong, lively personality that came across even in a brief conversation.

That morning, Anne had thrown corned beef into the slow cooker with an easy brown sugar/molasses/dijon mustard glaze, and it smelled warm and inviting when she went upstairs for dinner with Ben and Liddie after closing the library at five o'clock. She made mashed potatoes and a salad.

"You liked this, huh?" Anne gave Liddie a second small serving. Ben was already halfway through his seconds. Liddie and Ben both nodded.

"It tastes good with the mashed potatoes." Liddie shoved some potatoes into the gravy glaze from the corned beef and mixed them together with her fork. Some mashed potato pieces came dangerously close to the edge of her plate.

"Careful, Liddie, you don't want your food to fall after you've just mixed it all up, do you?"

Liddie mixed a little less vigorously.

"We made cakes today in school," Ben said. "I got to mix the batter."

"How did it turn out?"

Ben shrugged. "Okay, I guess. Yours are better, Mom."

"Thanks." She smiled. "How did your class bake them?"

"Mr. Layton brought in two toaster ovens. One was regular and one was con-vec-tion." He said the word carefully. "The convection oven was way faster."

"Did you have chocolate cake?" Liddie asked.

"Yeah, but it was kind of dry."

"I made mud pies at recess," Liddie said.

"I know. I scrubbed it from under your fingernails," Anne said. It had also stained the knees of her leggings, but by now, Anne was used to how hard her children wore their clothes.

"And how did that taste?" Ben teased her.

"Chocolaty," Liddie shot back, and the two of them laughed.

Anne loved seeing them tease each other. They had both had a tough time adjusting to life in Blue Hill right after they'd moved here, but with the help of good friends like Ryan and Cindy Jacobs, they were settling in just fine.

She was surprised to hear the doorbell ringing to their private entrance. She went to the intercom system. "Hello?"

"Hi, Anne, it's Tami and Stephan."

"Come on up." She buzzed them in, and soon they had entered through the doorway of their private back entrance to their living quarters.

"Sorry we're early," Tami said. "We have a favor to ask."

"Oh, sure," Anne said without thinking. Stephan's blue eyes sparkled, and Anne had a moment of misgiving.

"I'm afraid we have some bad news," Stephan said. "Shelby Truman found out that she tore the ACL in her knee."

"Oh no."

"Shelby scheduled her surgery for next week, but it means she won't be able to participate in the play."

"So we thought, maybe you could take her part?" Tami said.

Anne fought the impulse to groan theatrically.

"See, Mom? You can be in the play with us now," Ben said.

"Yay, Mommy!" Liddie raised her arms above her head, which unfortunately flung bits of potato at her brother since she was still holding her fork.

"Aack!" Ben grabbed his napkin and wiped his face.

Anne looked at them all helplessly. "You can't find someone else to do it?"

"Shelby was supposed to wear your aunt Edie's dress," Tami said. "We have a couple other women who might be able to take Shelby's part, but they're not the right size for the dress. It would take extensive alterations, which would be too expensive because we'd need to hire a professional seamstress and it would be hours of work. Plus, I didn't think you'd want to alter your aunt's dress so drastically."

Anne had to admit that while she had no problem loaning the dress to the theater club and even allowing small alterations, drastic ones would be harder for her to agree to since Aunt Edie had once worn the dress herself for a theatrical production.

"You're closest to your aunt Edie and to Shelby in size. Plus it's only a small part—you've seen that for yourself, since you've already been reading Shelby's part during rehearsals."

"And the character is a librarian," Stephan added. "It's perfect for you."

"Yeah, Mom," Ben added.

Anne had to admit she'd enjoyed reading the character's lines in rehearsals, and the part really was very small. And they seemed to be in real need…

"All right," Anne said with a sigh.

"Way to go, Mom!" Ben said.

"Thanks, Anne," Stephan said.

"Yay, Mommy!" Liddie crowed.

But Tami was the most ecstatic of them all. She rushed forward to embrace Anne in a fervent hug. "You are going to have so much fun! I can't wait!"

A part of Anne's brain registered that Tami was a little *too* excited about Anne taking the part, but she was distracted by Liddie, deliberately flinging potatoes at her brother, who protested loudly. "Liddie, please stop that right now," Anne said in a firm voice.

"Yeah." Ben wiped more potatoes off his shirt.

Liddie opened her mouth to protest, but Anne gave her a stern look, and she put her fork down.

"It's almost time for rehearsal to start, so we'll head downstairs," Stephan said.

"Would you mind unlocking the front door for everyone?" Anne handed Tami the key.

Anne managed to wash the dishes and even give Liddie a stern talking-to about throwing food before they went downstairs for rehearsal. Alex and Ryan had just arrived.

"Ryan, Mom's going to be in the play!" Ben burst out.

Alex smiled at Anne. "That's great. You're taking Shelby's part?"

"Yes, although I'm feeling guilty that the only reason is because she has to have surgery, poor girl."

Alex winced. "I heard."

"I hope she isn't in too much pain right now." Anne herded the kids toward the History Room. Ryan talked excitedly to Ben about something that sounded like "orange soldiers," and Anne was almost tempted to ask what that meant.

As they sat in their usual seats in the back of the room with the kids, Alex leaned close to Anne. "Did you read the entire script yet?"

"Not yet. I hope to, now that I know I'll be taking the librarian role."

Alex looked like he was about to say something but then changed his mind.

In rehearsal, Stephan announced that Anne was taking the librarian role, and everyone clapped and smiled at her.

This rehearsal ran even more slowly than the previous night because there was a complicated scene where several people spoke in turn, and the timing was difficult. They had to stop and start again several times because people missed their cues or spoke out of turn.

When Stephan finally called a halt to rehearsal, Tami looked disappointed. She was probably used to rehearsals running more swiftly with professional actors.

Tami was at Anne's side quickly. "Did you read the entire script?"

"Not yet. I will, though."

Tami gave her a bright smile. "Good. If you have any questions, just ask me, okay?"

"Sure." What was going on? Anne decided to read the rest of the script tonight. There was something both Alex and Tami knew that she didn't, and it made her nervous.

"Remember, everyone," Stephan said, "no rehearsal tomorrow night, since the library is open late, but be sure to be here on Friday night."

Everyone left and Anne locked up. She went upstairs to find Liddie dawdling over brushing her teeth.

"Come on, peanut," Anne said.

Liddie giggled but set to brushing with more vigor.

Anne always loved hearing her children's prayers, but tonight Liddie was especially long-winded. Anne was tempted to say something when Liddie began praying for Jesus to bless her schoolmates's neighbors's cats' fleas, but then Liddie wrapped up quickly with, "And Jesus, please bless everybody in the world tonight. Amen."

"Amen," Anne said a bit wearily.

When Anne went to Ben, he was reading an adventure novel in bed. "Have you finished reading the script yet?" Anne asked casually.

"Not yet. I will later."

She heard his prayers, then went to bed herself with the script.

Anne started getting an inkling of unease at the end of act two, when it was apparent that the librarian, her character, was showing signs of warmer feelings toward the gypsy, Alex's character. But he'd been flirting with all the women in the play, and really, he was such a charming fellow, who wouldn't respond to his compliments?

For a little while, it looked like the librarian might be the villain, but then the gypsy confessed to the crime. Anne was surprised. She would never have guessed he had done it, and why would he confess when there wasn't any evidence against him?

But the detective in the story revealed that the gypsy couldn't be guilty. The gypsy admitted he had confessed because he feared the librarian would be accused of the crime, and he had fallen in love with her.

Anne sat straight up in bed. She hadn't known there was a romance in the story.

And then she reached the one page in the script that she knew Tami and Alex had both been thinking of when they asked her if she had read the entire script. Anne gasped. She and Alex had to…? She reread the line again, but it was there in black and white.

Upon declaring his love for the librarian, and the librarian admitting her love for the gypsy, the two of them kissed!

CHAPTER ELEVEN

Anne spent most of Thursday alternating between mortification and worry over the play. The romance between her character and Alex's caused a flood of different emotions inside her.

When Wendy arrived to work, she noticed Anne's odd air of distraction. "Are you all right?"

"I'm fine," Anne said automatically.

Wendy gave her an exasperated look. "You're not all right. I can tell."

Anne's shoulders sagged. "I just don't know what to do about my part in the play."

"Oh. You mean the scene with Alex near the end?"

"I'm going to put Tami through the wringer the next time I see her. Now I know why she was so excited when I said I'd take the part."

"It's only a play. Don't you think it'll be… kind of fun?"

"No." Anne frowned down at the counter in front of her.

"But you and Alex were high school sweethearts."

"But we broke up when I went away to college. And I've been married and widowed since then. It makes things complicated."

"Do you feel you're betraying Eric?"

"Yes…well… no. I know Eric would want me to be happy."

"Are you still feeling the pain of losing him?"

"Lately the pain I used to feel every time I remembered him has dulled so that it doesn't hurt like it used to."

"Anne, that's a good thing. Eric wouldn't want you to walk around in pain."

"I guess I've been used to living with the pain for the past three years. It's strange to have my feelings change this way."

"Change is always strange. It's what I tell my kids all the time."

She shot Wendy a desperate look. "But kissing my ex-boyfriend in front of a room full of people seems pretty crazy to me."

Wendy grimaced. "I can see your point. Does it seem icky to you?"

"Not icky… just strange." Anne couldn't seem to get away from that word, but it perfectly described how she felt. "I'm worried that the situation will change our friendship. I don't want it to turn awkward and stilted."

"Alex knows this is just a play. He won't take it seriously."

"Maybe I can back out. There's still time to find someone else."

Wendy shook her head. "Stephan and I talked about it for an hour yesterday. You're the only person who has the same waist, height, and bodice size of your aunt. Anyone else would need at least one of those three adjusted in the costume."

"To be honest, I don't really want to have a dressmaker completely resize Aunt Edie's gown. I just feel as if I don't know what I'm getting into, and that makes me uncomfortable."

"It may not be as awful as you think."

Anne laughed. "That's what I tell my kids all the time. I should listen to my own advice for once."

Wendy reached over to give her a hug. "It'll all turn out all right."

Anne wished she could believe that.

After lunch, patrons started filing into the building. When Sheri Deveraeux arrived at one o'clock, Wendy offered to stay a little longer to help out, which Anne gratefully accepted. When the time came for Anne and Wendy to pick the kids up from school, they were still extremely busy.

"Why don't I pick your kids up for you today?" Wendy said.

"But the library is out of your way," Anne protested, even though she was in the middle of finding books for not one, but three different patrons.

"Sarah has a history paper on railroads and needs to look up some books in the History Room. Hannah needs to sit down and write her essay on *Julius Caesar*, and the library is as good a place as any."

"If you're sure..." Anne didn't want Wendy to be chauffeuring Ben and Liddie just because Anne was busy. Wendy had a busy life too.

"Not a problem. I'll get Ben and Liddie when I pick up my kids and bring them here with Hannah and Sarah."

"Thanks so much, Wendy." Anne gave her a grateful smile before hurrying away to find one of the books she needed for a waiting patron.

By the time Wendy returned with Ben and Liddie, the rush had slowed down. Sherri gave an exaggerated sigh and swipe across her forehead.

Anne smiled at her. "I know what you mean."

"Hi, Anne." Wendy hustled in the front door with all seven of her kids and Ben and Liddie.

"Mommy!" Liddie raced into the library waving a booklet. "I made an ABC nature book."

Anne attempted to admire her book, but after a few scant seconds, Liddie darted back to Justin. "Are you staying for snack?"

Anne said, "Why don't you take all your kids upstairs for a snack? I have plenty of cookies and fruit."

When Wendy hesitated, Emily and Justin pleaded with her, "Pleeeeeease, Mommy."

"Oh, all right. Thanks, Anne. Are you sure you're not too busy?"

Sherri shook her head. "You just missed the last of the big rush. The only people in the library right now are Betty Warring and Nellie Brown in the Nonfiction Room, and Claire Daniels just arrived a few minutes ago. I think she's in the Fiction Room upstairs."

Leaving Sherri at the now-quiet front desk, Anne went upstairs with Wendy and all the kids. The kitchen seemed loud with all the children, but Wendy's kids were respectful of Anne's home. The older kids ate in the living room while the younger ones ate at the kitchen table.

While they were supervising the children, Wendy leaned closer to Anne. "I don't want to worry you, but I saw something a little weird."

"What?"

"When I left the library to pick up the kids and also when I came back, I saw a guy in a car across the street. I thought he was waiting for someone in the library, but Sherri mentioned there are only three library patrons here right now. So the man across the street can't be waiting for any of them, can he? Betty and Nellie live by themselves, and he didn't look like Claire Daniels's husband."

"What does he look like?"

"He seems short. Dark hair. In a gray car."

A chill passed through Anne's shoulders. That sounded like the man Tami thought had been following her in town, and whom Anne had seen twice. "Is he just...hanging out there?"

"He was looking at the library a lot. That's why I thought he was waiting for someone inside."

"I'm going to go look." Anne went downstairs, trailed by Wendy. They paused at the front door. The gray car parked across the street looked a lot like the car Anne had seen on two previous occasions.

"I think I'll ask him if he's waiting for someone," Anne said.

"I'll come with you."

Anne was grateful for Wendy's support, even though this was Blue Hill and it was in broad daylight for all the neighbors to see. As she exited the library, a cool soft breeze wafted over her, smelling like wet earth and green grass.

However, as she and Wendy made a beeline for the car, the man at the wheel spotted them. He fired up the engine and in moments the car had moved off. Anne hadn't gotten a good look, but she was fairly certain it was the same man she'd seen.

"I think I've seen him a couple times around town," Anne said.

"Well, it's not a crime to be hanging around, and the library is a public building. But it did seem strange."

They went back inside in time to prevent one of Wendy's twins from spilling his glass of milk. After snack time, Wendy took her younger children home while Hannah and Sarah went to different rooms in the library to do their papers. Liddie went to the Children's Room to draw on the chalkboard wall while Ben sat in the living room doing his homework.

Unfortunately, the lull in patrons that afternoon gave Anne too much time to think about rehearsal tomorrow evening. She considered calling Alex but didn't want to talk about her concerns over the phone. And half the time, she felt silly about her worries and didn't want to bring the subject up with Alex at all.

When Anne went upstairs to have dinner with Ben and Liddie, she found Ben dozing in front of the television, with Liddie snuggled up beside him on the sofa. Anne paused a moment in the doorway to look fondly at the two of them. *Lord, I pray they will always take care of each other and be a good brother and sister to each other.*

"Who's ready for dinner?" she called to the two of them.

Liddie wakened immediately, jumping off the sofa. "Me! Me!"

Dinner was leftover corned beef, but Anne livened it up with heat-and-serve dinner rolls spread with honey butter and a colorful vegetable side dish of corn, peas, and diced carrots. Liddie was highly entertained by eating all the carrots first, then the peas, then the corn. Ben used his roll to scoop up the gravy on his plate.

As they finished dinner, Anne said, "I have to go back downstairs since the library is open late tonight. What will you two do?"

Ben said, "I think I'll read the play."

Anne felt a twinge of apprehension. What would he think when he reached the part about the kiss? He'd probably think it was gross—he was still at an age where he thought girls had cooties.

Liddie said, "Ben, watch a movie with me."

"What are you going to watch?" he asked.

"Let's watch Spider-Man."

Ben's expression lightened at the suggestion of his favorite character. "Okay."

Anne headed to the front desk just in time before Sherri's shift ended and she left for the day. "What are your plans for tonight?" Anne asked.

"I'm going with a couple friends of mine to catch a movie." Sherri named a romantic comedy that had just been released in theaters.

"Sounds fun. Thanks for volunteering today."

After Sherri left, several students came into the library, taking advantage of the extended hours on Thursdays, but they didn't need much help beyond checking some books out. Anne went through the script in her free time, but it only made the knot in her stomach tighten painfully. So Anne retrieved the biography on Hugh Bettridge, and in between helping patrons, she continued reading.

The biography moved on from Bettridge's childhood to his first successes in the London theater. In his twenties, he once spent an entire summer in an isolated cottage in Scotland that belonged to an aunt, finishing his play, *A Shadow's Bliss*. He didn't bother to shave, and when he returned to London, he had grown a thin mustache and narrow beard that naturally tapered into longer strands at his chin, making his chin look pointed. His hair had grown longer in the back and sides, and he had a very high, round forehead thanks to a prematurely receding hairline. His friends teased him since he looked like the posters of William Shakespeare that Bettridge liked to collect, and they began calling him "Billy." The nickname stuck when he decided to keep the mustache, pointed beard, and long hair.

Anne chuckled, remembering one summer when Eric had gone fishing for a week with his friends in upstate New York, and none of them had shaved the entire time. He returned looking scraggly but relaxed from his time away.

The story about Bettridge caused a nagging feeling in her mind, as if she ought to remember something, but it wiggled just out of reach...

"Hi, Anne." Beth Wilson came up with her five children and handed her a stack of books to check out. "I love that new Victorian mysteries display."

"Thanks." Anne saw the novel at the top of Beth's stack. "You'll love this series by Meredith Carruthers. Stephan Ullrick's wife is already on book three."

They chatted about different Victorian mystery series, but Anne didn't take too long in checking their books out because Beth's youngest, four-year-old Reggie, was already showing signs of boredom and had started running races with himself in front of the front desk.

"See you, Anne." Beth divided the books between her kids to carry, then herded them all out the front door.

Anne returned to the biography, reading about how Bettridge fell in love with a young actress named Miriam Chandler. The woman's name seemed familiar to Anne, as if she'd recently had a conversation with someone about a woman named Miriam, but she couldn't remember when or with whom. Maybe Wendy or Mildred?

Bettridge and his wife had two children, Lynne and her younger brother Charles, and they lived in London. Miriam gave up acting in order to stay home to take care of the children.

Bettridge began to receive critical acclaim for his plays, most notably *Lanterns* and *A Shadow's Bliss*. Both of those plays won numerous awards, and their runs in the theaters did modestly well.

His most famous play would be *Nanette*, which he began writing in the summer of 1961. But then on Christmas Eve of that year, his wife was driving home from delivering Christmas presents to her cousin when her car slid on some ice, and she was killed in a car accident.

Anne was horrified. Bettridge's children were only twelve and six years old at the time, and on Christmas Eve too!

She glanced at the clock and realized it was time for the library to close. Anne reluctantly tore herself away from the biography. She went to each of the rooms to let late patrons know they ought to check out their books now, but several of them dawdled. Anne finally ushered out the last patron, locked up, and shut down the computers, then headed upstairs with the Bettridge biography tucked under her arm.

Ben and Liddie were just finishing the Spider-Man DVD. Liddie was still awake, but she blinked sleepily at Anne as she entered the living room. "Time for bed," she said.

After tucking them both into bed and hearing their prayers, Anne headed to her own bed to continue the Bettridge biography at the tragic point at which she'd been forced to stop.

Hugh Bettridge was horribly shocked by his wife's death. He even stopped caring for his children for several days, and his close friends had to intervene. He spent four weeks in a hospital, and when he finally returned home, he had become a shell of who he had once been.

The spring theater season began, and Bettridge's friends forced him to a few small parties so that he wouldn't worsen his depression by sitting at home, but he had stopped writing *Nanette*, and many friends feared he would never be able to write again.

Anne yawned. She wanted to continue reading, but she was very tired and she was scheduled to meet Phoebe, Lynne Sallman's client, for coffee tomorrow. She set the book aside and turned off the light.

Anne wondered how the death of Lynne's mother and her father's depression had impacted her. She did not expect Lynne to call her back—after all, why would she wish to speak to a stranger about her famous father? Anne hoped that Phoebe might have heard rumors in the theater world and would know something about Lynne's father and the missing script.

CHAPTER TWELVE

O n Friday afternoon, Anne drove to the nearby town of Harrisburg to meet with Phoebe Ramsey, Lynne Bettridge Sallman's client. Anne had looked up the coffee shop, Fiona's Brew, online and printed out directions to get there.

The day started out with some fitful sunlight, but as Anne drove, the clouds completely obscured the sunlight. When she had found the coffee shop, rain had begun to fall, and she ran from her car in the tiny parking lot around the building to the front door of Fiona's Brew.

The door was heavy wood with glass panels, and she had to struggle a little to open it, but as soon as she entered, the warm smell of coffee and pastries wrapped around her like a soft blanket. Small square tables filled the front area, which were mostly filled with people, many of them working on their computer laptops.

Anne had seen Phoebe Ramsey's photo on Phoebe's Web site, so she recognized the playwright at a table near the far corner, typing away on a laptop. Phoebe's long, honey-gold hair had traces of red-gold, and she wore it with the sides pulled up into a clip at the back, and the locks flowing down over her shoulders in ringlets. She wore a yellow dress with ruffles of white lace at the collar and sleeves, making her look like a cheerful ray of sunlight in the midst of this rainy day.

Anne approached her. "Phoebe?"

The woman smiled. "Anne Gibson, right? So great to meet you." She held out her hand to shake Anne's.

"Thank you for driving out here to Harrisburg to meet me." Anne set her purse on the chair opposite Phoebe.

"Oh, it's not a problem. This is a great coffee shop to write in, but I don't come here often since it's a bit far. I usually write in a coffee shop only a half mile away from my house, and they're so used to me that the barista starts making my coffee order as soon as I walk in the front door." Phoebe chuckled. "Did you want to get some coffee?"

"Yes, I'll be right back. Can I get you anything?"

Phoebe gestured to her cup of coffee and a plate with a half-eaten chocolate croissant. "Nope, I'm good."

Anne made her way to the coffee counter. Phoebe was certainly friendly and talkative. She hoped the woman wouldn't mind chatting about her agent. Anne bought a cup of black coffee and couldn't resist adding a cranberry orange scone from the pastry case.

"Those scones are to die for," Phoebe said as Anne sat down. "The coffee here is very good—they roast their own beans—but I admit, I like the pastries even better."

Anne sipped her coffee and had to agree, the rich brew was excellent, strong, and flavorful.

Phoebe put her laptop away into a computer carrying case slung over the back of her oak chair. "I actually arrived an hour ago so I could get some writing done before you came."

"You can write with all this noise?" The coffee shop wasn't very loud, but there was a constant drone of voices from people chatting at nearby tables. Granted, not everyone was talking, for Anne saw that at least half the people in the shop were on their computers, but some tables had friends working on their laptops, and every so often, they would stop to speak to each other.

"Oh, I can write anywhere. I grew up with three brothers and two sisters, and now that I have my own family, I'm used to being able to focus and block out the noise. In fact, if it's too quiet, I have a hard time concentrating."

Anne laughed. "I love the quiet of the library, although I'm not very fond of when I have to remind people to keep their voices down."

"That must be a great place for you to write."

"I'm afraid I gave you the wrong impression. I don't write." Anne felt her cheeks redden. "I'm doing research into the Bettridge family because I just found out that my aunt, who recently passed away, may have been close to Lynne's father. I called Lynne, but I don't really expect her to return the call of a complete stranger. Since you're Lynne's client, I hoped you might know what is truth versus exaggeration in all the rumors about Lynne's father, Hugh Bettridge."

"Of course. The theater world loves to speculate. I guess because we're all artists. What did you want to know?"

"Do you know if Lynne or her father knew an Edie Summers?"

"I don't know, and, I've never heard of her. Was she an actress?"

"No, she worked as a director's assistant." Anne took out a copy she had made of the playbill Edie had sent to Mildred. "For Quentin Chandler, when he was directing the play, *Practice to Deceive* in London in 1962." She showed it to Phoebe.

The woman's eyes lit up. "Oh, by Montgomery Penn. I love his plays. I recognize Quentin Chandler, but I can't remember how..."

Anne suddenly recalled the Bettridge biography she'd read last night. "Is he related to Miriam Chandler, Lynne's mother?"

Phoebe snapped her fingers. "That's it. I read somewhere that he's Miriam's cousin several times removed, but he was also Lynne's godfather. He passed away a few years ago."

Anne then remembered Aunt Edie's letter to Mildred, and took it out of her purse. How had she not remembered it when she was reading last night? "In this letter, written in 1962, my aunt Edie mentioned being friends with a man named 'Billy.'"

"'Billy' was a nickname for Hugh Bettridge. Sometimes even Lynne refers to her father as 'Billy.' But is the Billy in the letter Bettridge or someone else named Billy?"

"I think it's Bettridge. My aunt writes about how Billy was still in mourning for his wife, Miriam, and the date of this letter is only a few months after Bettridge's wife died."

"There's your connection. Your aunt was working for Quentin Chandler, who I can tell you is Lynne's godfather, and this letter seems to say she knew Bettridge."

But it still didn't explain how Aunt Edie got hold of an unproduced play written by Bettridge. Why would he have given it to her? "When I was researching Bettridge, I read some rumors about a 'missing' play. Do you know anything about that?"

Phoebe rolled her eyes. "There have been rumors about that play ever since Bettridge died. I'm afraid I don't know anything about it, or even if it exists. People started buzzing about it again recently—maybe a year or two ago—when some director said he had gotten hold of it and was going to produce it."

"Roy Underwood. I read about that."

"Nothing came out of it, and I think Lynne would say something. I meet her about once a year—either she comes to the states or I go over to England. We have dinner together, talk about my career, that sort of thing. We've become friends enough that I think she'd tell me if her father's 'missing' play had turned up."

"Would she try to get it back if it did?"

"Oh, definitely."

Anne swallowed.

Phoebe continued, "I heard a rumor—so I don't know if it's true—that Lynne was in negotiations with some Hollywood producer to produce the 'missing' play if it ever turned up. You know that two of her father's plays were made into movies several years ago?"

Anne nodded.

"Lynne was the one who negotiated those contracts. She's mentioned them to me a couple times in conversation, and she's pretty pleased by them. She made sure they followed her father's play very closely and didn't take too many liberties."

"Is her brother an agent too?"

"No, he's a painter. He didn't follow in his father's footsteps at all."

"How long have you been Lynne's client?"

Phoebe thought a moment. "About five years. She's sold two plays for me. She's working on a movie deal for one of them. I hope it goes through. It's about a young British noblewoman who helps her brother with an injured stranger...." Phoebe chatted with Anne about her plays and writing, until the woman finally stopped herself self-consciously. "I'm sorry for going on like that, I don't often get to speak to people about my writing. Most of the time I'm by myself."

"I can see how that would be the case." Anne smiled.

"Anyway, I had better head home." Phoebe looked at her watch. "I have to get dinner ready for my husband. If you have any other questions, just send me an e-mail."

On the drive back to Blue Hill, Anne's mind circled around the possible ways Aunt Edie could have gotten the unproduced play from Bettridge. They had apparently been friends, and Aunt Edie had been working for Lynne's godfather.

When did Bettridge give the play to Aunt Edie? Anne hadn't found out anything about the "missing" play except that Roy Underwood had claimed to have it. Who would know anything about it?

When Anne returned to the library, Donna was just finishing checking in some returned books. "How was your coffee?"

"It's a great coffee shop. They apparently roast their own beans."

"*Ooh*. Where was it again?"

Anne gave her the printed directions she'd used to find the coffee shop. "Any problems while I was gone?"

"Nope. Wendy called to say she has Ben and Liddie at her house. They're making play dough."

"Liddie's probably enjoying that. Ben, maybe not as much."

"Ben's playing with Wendy's other kids."

"I had better pick them up so Ben can do his homework before dinner."

When Anne arrived at Wendy's house, Liddie's play dough creation was having a mock battle at the kitchen table with creatures created by Wendy's twins. Liddie's animal, which looked vaguely like a pink-and-purple horse, was trouncing the twins' blue-and-green blobs.

"Look, Mommy! It's a dragon."

"What a colorful dragon."

"He's eating the ants." Liddie pointed to the little blue-and-green lumps that the twins were churning out.

"What colorful ants."

"That's what's left of the two giant bears they made earlier," Wendy said.

"I can't believe you made play dough," Anne marveled.

"It's a super easy recipe, and it's completely healthy for the kids. Speaking of cooking, guess what? I got the high school cooking club to volunteer to help me get ready for the dinner play. They're coming in shifts, and they'll be helping me prepare in the days before the dinner, and a few of them will help me on that night."

"That's fantastic. How did you manage to do that?"

"They were already trying to figure out some type of community service project to do before the end of the school year. Good timing on my part, I guess."

"What's the menu going to be like?"

"I'm still planning it. Almost all the ingredients for the dinner will be donated to the community theater club, so it'll cost us very little. But I'm still waiting on a few businesses to get back to me on their donation lists."

"You must have twisted a few arms."

"The businesses were more than happy to donate stuff in exchange for advertisement in the playbill and at the silent auction."

Anne was aware that it was getting late. "Time for you and your dragon to clean up," Anne said to her daughter. "Where's your brother?"

"He's playing a video game." Liddie smashed her dragon's head between her fingers.

Ben was in the living room playing a multiperson video game with Emily and Christian. "Time to go."

"Aw, Mom," Ben said without taking his eyes from the TV screen. "Just a few minutes more?"

"Did you do your homework?"

Ben didn't answer her.

"Ben?"

"No." He pouted.

"Then it's time to leave," she said firmly.

Ben sighed heavily, but he reluctantly stood up, putting down his game controller. Anne was relieved he hadn't put up more of a fight.

"Thanks, Wendy." Anne herded her two children out the front door.

"Anytime!"

Anne returned to the library and settled Ben in the living room to do his homework. Liddie chose to amuse herself in the Children's Room, and Anne went downstairs to help Donna.

As they were stacking books to put away, Donna asked, "How's the play going? I'm so excited about it. I saw Wendy at the grocery store yesterday and bought two tickets from her."

The reminder of the play made Anne's stomach tighten. How in the world was she going to get through that scene tonight with Alex? She strived for a calm voice as she answered Donna. "It's going well, I think. Liddie and Ben are very excited for their small parts. They behaved well during the reading so far, but I hope they keep it up during the rest of the rehearsals. I'm worried they'll get bored in between their speaking parts."

But as the time to rehearsal slowly approached, Anne felt a tension across her shoulders. She closed the library and Donna left, but as Anne trudged upstairs, anxiety made her footsteps heavy. She took a deep breath to try to calm herself. It was only a play.

She fixed grilled cheese sandwiches and tomato soup for dinner. She asked Ben, "So did you finish reading the script?"

"No, I started reading a book on the Egyptian pharaohs that's really cool, so I haven't finished the script yet."

They finished dinner in time for Anne to let in the theater club members. When Alex arrived with Ryan, Anne gave him a tight smile in response to his "Hi, Anne."

He stopped to look at her. "What's wrong?"

"Nothing."

He gave her a thoughtful look but then moved toward the History Room.

Anne inwardly groaned. Why did she have to act like such a dunce?

She sat next to Alex as usual, with Ben, Liddie, and Ryan close by. But Anne couldn't help feeling anxious as the rehearsal started.

Tami arrived late. She gave Anne a quick thumbs-up as she hurried toward the front of the room. Anne grimaced at her friend's enthusiasm.

"All right, everyone," Stephan said. "Let's get started."

The place they had stopped at the last rehearsal was right before a section where the gypsy flirted with the librarian, so they began with an exchange between Alex and Anne.

"Look," Alex said as the wooing gypsy, "the moon has gathered her stars around her. She reminds me of your eyes."

"You'll not be taking me in with your silver tongue," Anne said woodenly.

Stephan gave her a pained look. "Remember, Anne, you're supposed to secretly like the gypsy, even though you're not falling for his flattery."

Anne repeated the line, but it sounded snappish. Alex gave her an odd look; however, Stephan didn't say anything, so they continued with the reading.

But the rest of the evening went the same way. Anne couldn't say any of her lines without sounding terrible.

At one point, Liddie whispered to her, "What's the matter, Mommy? Don't you like Mr. Ochs anymore?"

Anne stifled a groan. She was never going to get this right. Why in the world did she agree to this?

Alex, on the other hand, was relaxed and sounded the same as he had the last few rehearsals. Anne was baffled. It was as if he didn't even realize there was a kiss coming at the end. How was she going to handle the kiss? Would it change their friendship? Anne knew that realistically it shouldn't, but she couldn't help worrying about it.

Finally there came the kiss moment. Anne was strung as tight as a wire. How would she be able to do this?

"My darling, my love for you has grown to encompass every thought," Alex said in fervent tones.

Anne wondered how he could act so well with her, considering their past dating relationship and their present friendship. She took a deep breath, then read her lines. "I have loved you since the moment you first kissed my hand."

Now even Alex looked a bit uncomfortable. Then he leaned over to kiss her cheek.

His simple action seemed to release all her muscles, and she sagged in her chair. She should have known Alex would be respectful of her and not do anything inappropriate.

There were a few sweet sighs from the other actors at the romantic gesture. Stephan said, "That's fine for now, but the audience will want a real kiss on opening night, just a sweet kiss. You can do that, right? Didn't you two date in high school?"

Anne didn't understand why she felt so awkward when she and Alex had been high school sweethearts.

"No problem." Alex's voice was calm, but his expression when he glanced at her seemed apprehensive. Anne couldn't blame him, after her terrible performance.

The rest of the rehearsal went smoothly, and finally they were done with the read-through. "Great job," Stephan said. "We'll start tomorrow afternoon with regular rehearsals. I expect all of you to memorize your parts through act 1."

Alex leaned close to Anne. "Are you all right?"

"I'm…" She wasn't really sure how she felt. She wanted to demand how he could be so calm about this.

"Shut up!" Ben shouted.

Anne sprang to her feet in time to see Ben and Ryan getting into a tussle. She and Alex ran to separate them.

"What's going on?" Alex demanded from Ryan.

"He hit me," Ryan said belligerently. "It wasn't my fault."

"Yes it was," Ben said. "You wouldn't shut up."

"Ben, you are not supposed to be fighting," Anne said sternly. "I want you to apologize."

"No, I won't!" Tears sprang to his eyes. He was very upset at something, not simply angry at Ryan.

"Upstairs right now, mister."

Ben slunk away, his hands in his pockets. Anne looked helplessly at Alex. "I don't know what happened."

"Why don't I bring him back tomorrow? It'll give us both a chance to talk to the boys."

"All right."

No one embarrassed Anne with questions about the tiff. She saw them all out the front door and locked it, then headed upstairs. She'd sent Liddie upstairs to get ready for bed on the heels of her brother.

Anne went to Liddie's room first and heard her prayers, then went to Ben's room. He sat up in bed, his arms crossed, his face mutinous.

Anne sat on the edge of his bed. "Ben, honey, tell me what's wrong."

He didn't say anything, but his lower lip trembled.

"I promise I won't be mad."

He uncrossed his arms and his shoulders sagged. Anne could see him thinking. Then he said in a low voice, "Do you still like Mr. Ochs?"

"Of course I do."

"You didn't seem to like it when he kissed you."

"It was just a little awkward. He's still a good friend to me, just like Ryan is a good friend to you."

"Ryan was being stupid." Ben's voice regained some rebellion. "He was singing that stupid kissing song and I told him to stop."

"It was only a silly song." Anne stroked his head. "Can you tell me why it bothered you?"

His eyes were wide and confused. "I don't know. I know that's bad."

Anne put her arm around him and kissed him. "It's all right, honey. It's not bad to be confused." She herself was confused. She hadn't thought about how the scene would affect Ben and Liddie. She and Alex were friends, but it wasn't the same sort of relationship as the gypsy and the librarian in the play, and it might seem strange to her son, who was used to seeing Anne and Alex interact in a certain way.

"It was wrong for you to attack Ryan, though, even though he was doing something you didn't like. Will you apologize to him tomorrow?"

Ben gave a deep sigh. "Yes."

"That's my boy." She gave his shoulders a squeeze. "I'm proud of you." She couldn't help the welling of love in her heart for her young man, growing up so fast.

But she herself needed to figure out what to do. She certainly couldn't play the part the way she'd done it tonight! But what could she do to make herself relax? And how would this play affect her friendship with Alex?

Chapter Thirteen

Anne woke early on a sunny Saturday morning, before either of the kids arose. She brewed a cup of coffee and sat with her Bible out on the porch of the library. Now that the weather was becoming warmer, she would be able to enjoy more mornings like this.

She opened up to John chapter fourteen where Jesus was speaking to His disciples: *"All this I have spoken while still with you. But the Advocate, the Holy Spirit, whom the Father will send in my name, will teach you all things and will remind you of everything I have said to you. Peace I leave with you; my peace I give you. I do not give to you as the world gives. Do not let your hearts be troubled and do not be afraid."*

Anne sighed. She still felt worry over the play and Ben and Ryan. No, if she were honest with herself, she was more worried over how things were with Alex. Would they get more awkward? How could they smooth things over and make things the way they were again? Was it even possible? She didn't want to lose their friendship in any way.

Anne read the verse again and tried to feel some sort of peace, but she couldn't seem to still her racing thoughts.

"Mom!" Ben called from inside the house. "I need more toothpaste."

Anne realized she'd been sitting out here so long that her coffee had gone cold. She went inside, vaguely guilty that she'd been so caught up in her thoughts that she hadn't prayed this morning.

As she made pancakes for breakfast for Ben and Liddie, the phone rang. "Hello?"

"Hi, it's Alex. Is it all right if I bring Ryan over this morning?"

"Why don't you come over for breakfast? I'm just starting the pancakes."

Ben took Hershey out and then went upstairs to wash up. He had just wandered into the kitchen as Alex and Ryan rang the buzzer.

"Ben, Alex and Ryan are here for breakfast," Anne told him.

His face grew heavy.

"I expect you to apologize to Ryan, all right?"

"All right," he said in a low voice.

Ryan also seemed awkward as he entered the kitchen and saw Ben. The two boys scuffed their feet on the floor for a moment, then Anne said, "Ben," at the same time that Alex said, "Ryan." Anne and Alex shared an understanding look, then returned their attention to the boys.

"I'm sorry," Ben said at the same time that Ryan said, "I'm sorry."

"For what?" Anne said.

"I'm sorry for hitting you."

"I'm sorry for singing that song."

"Shake on it, boys," Alex said, and the two of them shook hands, like little men. It made Anne smile at the sight.

"Who wants pancakes?" she asked, and the two boys brightened. Ben went to get his sister, and then they all sat at the kitchen table while Anne placed the platter of piping hot pancakes in the center, along with maple syrup and butter.

"Alex, will you say grace?" Anne asked him.

He bowed his head. "Dear Heavenly Father, thank You for this good day. Thank You for providing this food, and for Anne cooking it for us. And thank You for our friendship with each other. In Jesus' name, Amen."

"Amen," they chorused, and dug in.

Alex's prayer somehow made Anne's heart a little lighter, especially after the worry she had battled earlier this morning. She hoped the two of them would be able to chat after breakfast.

The pancakes were a hit, although Liddie made a mess with her maple syrup, getting it all over her face, hands, and on the collar of her shirt. In a show of maturity, Ben said, "I'll help her wash and change her shirt, Mom." He took his sister upstairs. Just like watching him shake hands with Ryan, Anne felt a rush of pride and love for her son.

After breakfast, she sent the three of them outside with Hershey in the backyard while she and Alex cleaned up. He rinsed the dishes as she washed them.

"I'm sorry about last night," Anne said. "I feel like an idiot."

Alex smiled at her, and it lightened his blue eyes to the color of a summer sky. "It's all right, Anne. I understand."

"I just…that scene…" In her agitation, some soap bubbles flew up from where she was washing a plate.

Alex reached over to grab her fidgety hands in his large one. "Anne, it's all right. When I heard you'd taken the part, I guessed you hadn't yet read the ending of the script, and I wondered how you'd feel about it."

"I know it's silly of me to worry, because it's only a play, but I didn't want it to make our friendship awkward. But then my behavior last night made things awkward anyway."

Alex laughed and removed his hand from hers. She missed the calmness he had imparted to her.

"Anne, I hope you don't think I'm reading more into the play than what's already between us. I don't want you to worry about that."

Although she hadn't articulated it to herself, she had been worrying about that, and she shouldn't have. She should have known Alex would be sensible about everything.

"I respect you and I don't want anything to ruin our friendship now," Alex said.

"I don't want anything to ruin it either."

"Then let's just agree that even though our roles in this play are a little awkward, it won't affect how we interact with each other. It's been great for me to get to know you again, and Ryan loves your family—even though he and Ben have their occasional tiffs." Alex gave a rueful smile.

"Ben really does love Ryan too. His friendship has made it so much easier for Ben to transition to living in Blue Hill. Now he loves it as much as he loved living in New York."

"Ryan's come out of his shell a bit more too, because of his friendship with Ben. It's been good all around." Alex finished rinsing the last dish. "So, are we okay?"

"Yes. Thank you for talking to me about this. I feel better now."

"Don't worry about the play. Just pretend we're Mary and Joseph in the church Christmas pageant like we used to do." He grinned, and he looked like a teenager in high school.

Alex and Ryan left soon afterward since Alex had to meet with a potential client that morning and Anne had to open the library.

There were many people who came to the library but not many who needed her help. After Anne had taken care of books that people had returned, she sat at the checkout desk, in case anyone came up to her with a question, and finished the Bettridge biography she'd been reading.

It was a bit more interesting now that she understood how Aunt Edie must have met Bettridge. But Aunt Edie's relationship didn't seem close enough for him to have given her the "missing" play. Why would he have done that? Anne began to wonder if Aunt Edie had done something special for Bettridge, and he gave her the play in gratitude. And what a gift!

Unfortunately, the biography didn't mention much that happened during the year Aunt Edie was in England. After the death of his wife, Bettridge spent time recovering from his grief and eventually finished his most famous play, *Nanette*, in November or December of 1963.

The biography talked about his later plays and successes, and then Bettridge's death from a heart attack in the spring of 1990. A large percentage of his estate went to charity, with the full agreement of his daughter and son. The biography ended with a mention about the two movies made from Bettridge's plays, *Nanette* and *Lanterns*.

Anne finished the book in dissatisfaction. She had learned a great deal about Bettridge, but she hadn't gotten answers for the questions she was asking. The biography hadn't mentioned the "missing" Bettridge play, perhaps because there was no real proof it existed.

The writer of the biography, Dr. Harry Glendenning, was a professor of English at a New York university and on the board of directors for a nonprofit organization that supported performing arts programs in high schools. Would he have found information on the rumors about the "missing" play which he hadn't been able to include in the book?

Anne went online and found the university's Web site, then clicked through to the English department. She quickly found Dr. Glendenning's name and faculty page, which gave his e-mail address.

She composed an e-mail to send to him:

Dear Dr. Glendenning,

My name is Anne Gibson, and I am the head librarian at the Blue Hill Library in Blue Hill, Pennsylvania. I have just finished reading your biography on the life of Hugh Bettridge and found it fascinating. I recently discovered that my aunt Edie Summers was friends with Bettridge in 1962. I am curious about any information you may have about the "missing" Bettridge script that I have heard so much about. I am researching the script because I have reason to believe that my aunt Edie may have known something about it. Would you please contact me?

Anne had struggled over if she should mention her aunt's connection to the missing script, but she wanted the professor to know that she had more than a passing interest in it. He seemed conscientious of only writing about the facts of Bettridge's life in the biography, and she had a feeling he wouldn't respond to her e-mail if he thought she was simply a reporter or blogger looking to propagate the rumor about the missing script.

She included her contact information at the library and then sent the e-mail message.

She closed the library at one o'clock, then fed Ben and Liddie a late lunch just before the theater group was scheduled to arrive for rehearsal. It would be a longer rehearsal today since they would be able to have the library to themselves for most of the afternoon.

Wendy arrived first with her two kids, and she carried a large bag of toys and activities.

"What are all those for?" Anne asked.

"Since today's a longer rehearsal, I wasn't sure if my kids—or any of the kids, for that matter—would be able to sit still for all of it. I brought things for them to do in case I needed to take them out of the History Room for a little while. Since I'm not acting in the play, I can watch your kids too if they get antsy."

"You think of everything. Thanks."

"It's experience. We had a play a few years ago that my two oldest were in. I figured it was best to be prepared, just in case."

"Do you want to set these things in the Children's Room? That way they can entertain themselves with the books and chalk wall too."

"That's what I was thinking. I'll drop these off right now."

The kids went with Wendy to see what she'd brought.

Tami arrived, and she had a serious look on her face. "Could I talk to you?" she asked Anne.

"Of course." Anne drew her to the kitchen for some privacy. "What's up?"

Tami bit her lip and leaned against a counter. "This might be nothing, but I was a little spooked after I thought that man was following me last week."

"Do you mean that short, dark-haired man you saw? What happened?"

"Mom heard from several of her friends that a short, dark-haired man has been asking around downtown Blue Hill about Edie and a play manuscript."

Anne stared at Tami in shock. "The only way he could have known about Aunt Edie was through her note to Roy. How could he have found out about it?"

"I don't know. I never told anyone except you about the note I found."

"I told Wendy and Mildred, but they'd never breathe a word."

Tami swallowed. "Do you think he followed me here to Blue Hill?"

"You don't remember seeing him in London?"

Tami shook her head.

Anne rubbed her friend's shoulder. "Maybe there was something else hidden in another costume at Roy's estate auction. Or maybe it's not the Bettridge script at all but some other play he's referring to."

"But how likely would that be? You haven't found the script yet, have you?"

"I've looked everywhere, but I can't find it. I'm beginning to think she managed to get it to Roy before he died."

Tami rubbed her hands over her arms. "I'm just glad Aiden is arriving on Monday."

They heard feet tramping up the steps to the front porch of the library as more theater club members arrived. Anne gave Tami a quick hug. "Try not to worry about it too much."

When Alex arrived with Ryan, Anne felt a resurgence of her old worry, but he gave her a reassuring smile, and it calmed her. "Wendy's set up some activities in the Children's Room if the kids get too bored," she said.

"That's a great idea."

He and Anne didn't have many speaking lines in the first act. However, they stood on the stage at the front of the History Room with the other actors as they rehearsed, and Stephan often stopped everyone to adjust their positions and direct their actions so that they didn't block any other characters from the audience's view. With twelve adults and five children in that limited space, the choreography was tricky.

Alex's gypsy character was a gregarious fellow, interacting with both the other actors and occasionally with the audience. Despite feeling better about their friendship, somehow things were still strange for Anne.

Maybe it was because their talk this morning had made Anne appreciate even more how kind Alex was. The gypsy's mild flirtations with the librarian reminded her of their fun, sweet relationship in high school when they were dating. But it also reminded her of the playful relationship she'd had with Eric. It was what had made her fall in love with him, because he'd been comfortable with moments of liveliness.

At one point, Anne and Alex were crossing the stage and attempting to move out of each other's way. She'd move to her right, but the gypsy moved to his left. She'd move the other direction, and he moved with her.

"Anne, your movements are a bit wooden," Stephan said. "You're a mousy librarian, not expecting or wanting to be noticed, but you're in the way of this dashing gypsy. Look a little flustered."

Anne went back to stage right and Alex went back to stage left, and they tried the sequence again, striding toward each other. Alex was in character and had an amused look on his face, which made the corners of his eyes crinkle. Anne was aware of how close Alex was to her as they moved.

Alex said his line, "Now all we need is a fiddler playing a waltz. But would you dance with me, my darling?"

Anne spoke her line, but it came out sounding a bit strangled. "Don't call me your darling. And I would not dance with a rogue like you."

Stephan said, "Anne, while your character is rebuffing him, she secretly enjoys his flirtations, but she just doesn't want to show it. Try to inject a little amusement into her response."

They tried it again. Anne's frustration over her failed line made her sound irritated rather than amused. However, Stephan didn't stop the rehearsal, and they continued.

The kids were patient for most of the afternoon, probably because standing with the other actors and listening for their lines made the experience exciting. However, for the last third of the rehearsal, they began fidgeting, and Wendy took them upstairs.

When Ben and Liddie left the room, Anne seemed to do even worse. It flustered her to have Alex being more outgoing toward her, even though she knew he was just acting out his character. When she couldn't speak her lines very well, she grew more annoyed with herself, which only made things worse.

At the end of rehearsal, she breathed a sigh of relief. She thought that once she had a handle on her worry over her friendship with Alex, she'd relax and do a better job, but she still couldn't seem to unwind.

"I'm sorry," Anne said to Stephan. "Maybe you should find someone with more acting experience."

"You worry too much. We're all friends here, and no one is expecting an award-winning performance. You're pushing yourself, and it's making you stressed about something that isn't that big a deal."

"You're right. I don't know why I'm doing this."

"It'll be better as you get used to the play and rehearsals."

But as Anne said good-bye to Alex and Ryan, she thought perhaps her bad performance was because of a continued anxiety. Alex had allayed her fears about their friendship, but there was a different sort of fear that niggled at her now.

She was comfortable with Alex, and he was still an attractive man. During the rehearsals, she had started feeling hints of the same romantic awareness she'd had for Eric, feelings she hadn't felt since he died.

It disquieted her. She didn't know if she was ready to think about these sorts of things, and with everything going on with the play and Aunt Edie's script, her life seemed too complicated for her to want to examine her feelings right now.

But she was still in turmoil about these emotions. What should she do about them?

CHAPTER FOURTEEN

At church the next morning, Anne listened to Reverend Tom's sermon on Philippians 4:6–7: *"Do not be anxious about anything, but in everything, by prayer and petition, with thanksgiving, present your requests to God. And the peace of God, which transcends all understanding, will guard your hearts and your minds in Christ Jesus."*

Anne knew she needed to calm her anxiety, but she wasn't sure what she was anxious about. Her friendship with Alex? But hadn't he said they were fine? So why was she worried? About the whisper of attraction she'd felt for Alex at the last rehearsal? But why would that little thread of emotion upset her so much?

She was being silly. Alex was probably wondering why Anne was being such a basket case about the entire thing. It was only a play, after all, and it was all for the community theater club's fundraiser, not an award-winning production.

Anne realized that Reverend Tom was bowing his head for the closing prayer, and she hastily closed her eyes. She had spent the entire sermon worrying and thinking rather than listening! She prayed, *Dear Lord Jesus, why would I do something like that rather than learning from the teaching? Please forgive me for my wandering thoughts.*

After Reverend Tom dismissed everyone for coffee and cookies in the fellowship hall, Anne sagged in her seat for a few moments. Why did something silly like this play cause her to worry so much?

"Are you all right, Anne?"

She looked up to see Mildred's kind eyes as she stopped beside Anne's seat. "Hi, Mildred. I'm just thinking."

"You seemed a bit distracted during the sermon. I could tell your mind was a thousand miles away."

Anne groaned. "Things happening with the play are making me feel confused."

"It's all right to be confused sometimes. It could mean God is challenging us."

"I feel challenged, all right. I still haven't found Aunt Edie's script, although I think I know how she met the playwright." Anne told her about what she'd learned about Bettridge and the connection she'd made with Aunt Edie's letter.

"Imagine, Edie knowing a famous playwright and just blithely talking about 'Billy' in her letter as if he were nobody," Mildred said. "Wasn't that just like her?"

Liddie and Ben came into the sanctuary, released from children's church.

"Mommy, I want cookies," Liddie announced.

"Then let's go have some."

The two kids headed to the fellowship hall with Anne and Mildred trailing after them.

Anne said to Mildred, "I still don't know how Aunt Edie and Bettridge would have developed a close enough relationship for him to give her the play. I wonder if she did something for him."

"Edie wasn't one to accept payment or gifts in return for something she did for someone. She liked doing things out of the goodness of her heart. If he gave it to her, it was because he cared for her."

"Yes, that sounds more like Aunt Edie. I just don't know how I could find out what happened between them."

"The biography didn't mention Edie, I suppose?"

"I wish! But perhaps he did learn something but didn't include it in the book."

"Let's hope he e-mails you back so you can find out."

Anne was hopeful he would e-mail her back, since she had written a rather tantalizing e-mail message. But would he be able to help her understand her aunt's relationship with Bettridge?

* * *

Monday morning, Anne left the library in the capable hands of Remi and Bella and met Gwendolyn Ross in Deshler. Gwendolyn had a thirty-minute break from her shift at the hospital and asked if Anne would meet her on the grounds.

The back of the Deshler Community Hospital had a small area with clusters of trees and benches placed near crisscrossing walkways. The grass was a bright minty green, and the trees were well past budding and starting to come into full foliage. Summer was coming soon.

Anne had bought some coffee and a box of pastries at a local bakery, and as she sat on a bench near the back door of the hospital, the door opened and Gwendolyn Ross breezed out. She looked exactly like her photo on the Web site for the Deshler community

Theater—slender, with straight brown hair cut in a fashionable bob. She wore eye-catching turquoise blue scrubs in a fun print, and she carried a paper grocery bag.

Anne stood up and waved. "Gwendolyn? Hi, I'm Anne."

Gwendolyn's mouth pulled into a wide smile. "Hi. Thanks for meeting me at the hospital." Her low, husky voice carried well despite the noise from the nearby parking lot.

"I'm grateful you're taking time out of your busy day for me. I brought coffee and pastries."

"You're a doll." Gwendolyn sat next to Anne on the bench, her eyes already on the bag. "I didn't have more than a bite for breakfast."

"Help yourself."

Gwendolyn selected a chocolate croissant and stirred cream in her coffee. "Stephan said you wanted to talk about Collin Avery's plays? That reminds me, before I forget…" She handed Anne the paper grocery bag. "These are Stephan's hats. Please tell him thank you for letting us borrow them."

"Sure." Anne took the bag and set it down on the ground next to her. "I'm afraid Stephan misrepresented what I wanted to talk to you about. My aunt Edie died a few months ago, and I recently found out that she may have given a script to Roy Underwood, Collin's cousin. I wondered if Roy gave it to Collin."

At the mention of Roy's name, Gwendolyn made a moue of distaste. "Roy and Collin weren't exactly friends."

That confirmed the subtle clues that Roy's mother had given to Anne when she visited them. "So he wouldn't have shown the script to Collin?"

"I'm not saying that. Roy actually never struck me as being as competitive as Collin was. Collin always felt people were comparing them."

Considering Roy's outstanding successes in London compared to Collin's more mediocre ones in New York, Anne could understand how Collin might have felt. "You were all in drama club together, weren't you?"

"For our freshman year, and Roy's senior year."

"The two of them must have been very good."

"They had very different acting styles. They were both passionate about theater, but Collin would follow his whims when he was acting. It drove our director crazy."

"Roy wasn't like that?"

"Roy wasn't legalistic, but he followed the script exactly. He didn't improvise unless there was some emergency. One time, a stray dog wandered into the school theater because someone had left a door open. It was dress rehearsal for a scene where we were sitting at dinner, so we had real food. Roy was brilliantly funny in how he improvised his lines with this dog trying to jump up on the table."

"The director didn't stop the scene?" Anne grinned.

"He was going to, but Roy was hilarious, so he didn't. We were all dying laughing. Finally, Roy got the dog offstage to someone standing there, who managed to lure it back outside with a ham sandwich." Gwendolyn sighed. "I was so sad to hear Roy passed away last year."

"Did Collin go to his funeral?"

"Yes, even though he was in the middle of a production. He traveled to England three times during that production."

"Three?"

"He visited Roy about a month before he died." Gwendolyn frowned. "Now that I think about it, that was strange since Collin hardly ever talks to Roy. I think he was in London for something else, because he came back excited about something he couldn't talk about. Then Roy died, and Collin went to the funeral. And a month later, Collin attended Roy's estate auction."

"That's a lot of trips in two months." Anne wondered why Collin had gone to London the month before Roy died. Had Roy given the Bettridge play to Collin? But wouldn't he have produced it by now if he had it? Anne remembered how Flores Sanchez hadn't much cared for Bettridge's scripts. "I was reading about the rumors that Roy had a script by Bettridge."

Gwendolyn rolled her eyes. "Collin was so upset by those rumors, but he never wanted to talk about them. He's a huge Bettridge fan."

So would Roy have shown the Bettridge script to Collin because he was a fan, or would he not have shown the Bettridge script to Collin for fear his cousin would try to take it? "Was Roy a huge Bettridge fan too?"

"Actually, I'm not sure."

"I was talking to some other members in our community theater club, and while Stephan is a Bettridge fan, some others aren't."

"I'm not. His plays are a bit too depressing for me."

"I hope to watch the two Bettridge movies soon."

"Have a hankie handy. You'll need it."

Anne sipped her coffee. "So what's the new Deshler theater production going to be?"

They chatted about the Deshler theater group a bit, which was larger than the Blue Hill theater club. Their upcoming production was going to be a musical, *Some Brief Folly*, which sounded like it involved several different couples discovering they're in love and a possible murderer among them.

"I heard you're doing a Victorian mystery dinner play," Gwendolyn said. "That's different. I would think the dinner part must be difficult."

"Wendy Pyle is planning the dinner, and a lot of local businesses have donated food for the menu. We'll also have a silent auction to help raise more money than just the dinner."

"That's smart. I heard about the theater roof." Gwendolyn winced. She talked about some other ideas for fund-raisers that the Deshler community theater had done, and Anne stored the ideas away to relate to Wendy later.

"I'd better get back to work," Gwendolyn said.

"Thanks for meeting with me." Anne began collecting the trash. "So even though Collin saw Roy a month before he died, he never mentioned if Roy had given him a script?"

"No. Your aunt was a playwright?"

"It wasn't her play, it was written by a friend of hers. I'm worried since my aunt may have loaned the only copy to Roy, but he never returned it before he died."

"I can see how that would be worrisome. I can ask Collin about it, if you'd like."

"I'd appreciate that. I got his number from his aunt, but he doesn't know who I am."

"What was the name of the writer?"

Anne hesitated to mention Bettridge's name, especially with the rumors about the "missing" play right after Roy died. "I'd rather not say, to protect the privacy of his family. Roy got the script from Edie Summers."

"Protect the privacy of the family?" Gwendolyn had an odd look. "I'll ask Collin, but Roy may not have told him your aunt gave him the script."

"I wondered about that, but I doubt Roy has given many scripts to Collin, since they're not close."

They said good-bye, and Anne headed home. Because Collin was a Bettridge fan, if Roy had given Collin the Bettridge play, Anne doubted Collin would give it back to Anne now, just because Gwendolyn asked him about it. But if he had the play, wouldn't he have produced it by now? He could have explained that Roy gave it to him before he died. Or would Collin keep the script secret for some other reason?

Anne was driving up toward the library just as Tami was parking in front of it. She got out of her car and leaned over to peer into the silver Impala through the open window.

Anne gave her friend a rueful look. "Are you here to scold me after my performance yesterday at rehearsal?"

Tami smiled. "Of course not. But I am worried for you. What's up?"

Anne groaned. "I don't know. That's the problem. I thought I was fine acting with Alex, but I'm still feeling some weirdness between us. I'm pretty sure it's all in my head. I tried to tell myself to be professional, that it's only acting. Except I don't have a lot of experience in acting, so I felt insecure that I wasn't doing everything right. So then I tried to tell myself that it was all for the sake of the community theater club."

"No wonder you had such a martyred look on your face all during rehearsal."

"Stephan tried so hard to help me."

Tami gave her a sympathetic look. "Aiden's coming in today. Did you want me to ask him to help you out?"

"Of course. If anyone can help me, it's your actor husband. Will he mind?"

"Not at all. Can you come by my parents' house tomorrow morning? We have a family luncheon in the afternoon."

"That would be great."

"I'll see you tomorrow, then." Tami straightened and waved to Anne as she drove away to park her car.

Tami's offer made Anne feel better. Surely, Aiden could help her with her terrible acting. If only her feelings about Alex and worry over their friendship would stop hindering her performance during rehearsals.

When Anne entered the library, Bella looked up from the checkout desk. "Good timing. You just got two packages."

Anne unwrapped the first box. "That's quick, it's the DVDs of the two Hugh Bettridge movies that I ordered through interlibrary loan."

"Oh, Hugh Bettridge?" Bella looked at the titles. "We did *Nanette* for the community theater club a few years ago. I got the role of Ninion and had this fantastic death scene at the end."

"Your sister told me about that."

"Remi doesn't like Bettridge plays very much. She says they're depressing, but if you look at the symbolism, there's a lot of hope in the underlying message."

"I guess I'll have to look at the movie and see." Anne unwrapped the second box and found it was the VHS recording of Krista Underwood Bennett's famous play, *Time's Fool*. "It doesn't rain, but it pours. I ordered this almost two weeks ago and it's only arriving now."

"I've never heard of that play."

"It was famous before you were born, so that's probably why."

Remi arrived at the checkout desk with an empty book cart and caught sight of the Bettridge DVDs. "Be prepared to cry buckets."

"It wasn't that depressing," Bella protested.

"You had an epic death scene. What's happy about that?"

Bella rolled her eyes. "It was the juxtaposition of life and death. Nanette lived with greater wisdom about the value of life specifically because she saw how bravely Ninion died."

"Nanette and Ninion, huh? I had to do a paper on name derivatives when I was in high school," Anne said. "Those are both derivatives of my name, Anne."

"Really?" Bella's eyes shone. "I didn't know that. It gives so much more depth to the story now..."

Remi winked at Anne. "If you ask her, I'm sure she'd do Ninion's death scene for you right now, here at the checkout desk."

Bella gave her sister a sour look, but Remi just grinned back at her.

"I didn't know his other play was made into a movie," Bella said. "Can I check this out when you're done with it?" She held up *Lanterns*.

"Of course," Anne said.

"I can't believe you didn't know about this movie," Remi said to her sister. "You're almost as big a Bettridge fan as Stephan."

"Well, this came out when we were still in middle school," Bella said.

"Stephan mentioned that both these movies weren't very well publicized," Anne said.

"I wonder why?" Bella said. "Bettridge has won loads of awards for his plays."

"Maybe because no one wants to watch a depressing play?" Remi teased her.

"Nicholas Sparks's movies are blockbusters and a lot of his movies are sad," Bella said.

"Yeah, I guess so," Remi admitted.

The mention of blockbuster made Anne wonder about the financial success of Bettridge's movies. "Is there a way to find out how much the movie made when it released in theaters?"

"Oh sure." Bella went to the computer and pulled up an Internet browser. "Movies' gross earnings are usually up on the entertainment Web sites. You can search for a particular movie."

Anne should have known that web-savvy Bella would know about this. They had to sift through other movies with the word *lanterns* in the title, but they finally found the movie with the right release date. "The gross earnings were really low."

"Yeah." Remi was looking over her sister's shoulder. "How about *Nanette*?"

Bella began typing. "Here it is."

Nanette did a bit better than *Lanterns* but not by much. "Wow, those are dismal," Remi said.

"Here's the production cost." Bella pointed to the screen. "The movie barely made enough to break even."

Anne now wondered if the rumors about Lynne Bettridge Sallman wanting to make a movie from the "missing" script were really true. According to these numbers, her father's other two plays did not make a great deal of money as movies, so would she really have a third play produced into a movie? The chances of it making money seemed slim. She might still insist the script belonged to her family, but it seemed unlikely that she would want the script made into a movie.

The phone rang. "Hello, this is Blue Hill Library. Anne Gibson speaking."

"This is Consuela from Sanguinet Broadcasting. You had called earlier about getting a copy of an episode for one of our TV programs? We did have old copies of the show *Behind the Curtain* in our archive room, and we were able to make a DVD copy of the episode you wanted, number one-one-two. Did you still want to see it?"

"I would love to. How much would it cost?"

"Right now, it would only cost you the postage to send you the DVD of the one episode. However, we are in the process of digitizing our old programs to sell on DVD sets, and we would like you to think about buying the show, *Behind the Curtain*, for your library inventory when we release it. We would offer it to you at a substantial discount if you agree to add the episode to your library inventory and have it available through interlibrary loan to other libraries." She named a price that was very reasonable for the number of years the program had run. Consuela also listed several of the people who had been interviewed on the program, and even Anne recognized many of them.

"I would definitely like to think about it." Anne gave her the address for the library, thanked her, and hung up. Remi and Bella were looking at her with curiosity, so Anne explained about the TV program. Both girls seemed interested when Anne listed the names of the people interviewed.

"It would be really neat to have a program like that at the library," Remi said, "especially with the community theaters here and in Deshler."

"So do you think people would be interested?" Anne asked. "The studio is being very generous in giving me the episode I wanted to see, and since the price of the program is very reasonable, I'm willing to order it for the library if there's enough interest in it."

"With the amount of tickets we've sold for the Victorian mystery dinner play, it seems a lot of people in town like plays in general," Bella said.

"You can also see how many people bid on the New York theater tickets being donated to the silent auction," Remi said. "Tami O'Brien apparently knows someone in a theater in New York who agreed to donate the tickets for the silent auction."

"I want to ask her about it at rehearsal tonight," Bella said.

The reminder made Anne worry about the rehearsal. If she tried really hard, would she finally be able to relax?

* * *

The rehearsal that night went great for everyone else, but Anne was still hopelessly stiff. After their scene, Alex leaned close to Anne. "Are you all right?"

"I really don't know what's wrong with me."

"You're not still worried about our friendship, are you?"

"No." She didn't want to admit to him that their comfortable relationship was what made her worried. Every time she saw him, there was that whisper of attraction she felt, which she hadn't been aware of before. Yet he was still the same Alex who was her friend. Why couldn't she stay the same? "I'm meeting with Tami's husband, Aiden, tomorrow."

Alex looked over at Aiden, who had accompanied his wife tonight and helped with acting and blocking. "He's a good actor. I'm sure he'll be able to help you."

One of the other actors waved at Alex. "Alex, we have a question about the set."

Anne took the opportunity to go up to Stephan. "I'm so sorry."

"You're worrying too much about it. If you relaxed a bit more, you'd be fine."

"Aiden said he'd help me tomorrow."

"That's a great idea. All you need is a few tips to boost your confidence and make you more comfortable."

Anne nodded, but what if it took more than a few tips to help her? Tonight she'd been marginally better, but she was still too awkward. Was she still anxious about the kiss at the end? How could she approach this with a more distanced, professional attitude?

At bedtime, Liddie fell asleep almost as soon as her head hit the pillow. In contrast, Ben seemed wide awake when Anne went in to hear his prayers.

After praying, he looked down and fiddled with the edge of his bed sheet.

"What is it, sweetie? Something on your mind?"

He nodded slowly. "It's about the play."

Anne had an inkling about what he wanted to talk about. "What about it? Do you like your part?"

He nodded again. "It's not that. It's… it's your part."

"The librarian?"

"Yeah. And the gypsy."

"Does it make you uncomfortable? Seeing me and Mr. Ochs acting those parts?"

"Sort of." He scratched his head. "It's kind of weird."

"It's a little weird for me too. But I remind myself that it's only playacting, and it's all for the community theater club fund-raiser, so it's for a good cause."

"I guess that's a good way to think about it."

"Do you feel okay with Mr. Ochs?"

"Yeah. He's nice. And I like Ryan a lot." He hesitated, then he said, "Do you miss Daddy?"

Anne folded her arms around him. "Of course I do. He's up in heaven, but if he were here, he'd say he was very proud of you, Ben."

"I'm glad he's happy in heaven. I think he only wants us to be happy here too."

What a precious word of insight from the mouth of her child. Anne squeezed her son tight. "I think you're right." She prayed, *Lord, thank You for watching over my children and for helping Ben to be filled with Your wisdom.*

Anne left her son in bed but wandered downstairs to the darkened library. She was frustrated over her inability to act naturally in her scenes with Alex. Maybe if she watched some good actors, she'd be inspired.

She grabbed the VHS tape of Krista's play and went to the VHS player available to the patrons for the library's small video collection. She popped in the tape and settled back to watch the play.

Anne laughed out loud at several parts, and at others, she teared up at the poignancy of the lines. The witty dialogue was weighty with meaning behind the humor.

She would have to watch the DVD of Bettridge's plays to be certain, but from what she'd learned, his plays were much more serious than Krista's and were probably targeted to a different audience too.

That being the case, Krista could never pass off a missing Bettridge script as her own writing. But would she want the missing script for some other reason?

CHAPTER FIFTEEN

On Tuesday morning, after opening the library, Anne left Donna Slade to man the front desk while she stepped out to go to Tami's parents' house. Their brick house lay on the outskirts of Blue Hill, a long, single-story building curved around an inner courtyard. Anne remembered happy barbecues in the courtyard with Tami and their friends on long summer nights.

Mrs. Bates, Tami's mother, opened the front door to Anne's knock. "Hello, Anne, come on in." She stepped aside so Anne could enter the tile-floored foyer. "Aiden and Tami are setting up in the courtyard."

Anne made her way through the house to the door opening to the central courtyard.

"Hi, Tami, Aiden."

Aiden was tall with blue eyes and red-blond hair. "I didn't get a chance to talk to you last night." He had a wide smile and even features, and his Irish accent gave him a bit of dash.

"Thanks for helping me today. I'm afraid I'm going to be a real challenge for you."

"Don't listen to her, Aiden," Tami said. "She just needs to learn a few tricks to relax."

"Trust me, m'dear, an actor always likes a good challenge." He winked at Anne.

Tami rolled her eyes. "I had to marry a man with plenty of blarney."

"Now, you don't listen to her, Anne." Aiden put his arm around Tami and kissed the top of his wife's head. "The blarney is how I caught her in the end."

"I heard you just arrived from London yesterday," Anne said.

"Yes, I had to stay a couple weeks extra because of the production I was acting in," he said.

"You weren't in the same production?" Anne looked from Tami to Aiden.

"No, the producer I work for was doing a different play," Tami said. "Aiden got a major role in another play, so he didn't try out for any parts in mine. Mine ended early, so I came here while he finished up."

"So Tami tells me you met in a play she was working on... what was that like?" Anne asked.

They all chatted for a while about Tami and Aiden's romance, which grew slowly over a couple of years as Aiden happened to get parts in the plays that Tami's producer worked on, and their active social life in London.

"Shall we get started?" Tami gestured to where they'd angled the barbecue grill in front of two lawn chairs. "The grill is the fireplace, and these two chairs can take the place of the leather chairs in the library. Let's go through the scene you had last night. Aiden will read Alex's parts."

They went through the lines. Anne thought that perhaps because it wasn't Alex standing next to her, she might have an easier time, but she kept imagining Alex's face and voice, and it made her mess up her lines or say them in a hollow, stiff voice.

Aiden immediately picked up on what Anne's problem was. "Instead of being in character, you're thinking too much about other things. You have to focus on emptying your mind and entering into the character entirely."

"Yes, you're right. I'm just not sure how to shut off my brain."

"That's where I come in." Aiden proceeded to coach her on various tricks for shedding Anne Gibson and putting on the librarian character in the play.

"Anne, you're entering into your character better, but your body language is still a bit tense," Tami observed. "You look like you'd rather run away than talk to this handsome gypsy. Maybe we should address what you're worrying about, if you're up to talking about it."

Anne bit her lip. "It's rather embarrassing."

Tami laughed. "No less embarrassing than when I slipped and skidded all the way down the hill on my bum in the mud."

"Now, why didn't I hear this story?" Aiden asked.

"You have more than enough embarrassing stories of your own." Tami grinned at him.

Anne smiled. "Okay, in contrast with your mud incident, I suppose this isn't all that embarrassing. I'm just worried about what Alex is thinking as we're doing this scene. We're just friends, now, and a lot has happened in our lives in the years since we dated in high school. Flirting with him as the librarian character feels strange."

"You're still thinking of yourself as Anne and not the character," Aiden said. "Here's a trick to clear your mind so you can get into character."

By the end, Anne was doing better. However, she still worried how she'd do with Alex in front of her and not Aiden.

Also, she hadn't confessed that the faint hint of attraction she felt for Alex when they were doing their scenes also worried her. When they were just talking, things were the same, but somehow when they were speaking their lines, Anne felt different and knew that was contributing to her tenseness. She did her best to try to relax.

"You'll do fine tonight," Tami said.

"The techniques might feel odd at first," Aiden said, "but the more you use them, the easier they'll get. After a while, you'll be more comfortable, and that will help you to relax more too."

"Thanks to both of you," Anne said. "I feel better about tonight. I was worrying I'd screw everything up again."

"Try not to worry," Tami said. "I know it's hard, but it's at the root of your problems."

Anne said good-bye to them until rehearsal later, then headed back to the library. Donna's shift ended at noon, so Anne had enough time to gobble a quick lunch and take over at the front desk.

There was a lull after noon, and Anne was stacking books to take back to the shelves when the phone rang. "Hello, Blue Hill Library. Anne Gibson speaking."

"This is Dr. Harry Glendenning."

The author of the Bettridge biography! "Dr. Glendenning, thank you for calling me back."

"Call me Harry, please. Dr. Glendenning always sounds like a tongue twister." He had a jovial voice, as if he spent a great deal of time laughing. "I apologize for not calling you sooner, but I wanted to check my notes before speaking to you. Your e-mail intrigued me, to say the least."

"I hope I didn't sound too sensationalistic. I know there's been a lot of speculation about the missing Bettridge script."

"Unfortunately, yes. However, when you mentioned the date your aunt was friends with Bettridge, that definitely piqued my interest. From my interviews with Bettridge's friends, he might have written that 'missing' script either in the summer of 1962 or the summer of 1963."

"My aunt Edie met him in early 1962. I have a letter she wrote to her friend, Mildred, that mentions Billy and how he recently lost his wife, Miriam."

"That certainly has a ring of truth. Most of Bettridge's friends referred to him as Billy rather than Hugh, and he would have been introduced to new people as Billy."

"My aunt worked as director's assistant for Quentin Chandler in the spring of 1962. I believe Quentin was Lynne Bettridge's godfather?"

"Yes, Quentin was a cousin to Miriam Bettridge. I didn't mention it in the biography since the book was about Bettridge and not his wife."

"I noticed you didn't mention the missing script in your biography either."

"I don't have any hard facts. I didn't want the biography to have the flavor of a gossip magazine."

"I understand. It's what made me mention the missing script and my aunt's involvement to you."

"I'm glad you trusted me. Your e-mail was one of the most exciting things I've read in a long time."

"How did the rumor about the missing script start?"

"I'm not sure. When I interviewed Bettridge's friends and family, several of them mentioned that Bettridge had once joked about writing a play that would be released posthumously. However, no one can tell me when Bettridge said this. It was just something all his friends were saying after his death. And obviously, after his death his lawyer and his family didn't mention anything about a play to be produced posthumously."

"So that's how the rumor started?"

"Not entirely. I figured out a timeline for when almost all of Bettridge's plays were written. He worked on *Nanette*, probably his most famous play, from approximately July 1961 until he finished it in November 1963. I interviewed two of his closest friends, the ones who took care of his children for him in early 1962 after the death of his wife and who had him committed to a hospital for his depression. When he returned home, he didn't write for a few months, then slowly started working on *Nanette* again. However, his close friends both told me that he holed up in a friend's summer home in Derbyshire, writing what he called a 'special' script either in the summer of 1962 or the summer of 1963—their dates do not correspond, which was another reason I didn't include it in the biography."

"Did he ever explain what he meant by a 'special script'?"

"Apparently not. But both friends told me that when the special script was done, he never gave it to anyone to produce, he simply went back to working on *Nanette*. One of his friends asked him about the script later, and Bettridge said it was 'in safekeeping.'"

In safekeeping with Aunt Edie?

"Bettridge mentioned his 'special script' to a few of his other friends, so they knew about it but not what happened to it. No play was found in his personal effects after his death."

"None of the people you interviewed mentioned Edie Summers?"

"I'm afraid not. However, many of them were older when I did the interviews, and their memories weren't as sharp."

But surely if Aunt Edie was a good enough friend that Bettridge gave her a script, someone would have known about it? "Is there any way I could speak to the two close friends who knew about Bettridge writing the 'special script' in Derbyshire?"

"I'm afraid not. Both of them desired anonymity from the biography. One of them is a peer and wished to have privacy for his family — he was the one who loaned the summer home to Bettridge to write in the summers of both 1962 and 1963, which is why that special script could have been written in either year. It was also why I didn't mention the summer home in the biography. The other is a wealthy philanthropist who also wished for privacy — he and his wife took care of the children when Bettridge was in hospital."

Anne sighed. "I'm afraid I don't have much. I have two letters. One was a note found by a friend of mine, which mentions the missing Bettridge script." Anne read the note to Roy Underwood that Tami had found.

"A few months before he died, Roy Underwood did say he had the missing Bettridge script," Harry said. "The Bettridge biography had been published by then, but I still tried to interview him. I got an appointment, but he died in the interim."

"How disappointing."

"Roy wasn't one to propagate rumors, so I was inclined to believe he had the real thing. However, there was no proof."

Anne next read the older letter from Aunt Edie to Mildred in 1962. Harry seemed excited because the two other people mentioned in the letter, Prudence MacTavish and Raymond McConnell, were little-known contemporaries of Bettridge, and only someone at those parties would have known that Bettridge was friends with them.

"But I don't know how Aunt Edie would have gotten the script," Anne said.

"I can keep digging in my notes to see if I uncover something. You don't think the note was forged?"

"I don't think so. The note writer says for Roy to meet her in Blue Hill and she'd loan him the script. If it was forged, they'd have wanted Roy to send money and they would mail it without seeing them face to face."

"That's true."

"I'll keep looking for the script." Anne thanked the professor and said good-bye, but she hung up the phone in frustration. Why would the playwright give Aunt Edie his play? If it was supposed to be released after his death, why wouldn't he give it to his lawyer instead of Edie? And if she had the play, why didn't Aunt Edie release it when he died?

Aunt Edie, where did you hide it?

* * *

On Wednesday afternoon, as Anne was about to leave to get Ben and Liddie from school, the front door flew open and a man strode in. Anne recognized him immediately—Collin Avery. But what was he doing in Blue Hill?

"I'm here looking for Anne Gibson." His high voice echoed off the walls of the entrance foyer.

"I'm Anne."

"Collin Avery." He gave a sycophantic smile that revealed a great deal of long teeth. He thrust his hand out at her.

"Hello." She rather limply shook his hand.

"Gwendolyn told me all about your delightful coffee break on Monday." He was markedly different from when Anne had spoken with him on the phone. Gone was the brusque tone and instead he seemed to almost be simpering at her.

"I'm glad she spoke to you."

He drew in close to her, ignoring Mildred at the front desk. "I hear you may have something I am most interested in. Is there somewhere we can speak privately?" He gave her another toothy smile.

"Sure." Anne led him to the kitchen, which was only semiprivate, but some inner alarm at his slick personality made her distrust being alone with him.

"I know you want to keep this hush-hush, and I am completely fine with that. Just please tell me this is not a hoax." He looked pleadingly at her.

"I'm afraid I have no idea what you're talking about."

"Is it money? Because I can spare no expense."

"Mr. Avery—"

"Collin, please." He smiled.

"Collin, I really am very confused."

"You did meet with Gwendolyn on Monday, right?"

"Yes. She offered to speak to you about a script my aunt might have loaned to Roy. Did he show you any script before he died?"

"No, but he was going to." He lowered his voice to a theatrical whisper. "The missing Bettridge script?"

"Why would you think I have the Bettridge script?" Anne asked warily. "All I said was that my aunt had a script from a friend."

Collin gave her an annoyed look. "Roy didn't deign to speak to his lowly cousin across the pond unless it was to spout some new award he'd won." His voice was dark with a deep-seated bitterness.

That didn't sound like the Roy Anne had heard about, but Collin's perception may be tainted by jealousy.

Collin continued, "But the one time he spoke to me was a month before he died, telling me about the Bettridge script. So don't try to tell me you don't have it, because I know you do. There was only one script Roy would have shown to me, and that was it."

"But I don't have it. I've looked and I can't find it."

Collin's face contorted, first into despair, then into anger. "What do you mean, you can't find it?"

"All I know is that my aunt was going to loan the script to Roy. I don't know if Roy got it from her or not, but it's certainly not anywhere in this house."

Collin began pacing in the small kitchen with rapid steps. "You have to be lying. The script can't be anywhere except here."

Anne didn't appreciate being accused of lying. "Mr. Avery, I think you should leave."

Instead, he loomed over her. "You're keeping property that should belong to me."

"Anne?" Mildred's sweet voice rang loudly from the open door to the kitchen. "You're needed at the front desk."

At Mildred's voice, Collin straightened and looked as if he'd been caught with his hand in the cookie jar.

"Mildred, Mr. Avery was just leaving," Anne said firmly.

"Just in time, because we're getting quite busy," Mildred said, still in that sweet voice.

Collin gave a huff of frustration, but then he spun around and left the kitchen with those same rapid footsteps, which seemed to be his only speed of walking. Anne and Mildred followed him, and before he got to the front door, he turned and said to Anne, "This isn't over—"

"Good-bye, Mr. Avery," Anne said in that strict, loud voice she used for difficult patrons. Working in her old job at the New York library branch, she was used to the occasional unhappy patron.

She breathed a sigh of relief as the front door closed behind him, then turned to Mildred. "How did you know I needed rescuing?"

"I couldn't help overhearing." Mildred leaned closer. "Was he talking about Edie's script?"

Anne nodded. "He got very upset when I said I didn't have it. But at least it indicates that he doesn't have the script."

"Did you find out yet how Edie might have gotten the script? I've searched for more of her letters from that year, but I'm afraid I can't find them."

"I think that if Edie had told you about the script in a letter or in person, you'd probably remember because it was so precious to her. I know how she might have known Bettridge, but I still can't figure out why he would have given the play to her." Anne looked at the clock and gasped. "I've got to go pick up Ben and Liddie."

"Go ahead, I'm here to watch over things."

Anne ended up walking to school to pick them up since she would have had to wait in the carpool lane for them anyway. Liddie was waving a stick which had attached to it several paper fish dangling on strings. "Mommy, I fished for words today! I was the best fisherman in class!" Liddie's paper fish had various short words on them, which was apparently a fun way to hone her reading skills.

"Congratulations."

"Miss Reed said she 'spected no less from me cuz you were the town librarian."

Anne laughed. "I would hope you'd love to read regardless of if I were the town librarian or not."

Ben walked up at a slower pace. "Hi, Mom."

"Did you have a good day?"

He gave a one-shoulder shrug, which Anne suspected she'd see a lot more of as he got into his teens. "It was that exciting, huh?"

Ben gave another shrug, but he smiled.

Back at the library, after Ben took Hershey out, he sprawled out on the living room floor to do his homework. Liddie lay next to him with her crayons, coloring her word fish.

Anne returned downstairs, and for the rest of the afternoon, the traffic in the library picked up considerably. Anne was grateful for Mildred's help.

Anne was also excited to receive a package in the mail with the DVD of the episode of *Behind the Curtain*, where Krista Underwood Bennett had been interviewed about seventeen years ago. She hoped to have time to watch it tomorrow night, since there wouldn't be rehearsal at the library on Thursday.

A few minutes before closing, she was surprised to see the elderly sisters Betty Warring and Nellie Brown returning to the library. They had checked out a biography only a few hours ago, just after Anne had returned with the kids.

Betty set the book they'd checked out on the table. "I'm sorry, Anne, but we have to return this book."

"Oh no. What's wrong with it?"

Betty flipped open the pages and Anne saw a piece of banana, recently smashed in between the pages. "Yuck! Yes, I can see why you needed to return it."

"We didn't notice when we checked the book out, but then Betty kept saying she smelled banana," Nellie said.

"I told her we should just read around it, but she wouldn't have it," Betty said, thumping her cane for emphasis.

"Of course not. It's good you brought this back to me right away." Anne wasn't sure the book was salvageable with the icky banana soaking into the adjacent pages. She may have to order a new copy. "Why don't you two pick something else to read?"

"But the library's about to close," Nellie said.

"Don't worry about it. We can stay open until you pick something. Oh, wait a minute, why didn't I think of it before? I have the perfect biography for you, which I just finished. Let me go get it." Anne headed upstairs to their living quarters to get the Bettridge book.

As she entered the locked door to their living quarters, Ben met her with wide eyes. "Mom, did you try to come in here about fifteen minutes ago?"

"No."

"Someone rattled the doorknob like they were trying to come in." Ben had pitched his voice low.

Anne's heart sped up. "You're sure someone didn't accidentally try to open the door because they thought it was a library room?" It was a troubling thought because their locked door clearly indicated it was into the private quarters.

"Whoever it was kept turning the knob, and it sounded like they ran into the door to try to get it open. Hershey barked like crazy. Liddie just laughed at him, but I was worried cuz I know you have your key. But I didn't want to go outside in case they were there."

Anne didn't want to show her fear to Ben, but she couldn't resist putting an arm around him. "You did exactly right."

"I'm sure glad Mr. Ochs put the lock on that door. I knew it was good and strong."

"Me too. You're okay?"

"I'm fine, Mom." Ben pulled away from her, a brave look on his face that only made her want to hug him again.

Anne went to get the Bettridge biography from her bedroom, then carefully locked the door to their private quarters. She tried the handle and was reassured how solid it was.

She pasted on a smile when she went downstairs to give the book to Nellie and Betty. Mildred gave her an odd look but didn't say anything in front of the two sisters. However, after they'd checked out the biography and left the library, Anne heaved a sigh as she firmly locked the door behind them.

"Anne, are you all right?" Mildred asked. "You had the strangest expression."

Anne told her what Ben had said, and Mildred's face grew troubled. "But why would anyone want to do that?"

"I thought maybe someone might be after the script."

"To try looking for it?"

Anne nodded. "Collin Avery just arrived in town today, and he thinks I have the script. And now that I think about it, Tami and I have been concerned about a stranger asking around town about Aunt Edie and a play manuscript."

"How would he know about it? I haven't spoken of it to anyone."

"He originally seemed to be following Tami around town, so perhaps he found out about the play in London and followed her from there."

Mildred gave her a serious look. "You need to be careful, Anne, especially with your children."

"I know. I had a terrible fright when Ben told me."

As they continued to close up the library, Anne silently prayed, *Lord, please protect my children. And please help me to find this script so I can get rid of the threat to my family.*

Chapter Sixteen

O n Thursday afternoon, Anne was putting up a flier on the display case near the front door when she heard loud voices from the front of the library. She peered through the front door and was surprised to see Tami and Collin Avery on the sidewalk.

"The play is absolutely phenomenal. It's right up Gideon's alley." Collin's voice carried clearly.

"Then I'm sure Gideon would be happy to talk to you about it." Tami's voice sounded strained to Anne, and she looked nervously toward the library as if anxious to get away from Collin.

"There's the problem, you see? Because Gideon's secretary doesn't know me and doesn't know to forward my messages to him." Desperation edged Collin's tone, and Anne could see the anxiety in his face. It made her feel a little sorry for him, despite how he had acted toward her yesterday. "If you could just talk to him…"

Anne decided to intervene rather than eavesdrop. She opened the front door. "Tami, there you are." She gestured urgently for Tami to come inside. "I was waiting for you."

Tami had the expression of someone saved from the guillotine. "I need to go, Collin. Good-bye." She bolted up to the library door and Anne shut it behind her.

Tami hugged Anne. "You are a treasure. He has been following me all the way from downtown. I couldn't get rid of him."

"What did he want?"

"He wants me to get my boss, Gideon Rossiter, to produce some play and hire Collin as the director."

"Do you think your boss might be interested?"

"Gideon doesn't like it when people don't go through the proper channels. If Collin did contact his secretary first and Gideon rejected the project, then he won't appreciate being bothered about it a second time."

"I get the feeling this happens to you often."

"Usually not from someone as aggressive as Collin."

Anne peeked through the front door. "It looks like he's gone."

Tami heaved a sigh. "I'll wait a few minutes and then head to my cousin's house. Aiden's already there, but I was running an errand for my mom." She held up a pint of ice cream she'd picked up. "I was going to text Aiden for help."

At that moment, Tami's cell phone rang. "It's Aiden. He's probably wondering where I am." She answered the phone, and Anne moved to the checkout desk to give her privacy.

After Tami hung up, she went to the desk. "Aiden says hi, and said that you were much less stiff at rehearsal last night, but you should still be practicing those techniques he gave you."

Anne groaned. "I'm never going to get this right."

"Sure you are. You just need more time to get used to working with Alex."

"We had a talk about our friendship, so I feel like I can't tell him that I'm still worrying about it."

"Why are you worrying about it?"

Anne bit her lip. "I'm not sure. When we're rehearsing, things just feel strange between us."

"He obviously doesn't think so."

But Anne had married someone else and then lost him, and Alex hadn't had that kind of experience. Maybe it was easier for him to deal with the romantic mood of the play because it simply reminded him of high school. But for Anne, the romance reminded her of Eric, as well as her time dating Alex, and it felt odd.

However, she didn't want to burden Tami with her problems. "Like I told you, it's all in my head. Tell Aiden I'll work on the exercises he gave me."

"I'd better go before the ice cream melts. Thanks!" Tami left the library after first looking up and down the street.

When Anne closed the library at eight o'clock, she had to admit she was rather relieved there was no rehearsal tonight. Her worry was causing them to be stressful.

Anne spent some extra time snuggled with Liddie in bed reading a book. She felt she had neglected her children for the past week because of the play, and they had been very patient with her. They weren't required for all the rehearsals, and Wendy had been fantastic about keeping the children occupied in the Children's Room while the adults rehearsed.

When Liddie began yawning, Anne closed the book. "Time for prayers."

Liddie folded her hands and prayed, "Dear Jesus, thank You for Mommy and Ben and Grandma and Grandpa in Florida..." She went down the list of her loved ones and even prayed for Hershey and the future cat she wanted to get when she was old enough. Finally she said, "And Jesus, please be with Mommy because she seems worried about the play. Amen."

Anne gave her daughter a hug. "Thank you, Liddie. I am a little worried."

"You should talk to Rev'rend Tom," Liddie said. "He always makes me feel better."

Anne realized she hadn't even thought about asking for help from Reverend Tom, which was unusual. "You're right, sweetie, I'll talk to him on Sunday." How wonderful for the Lord to remind her of the help Reverend Tom could give to her, through the mouth of her little girl.

Ben was in bed, hunched over his book as if ready to bolt out of the covers. He looked up as Anne walked in. "Can I stay up just a little bit longer? I'm almost done with this book." His eyes shone as he showed her the book on the ancient Egyptians that he had told her about a few days ago.

Anne couldn't help loving how avidly her children enjoyed books. "All right, but go to bed as soon as you're done. And no complaints if you're tired tomorrow morning."

"Thanks, Mom!"

She prayed with Ben, then left him to the Great Pyramid and the Sphinx. She popped the DVD of Krista's interview into the player in their living room and settled down to watch.

It was amusing to see the dated hairstyles and clothing from almost two decades ago. The picture quality was not as good as she was used to from modern shows.

The episode interviewed three guests in the half-hour program, and Krista was the second interview. The first guest had been an award-winning actor who had just started a new play that opened the weekend before.

Krista looked much like the photos Anne had seen of her online, although with longer hair in a darker color than her recent photos. The show's host started off with some warm-up questions about her most recent play, being performed at that time off Broadway. Krista had a great deal of confidence on camera, and she answered the questions with a seriousness and yet an intensity that showed how passionate she was about the writing of the play.

"How do you feel about the actors chosen for this play?" the host asked.

"They're wonderful," she replied. "They have terrific timing and bring the characters to life in a way that reflects the issues each of them are going through. The humor only enhances the issues of loss, betrayal, and friendship in the story."

"How do you like working with the director?"

"He really understands the message I want to convey in the story about the depths to which betrayal can affect us even years after the fact."

Anne noticed she always brought the conversation around to the messages and issues she wrote into the story.

"Let's talk about some of the criticism voiced about the play," the host said. "Some critics say that the humor falls flat because there's an underlying bitterness to the writing."

Krista's shoulders stiffened, but she responded in a neutral voice. "I wrote the play to cause the audience to examine their own lives, and so each person—audience and critics alike—will have different emotional reactions to the story."

It was a good answer, but Krista's body language was uncomfortable, and there were harsh lines alongside her mouth. Anne wondered if there was some underlying issue in Krista's own life that had perhaps leeched into the writing of the play.

"How about your future plans?" the host said. "There are rumors flying that you intend to move from writing to producing. After all, your brother, Roy Underwood, and your cousin, Collin Avery, are both directors."

Krista laughed easily. "Most people don't realize this, but I did venture into producing for my last play. However, the responsibilities weren't to my taste, and the time involved took away from my family commitments. Plus, I just missed writing."

"How about directing?"

"I have no head for the organizational skills and people skills needed to be a good director. I leave that to Roy and Collin."

"So, no hope of a career change for you?"

"No. I just love writing too much."

The interview finished soon after that, and Anne shut off the DVD player. So, assuming Krista hadn't changed her attitude about her writing and the responsibilities involved in producing plays, she probably wouldn't want the Bettridge play in order to produce it herself. And Anne had already seen in her plays that her writing style was very different from Bettridge, so she would be unlikely to try to pass the script off as her own.

Was there another reason for her to want the play? Would Krista need the money she'd receive if she could auction it off or sell it privately? Would it cause Krista to take the script from her brother?

* * *

On Friday afternoon, as Anne was about to leave to pick up Ben and Liddie from school, the phone rang. It was Alex.

"Hi, Anne. I hate to ask you this, but could you pick up Ryan today from school and keep him with you at the library? There's a problem at my work site today and I can't get away."

"No problem. Is it all right if I take him out for ice cream?"

"He'd love it. Thanks a bunch. Why don't I bring dinner to the library? We can eat just before rehearsal today."

"That sounds good, but you don't have to."

"It's the least I can do. Pizza sound good?"

"The kids would give an enthusiastic yes."

"And you?" There was a teasing tone to his voice, and Anne was reminded again of the romantic mood of the play.

She shook it off — she was letting this play affect her too much. "I wouldn't mind, but I'll make a salad to go along with it."

"I'll take some of that. Okay, thanks!" He hung up.

Sherri Devereaux was volunteering at the library that day, so Anne turned to her. "Would it be all right if you held down the fort for a little longer so I can take the kids for ice cream?"

"Sure," Sherri said. "It's not like we're super busy, anyway."

"It might get busy later, but I'll try to be back soon."

When Anne picked up Ben and Liddie, she waved to Ryan too. "Your uncle asked me to pick you up and take you to the library this afternoon."

"Cool!" Ben said to Ryan. "I can show you that new computer game."

"After you both finish your homework," Anne said.

Both boys groaned a little, but they were obviously happy to spend more time together, for which Anne was grateful. They had formed such a good friendship, and it made her feel better about Ben and his easing into life here at Blue Hill.

"How about ice cream for everybody?"

Predictably, all three kids hooted their acceptance of that idea.

Anne walked with them to the drugstore and the ice cream fountain counter, where the boys both picked chocolate while Liddie ordered her cone of strawberry. Anne was trying to decide between mint chip and strawberry when suddenly Tami rushed into the drugstore and hurried up to them. She looked rather flustered, and she was panting.

"Are you all right?" Anne asked anxiously.

"Is it okay if I stick with you for a little while?" There was a hunted look in Tami's wide green eyes.

"Of course. Want some ice cream?"

"Sure. Anything."

Anne ordered mint chip for herself and Tami, remembering that her friend liked that flavor, and they all sat down to eat. Tami simply played with her ice cream with her spoon for a few minutes, and Anne leaned close to ask in a low voice, "What's wrong?"

Tami whispered, "Collin Avery's been harassing me. Everywhere I go, he seems to pop up to ask me again and again to talk to my boss about his play. He just tried to waylay me on my way out of the post office, and so I ducked in here to avoid talking to him."

"I thought you told him to talk to Gideon's secretary?"

"I did, but the man has selective hearing and completely ignores my refusals."

Anne's lips tightened at Collin's rude behavior. It hinted at the type of personality who would try to get into the locked portion of the library in order to look for the Bettridge play himself because he still believed Anne had it hidden away. "Tami, I think you should talk to Gideon and tell him you're being harassed. Maybe he can help, or find out why Collin is being so insistent."

"I don't want to seem like I'm tattling."

"Collin's not your brother. He's a potential director that your boss might be thinking of working with."

"It makes sense when you put it that way. Okay, I'll e-mail him." Tami's shoulders relaxed and she was able to enjoy her mint chip ice cream with relish.

They said good-bye to Tami on the sidewalk as she went to her car, and Anne and the kids headed back to the library. Anne made Ben and Ryan do their homework in the living room, and Liddie, wanting to be near them, lay on her stomach with her coloring books and pencils.

Anne and Sherri had a busy afternoon, but during a lull, Anne remembered the DVD with the interview. She went upstairs to get it from the DVD player and found Ben and Ryan finishing up their homework.

"Can we play computer games, Mom?" Ben asked.

"All right, but include your sister," Anne told him.

Anne took the DVD back down to the front desk and wondered what she ought to do with it. She leafed through the packet that the studio had included with the DVD, which included information on the entire series and the other people interviewed by the show during its five-year run. She was surprised to see

Roy interviewed at one point and wondered if she ought to watch the episode. But the date was before Aunt Edie had written to him, and Roy was unlikely to mention anything not already public knowledge about his relationship with his sister and cousin.

She decided to enter the DVD into the library's collection and tell the theater club members about it in case any of them might want to see it. Had Krista's parents seen the interview when it aired? Would they want to see it?

Anne gave them a call, and the Underwoods said they'd love to borrow the DVD. Anne arranged to drop the DVD off tomorrow morning at nine o'clock, which would give her enough time to get back to the library to open it.

Tomorrow might be a good time to get more information about Collin and Krista, now that she knew more about them. It was obvious Collin didn't have the script, but would Krista have a reason to take it from her brother? Would her parents know?

Alex arrived with a pepperoni and a cheese pizza, and after praying, the two boys fell upon the pepperoni as if they hadn't eaten in days.

"You may want to slow down to breathe," Anne teased them.

"I remember eating like that up until my twenties," Alex said.

"And then what happened?"

"I started getting a gut." Alex slapped his flat stomach. "My crewmen started teasing me."

"Dieting by peer pressure?" Anne said with a grin.

"And I discovered I could save more money when it wasn't all going into food. A moment of realization for a single young man."

Laughing with Alex like this was nice. Anne didn't understand why she couldn't be this relaxed during rehearsals. Just the thought made her stomach tighten. Well, she'd speak to Reverend Tom on Sunday. He'd be able to help her, wouldn't he?

CHAPTER SEVENTEEN

Wendy was scheduled to volunteer on Saturday, and she was more than happy to come by early in order to watch the kids for Anne while she dropped the DVD off at Krista's parents' house. She came armed with colored paper and ribbons.

"I hope you don't mind, I'm going to put your kids to work to help me with the table decorations for the dinner play," Wendy said.

"Feel free," Anne said. "Just be aware that Liddie turns into a hurricane near glitter."

"So are my twins, so I purposely did not include any glitter." Wendy grinned.

Anne headed to Deshler to the Underwoods' home once more. Blanche Underwood welcomed her with a wide smile. "I so appreciate your bringing the DVD by for us." She ushered Anne into the bright living room, where Wilfred was still sitting with his knee propped up. "We watched the show when it aired years ago but would love to see it again. Have a seat. I've just set out the coffee and muffins."

"Oh, you don't need to do that," Anne said.

"Don't be silly. It's just me and Wilfred, and we love company."

"Blanche gets as cranky as a wind-up toy," Wilfred said to Anne in a whisper meant to carry to his wife, but she only rolled her eyes at her husband.

Anne laughed. "In that case, I'd love coffee and muffins."

"You take it black, don't you?" Blanche poured coffee and served muffins all around while Anne asked Wilfred about his knee.

"Still sore," he said with a touch of crankiness himself. "And my tulips are going to all die if I don't get out to the garden soon."

"Did you speak to Krista and Collin yet?" Blanche asked her.

"I spoke to Collin, but when I called Krista, a woman answered and at first I thought it was Krista."

"That was probably Mitty, their housekeeper," Blanche said.

"Housekeeper? That must be nice," Anne said with a smile.

"Mitty's been with Krista's family for over a decade. They hired her when Krista's husband bought their home on Fifth Avenue."

Only the most wealthy people could afford homes on New York's Fifth Avenue. "What does Krista's husband do?"

"He's an investment banker," Wilfred said. "Worked hard for his success too. He came from a poor family in the Bronx."

"It's a wonderful success story," Blanche said.

Anne could see now that Krista didn't seem to have any reason to want the Bettridge script. She wouldn't pass it off as her own writing, she wouldn't want to produce it, and she had no need of the money it would bring to her if she sold it.

Collin didn't have the script in his possession either. So where could it possibly be?

* * *

As rehearsal time approached that afternoon, Anne's palms began to sweat, and she kept wiping them on her slacks. They were supposed to rehearse the kiss scene today, and Anne wasn't sure she could do it. What would she feel when Alex kissed her? What if she started thinking of him as more than a friend? What would he think of her after their kiss scene? Why couldn't she just be cool about it all and separate the play from their friendship? What was wrong with her?

"Mom, are you okay?" Ben was looking at her oddly. "You look a little sick."

Great, now she was worrying her nine-year-old son. "Thanks for thinking of me, sweetie, but I'm fine."

After the library closed at one o'clock, Anne opened the front door to let in the theater club members. Tami was one of the first to arrive, and she took Anne aside. "I spoke to Gideon about Collin. Apparently the producer for his last play backed out a few months ago and he hasn't been able to find another one. He's been desperate to find a financial backer for his new production."

"I suppose his desperation is what's making him so aggressive."

"If he really did have the missing Bettridge script, he'd be telling everyone he has it and he'd be swimming in offers."

"But he knew Roy had it. Which means maybe Aunt Edie gave it to him before he died."

"But then where would it be?"

"That's still the million dollar question."

The door opened and Alex arrived with Ryan. "Hi, Anne, Tami." They headed to the History Room.

Tami leaned close to Anne. "How are you feeling about the rehearsal today?"

"I'm trying not to have a nervous breakdown."

Tami stared at Anne. "Really?"

"No, I'm joking. Although I am a bit tense about it."

Tami put a hand on Anne's shoulder. "I think you should trust in how much Alex respects you. I think he understands you better than you think. He'll make the scene go smoothly. Just wait and see."

Anne found that Aiden had been right, and the more time she spent doing the rehearsals with Alex, the more comfortable she was becoming. She certainly wasn't as horribly stiff with him as she was the first week. She wasn't quite as relaxed as Alex was, though. It was as if he kissed librarians every day of the week.

Finally came the kiss scene, and Anne found her back as straight as a poker. She couldn't seem to unclench her jaw either. She said her lines in a strangled voice.

Alex didn't hesitate. He swept her back into a romantic dip, but when he kissed her, he smacked her lips as if kissing his nephew good night.

Everyone laughed, including Anne. "Nice touch," she said as he put her back on her feet.

"I told you, I love how being in a play lets you ham things up."

"Run through that again," Stephan said, his eyes twinkling. "Anne, a little more feeling this time?"

The tension had been broken, and Anne found herself saying her lines more naturally. Alex again dipped her for the kiss and pecked her lips.

She felt a tiny spark, and then it was gone. Alex was grinning at her like always, but suddenly Anne felt something different. And it was a little scary.

She was able to finish the scene credibly, but she kept that tiny fear deep inside her. What was happening to her? And more importantly, what should she do about it?

* * *

On Sunday morning, Anne took Ben and Liddie to cookies in the fellowship hall and steered them toward Wendy and her brood.

"Wendy, would you keep an eye on Ben and Liddie? I need to speak to Reverend Tom," Anne said.

"Sure. Take as long as you like."

Anne waited while Reverend Tom spoke about the next men's Bible study meeting with Mr. Willet. Before leaving, Mr. Willet said to Anne, "I'll be by the library sometime in the next week or two. I have a question about an old mystery book I'd like to read, written by an author from the Victorian period."

"Sure," Anne said. "I'm always happy to help a reader find the book they want."

"I figured you'd say that." Mr. Willet winked at her, then left.

"Anne, how may I help you?" Reverend Tom said.

"Could I talk privately to you? I could use some advice."

"Of course." He steered her toward his office, and he closed his door.

Anne sat across from Reverend Tom. "I'm really not sure where to start."

"Start at the beginning. I like long stories." His eyes twinkled.

Anne talked about the play and being roped into the librarian part. "The ironic thing is that I took the part because of the problems they would have had with the Victorian dress, but I haven't even worn it yet," Anne said ruefully.

She talked about her shock at finding out about the kiss at the end of the play, and how it made her very stiff and awkward in her acting.

"Did you talk to Alex about it?" Reverend Tom asked.

"Yes, and he was really great about respecting me and not wanting our friendship to suffer from this situation. I thought things were fine between us, but then at the next rehearsal, I... felt something. Not a big thing, but something that reminded me of my early feelings for Eric, and of how I used to feel with Alex when we dated in high school. And it made me feel strange and scared too."

"How have rehearsals been since then?"

Anne told him about how Aiden had given her tips for relaxing and getting into character, but she couldn't seem to separate the librarian role from herself. "I don't know what's wrong with me."

Reverend Tom reached over to clasp her hands in his. His touch was warm and reassuring. "There's nothing wrong with you. I think anyone would be confused and a little frightened if they were in your shoes."

"I don't want to ruin the play, and I don't want to ruin my friendship with Alex, but I'm afraid I'm doing both."

"I doubt you're really ruining anything. And you're not giving Alex enough credit. He's a kind, sensitive man who wouldn't want you to be feeling all this anxiety about the situation."

Anne took a deep breath. "Yes, you're right."

"Have you prayed about this?"

Anne thought back and realized she hadn't. "I read my Bible every day, but it seems as if every time I tried to pray about the play, my thoughts were racing."

"It seems to me that you're trying to handle this entirely on your own. One of my favorite passages is Matthew 11:28–30: *'Come to me, all you who are weary and burdened, and I will give you rest. Take my yoke upon you and learn from me, for I am gentle and humble in heart, and you will find rest for your souls. For my yoke is easy and my burden is light.'*"

Just hearing the scripture verses made Anne feel a stillness under her breastbone, the peace that comes from the Lord.

"My suggestion is for you to pray over this situation involving Alex," Reverend Tom said. "Allow your heavenly Father to help take the burden off your shoulders."

"I guess I've been trying to deal with this on my own."

"God wouldn't want you to do that. He loves to take away our burdens." Reverend Tom squeezed her fingers. "May I pray with you right now?"

"Yes, please." Anne bowed her head.

"Dear Heavenly Father, we thank You for Your hand over Anne. You love her and only want what's best for her. Please give her Your infinite wisdom about this situation and spread Your peace over her so that she can know what You want her to do. In Jesus' name, Amen."

"Amen," Anne whispered.

Reverend Tom stood, but he placed a hand on Anne's shoulder. "Why don't you stay here for a little while and pray?"

Anne nodded gratefully, and the pastor left his office, closing the door behind him.

Anne prayed, *Lord, please forgive me for not coming to You sooner. I've been so caught up in my own worry that I didn't even stop to talk to You about it. I know You must have been waiting for me to ask You for help.*

But she was coming to the Lord now. *Please help me to completely surrender my worry to You.*

She took a deep breath, and it was as if she could feel the stress leaving her body. Her shoulders relaxed, and it was as if she had been holding them tight for weeks without realizing it.

As she prayed, she was reminded of happy memories of Eric—their first date, their first kiss, the night he proposed to her. She missed him, but she was able to revel in the joy of those memories and was thankful for the time she had with him.

And suddenly, the whisper of attraction she felt for Alex didn't seem so awkward anymore. It wasn't something for her to worry about. God had taken her worry, and He would take care of everything.

* * *

When Anne returned to the fellowship hall, the first person she saw was Mildred, who was speaking to Helen Smith, the president of the church board. Helen was speaking earnestly, and Mildred looked surprised, then embarrassed. Helen pressed an envelope into Mildred's hand before moving away.

"Everything all right?" Anne asked.

"Oh yes. Helen gave me this card." Mildred opened it and found a gift card and a thank you note. "How nice of them."

"Who is that from?"

"The women's sewing group. They said I've baked something for them for each of their meetings for the last six months. They were so grateful they got together and got me this gift card to Coffee Joe's. And look, they all signed the thank you note." Mildred showed Anne the thank you card, which had a quilt pattern on the front and the words, "Thank you sew much."

"That's cute. And such a thoughtful gift."

"They're a nice bunch of girls. I enjoy baking for them. I didn't realize how often I'd done it."

"A couple weeks ago when you gave me Aunt Edie's letter and playbill, I remember you had to leave to bake cakes for them." As Anne looked at the note, she had a sudden thought. "It just occurred to me. If Bettridge gave Aunt Edie the script, wouldn't she have received a card or note from him at the same time?"

"I would think so."

"I've been trying to consolidate all of Aunt Edie's notes and letters whenever I come across them in the attic, so there are already a bunch of them in a box. Maybe Bettridge's note to Aunt Edie is there."

"I have a feeling you'll be searching the attic today."

Anne collected Ben and Liddie and headed home for an early lunch. She had a few hours before the play rehearsal that afternoon, and she wanted time to look through Aunt Edie's notes.

After a quick lunch of tuna salad sandwiches and potato chips, Anne sent Ben and Liddie to play outside with Hershey in the backyard, thanking the Lord for a sunny day. They'd been spending a lot of time close to home lately because of the play rehearsals, so some time in the yard would be good for them.

Anne entered the dusty attic and reflected that she'd rather be out in the yard too. She gave a mighty sneeze, then quickly went to the box where she'd been collecting Aunt Edie's notes.

The box was large and very full. Unfortunately, many notes didn't have envelopes, where she could have seen the sender in the return address. The shorter notes often weren't signed by anyone, and on other letters, the signatures were just scrawls on the page. Aunt Edie must have known who they were, but Anne certainly couldn't figure it out.

After looking through only a fraction of the box, Anne stopped in frustration. She could only identify the writers of a handful of the notes. How would she ever figure out which note was from Bettridge?

Perhaps Dr. Harry Glendenning had a copy of Bettridge's handwriting? That might be a more efficient way to search, with less time wasted. Anne decided to hold off until she could get a copy of Bettridge's handwriting.

She went downstairs and sent an e-mail to Dr. Glendenning, asking if he could send her a scanned picture of Bettridge's writing. Otherwise, it was back to sorting through the boxes for a note from Bettridge. She didn't know how else to figure out how and why Bettridge would entrust a special manuscript to Aunt Edie. Looking for a note was a long shot, but Anne was running out of options.

CHAPTER EIGHTEEN

On Monday, the library was a bit busier than normal because the first of the silent auction items began arriving. Wendy popped in and out of the library throughout the day, each time with a new item in her arms, which she set up in the Nonfiction Room. Anne had helped her shove the table against the wall, and Wendy displayed the auction items in a neat row.

"I'm so impressed with the auction," Anne told Wendy as she bustled in that afternoon. "You didn't want to wait until you had all the items before setting them up at once?"

"Having everything up one by one garners interest, don't you think?" Wendy set up a flier of an auction prize of ten pizzas.

"You're right, more and more people have been coming in just to see the auction. They've also been checking out books."

"That's great." Wendy set out a basket of assorted teas and a china teapot. "Where're the kids?"

Anne had volunteered to pick up Wendy's kids from school today, since Wendy was so busy gathering the auction items from the local businesses. "The older ones are in the library somewhere studying, and the younger ones are all in the backyard playing with Hershey and a scuffed old soccer ball. The game sounded something like, 'keep the ball away from the dog unless he's chasing you, in which case give him the soccer ball to gnaw until he gets tired of it and then steal it away from him.'"

Wendy laughed. "Sounds complicated."

"Any more items to bring in?"

"One or two more, but I'll wait until we have rehearsal tonight. I'd better get my brood home. I have to feed them before we come back to the library for rehearsal."

The kids were disappointed to end the game, but Anne pointed out that the library would be closing soon anyway. They trooped out the door with their mom, and Anne began the process of closing the library for the evening. Then it was upstairs for a quick dinner of spaghetti and meatballs with Ben and Liddie.

"Liddie, let's change your shirt before the theater club arrives," Anne said.

"But Mommy, I'm polka-dotted." Liddie pointed to the red sauce dots all over her shirt from slurping the pasta.

"Why don't we change into your pink polka-dot shirt? Then you can have pink dots instead of red."

Liddie thought about it for a moment. "Okay."

Rehearsal on Sunday afternoon had involved more of the sections where the kids had speaking parts, so Anne and Alex hadn't had to act out their parts very much. Tonight, however, they'd be back to rehearsing their lines together. Anne hoped that the newfound peace she'd received from the Lord on Sunday would continue to remain with her.

Rehearsal went great. Anne prayed silently as she was on stage, waiting for her cues, and when she finally spoke her lines, she managed to deliver them sweetly and without stiffness.

"Good job, Anne," Stephan said after her segment.

When rehearsal ended, Alex gave her a thumbs-up. "The dinner play night will be fun."

Anne smiled at him and sent a grateful prayer up to the Lord for helping her.

Even as Anne put Liddie to bed, her daughter murmured, "Mommy, you were happy tonight."

Had she really been so uncomfortable that her daughter had thought she was unhappy? Anne paused to pray, *Lord, please continue to help me so that I don't worry my own children.*

Anne put in the DVD for the movie made of Bettridge's play, *Nanette,* and settled in to watch. While she'd read the biography and read about the play, she felt faintly guilty that she hadn't yet watched the play itself.

It was a bittersweet story about two sisters, Nanette and Ninion, whose parents were wealthy socialites. Ninion was secretly in love with a young man of whom her parents disapproved, and her parents arranged for the man to be falsely accused of setting a fire and arrested. He died in jail, and soon after, Nanette and Ninion's parents died in a fire, leaving the girls penniless.

Nanette was full of life and fervor while Ninion was quiet and responsible. Nanette reacted wildly to the troubles in her life. She got a job as a sales clerk in London but spent all her money partying and getting into trouble with her friends. Nanette flirted with a young man, Wentworth, who was jaded and cynical, but genuinely in love with Nanette, although she didn't know it. She had many boyfriends, which broke Wentworth's heart.

Ninion got a job as a nanny working for Walter, a widower with two children, a boy and a girl, and she tried to help Nanette to curb her wild ways. Walter's friends accused Ninion of having feelings for Walter, but a poignant scene showed that Ninion was still pining for the man she loved, who was now dead, and Walter was not only still grieving his dead wife, but also closed to any type of love or relationship, including a closer relationship with his children. Ninion and Walter became good friends, and she tried to help him out of his depression. Several of the things that Ninion said reminded Anne of Aunt Edie's good advice and warm heart.

When Nanette fled an abusive boyfriend, Ninion enabled Nanette to find shelter with Wentworth, and she soon realized that there was attraction between Walter and Nanette. However, in the midst of helping her sister, Ninion was exposed to a sick child and she herself fell ill.

Nanette's abusive boyfriend found her and when Wentworth tried to protect Nanette, the boyfriend killed him just before being arrested. Walter was shocked by the selfless death of the young man.

Just before Ninion died, she entreated Walter to continue living for the sake of his children, and to have hope that he could feel love again. Nanette had a tearful good-bye with her sister just before Ninion died.

The end of the movie showed Nanette turning to Walter for comfort, but then they embraced his two children as well, showing the hope for the future that all four of them would eventually find peace and happiness with each other. The last line of the movie was Walter saying of Ninion, "In sharing her heart, she helped to heal mine."

Anne cried buckets during the movie and could understand what everyone had said about Bettridge's writing. It was very emotional but also emotionally draining.

As she went to bed, Anne wondered if Walter's character mirrored Bettridge's experiences during the dark time after his wife died. The sadness of the movie brought up memories of how she'd struggled to cope after her husband died, and it made her feel melancholy. She wasn't sure she liked that, because she had been taking steps forward in this new life here in Blue Hill, letting the grief subside rather than consume her.

She knew Eric would want her to move on, but tonight, she lay in bed and missed him horribly.

* * *

On Tuesday morning, the poignant sadness of the movie still wrapped around Anne like a cobweb shawl. It didn't help that the clouds unleashed a chilly drizzle. She shook the somber mood off with difficulty as she had breakfast with the kids and drove them to school, but Liddie still noticed.

Just before running off to her classroom, she turned to Anne and said, "Mommy, maybe the sun will come up later and it'll make you feel better."

Anne felt a pang of guilt that she'd let her mood affect her children, and she resolved to be a cheerful librarian today.

The drizzle possibly caused the library to be sparse of patrons, but Anne used the time to keep up with paperwork and look through some new catalogs that arrived in the mail that day. She was at the checkout desk when the phone rang.

"Hello, Blue Hill Library. Anne Gibson speaking."

"Hi, this is Krista Bennett."

Roy's sister. Anne had almost forgotten that she'd left a message for Krista to call her when she returned from her writing retreat. "Hi, thanks for returning my call."

"I'm sorry I was out of pocket for so long. Mitty gave me your message only this morning. I was at a writing retreat finishing my last play."

"I hope you got it done?"

"Last night, and so I came home today."

Anne winced. "I hope I didn't make my message sound urgent. I wouldn't have wanted you to call me back if you're still busy getting settled in."

Krista chuckled. "Trust me, after two weeks of writing, I'm anxious to speak to a live person rather than the characters in my head."

Anne laughed. "I wanted to ask a question about your brother, Roy. I recently found out that my aunt Edie knew him quite well." Anne no longer suspected Krista of wanting or taking Aunt Edie's script from Roy, but maybe Roy mentioned it to his sister.

"Yes, he told me about his friendship with Edie."

Anne smiled inwardly. At last, she'd found someone who had heard of Aunt Edie's and Roy's friendship. "I didn't know until a few weeks ago that she might have given him a script she owned, just before he died."

"A script?" Krista inhaled sharply. "Wait, do you mean the Bettridge script?"

Anne's heartbeat jumped. "Did Roy tell you about it?"

"Yes, he called me about it because he was so excited to discover that Edie had it."

"I'm afraid I can't find it. Do you know if Aunt Edie gave it to him?"

Krista sighed. "I don't know. I'm assuming not, since we didn't find it among Roy's things after he died."

"Roy didn't mention a trip back to the states to pick up the script, perhaps?"

"I didn't speak to him about the script after he told me about it. No, wait." Krista paused. "He did tell me when he'd spoken to Collin about it."

"Yes, Collin thought I had it."

Krista groaned. "Collin's extremely disappointed. He was pinning all his hopes on coproducing it."

"Coproducing?"

"Roy offered to coproduce the play with Collin, since Collin loves Bettridge's writings. Collin told me he could hardly wait for Roy to get the script."

"Did Collin know when that was going to happen?"

"Actually, I think Collin mentioned something about later that year, probably after Roy's last production ended. But Roy didn't tell me anything about when he was going to get the play, so I'm not certain if that's true or not."

However, that made sense. It would have been reasonable for Roy to wait until his schedule freed up before he flew to Blue Hill to retrieve the play. He could trust Aunt Edie to keep it for him until then. Roy certainly hadn't expected to die so suddenly.

"So Edie didn't tell you where she put the play?" Krista asked.

"I'm afraid not. I didn't even know she had it."

Krista sighed. "Poor Collin."

"He's, um… here in Blue Hill."

"Uh-oh." Krista sighed again. "I know he's a bit abrasive, and he's probably even worse now because of his disappointment. But his manner is because he's insecure inside. He's always been that way."

Anne remembered that moment she felt sorry for him, and she could understand why Collin had acted the way he had while in Blue Hill. "I appreciate your telling me that."

"I wish Roy had told Collin where the play was. He only said that a friend had found it."

"I'll keep looking for it." However, Anne wasn't hopeful.

"It's been missing for this long, maybe it just wasn't meant to be found and produced. Roy mentioned that the story was 'special.' At the time I thought he was just referring to the fact it was so mysterious, but now I'm beginning to wonder if he meant something else about the plot."

"That's an interesting thought," Anne said. Was that why Aunt Edie had made the script so hard to find?

At that moment, a patron came into the library and looked expectantly at Anne. "I'm afraid I need to go," she said to Krista. "Thank you for calling me back and telling me all this."

"I hope you find the script." Krista said good-bye and hung up.

Anne helped the patron find a book on knitting which she wanted, then returned to the checkout desk. Krista confirmed what Anne already suspected, that Roy hadn't gotten the script from Aunt Edie.

She would keep looking for it, but she didn't have a clue where it could be. Where would Aunt Edie have hidden it? And why would she hide it so thoroughly?

* * *

Anne knew her smile was tight as she opened the library door on Wednesday night for the theater club. They were going to rehearse the kiss scene again.

She'd been doing well at rehearsals for the past couple nights, praying to God for help, but the kiss scene made her more nervous than all the light flirtations had been between the gypsy and the librarian character. Would she mess up? Revert back to her old stiffness?

Lord, please help me with tonight.

Alex came in with Ryan last, and while he gave her his normal smile, there were worry lines around his eyes.

"Are you all right?" he asked her in a low voice as Ryan, Ben, and Liddie raced ahead of them to the History Room, laughing and chattering with each other.

"Oh, I'm fine," she said a little too brightly.

He gave her a concerned look.

She could hardly expect him not to notice her stiffness for the past couple weeks. "I'm a little nervous, but I'll do my best."

"I don't want you to have to suffer through it, you know." The corner of his mouth quirked up. "I hope it's not as if I'm forcing you to eat brussels sprouts."

Anne laughed. "No, definitely not brussels sprouts." She tilted her head. "Maybe more like spinach."

Alex grimaced and Anne laughed again. "I know I've been uncomfortable, but I think it's just nerves. I haven't acted since high school, and these roles certainly aren't lambs and shepherds from a Christmas pageant."

"Is there anything I can do to make things easier for you?"

"Just be yourself." Anne laid a hand on his arm. "I really am glad you're such an understanding friend."

A faint line appeared between his brows for a second, but then it was gone. "I'll always be your friend, Anne." He headed into the History Room.

During rehearsal, Anne could tell that some of her former stiffness had returned, and she took deep breaths to get her shoulders to relax. *Please Lord,* she prayed, *help me do a good job.* Aiden gave her an encouraging thumbs-up anytime she glanced in his direction, which buoyed her spirits.

It might have been Anne's imagination, but it seemed the majority of the cast members held their collective breaths during the buildup to the kiss.

Alex delivered his line with a bit less romantic fervor than previously, and the lines of worry had reappeared around his eyes. Anne spoke her line, which didn't sound too bad, although it didn't sound like a woman in love either.

Then he swept her up into a dip, just as he had at a previous rehearsal. Anne couldn't help but smile, and when Alex kissed her, his lips fell to the side of her mouth. Because of the angle of their heads, to the audience it looked like a regular kiss.

Alex's thoughtful gesture warmed Anne's heart. Why had she been so nervous? Didn't she trust Alex's friendship and kindness? During all of the rehearsals, he'd always done what he could to help her feel comfortable. Of course he'd do the same for this scene that she'd been worrying about.

Lord, thank You that Alex is such a good friend.

Anne smiled up at him when he straightened and set her back on her feet. "Thanks," she said in a low voice.

She was surprised because he hesitated, as if conflicted about something, but then he grinned at her. "I definitely know how to sweep a lady off her feet."

"Let's try that again from page eighty," Stephan said. "Give it a little more romantic *oomph*, could you?"

Anne and Alex both added more *oomph* to their lines, and again, Alex swept her into a dip and kissed the side of her mouth. Stephan seemed pleased with the scene and didn't stop the play, so they continued with the rehearsal.

Anne then noticed that Ben, standing with the other children to the side, was frowning at Alex, then her, then back at Alex. She remembered her conversation with Ben after the first time Alex had kissed her in rehearsal. He had seemed all right after they talked, but were his feelings shifting in a different direction now?

They finished the run-through of the play. "Remember, we have no rehearsal tomorrow night because the library is open late," Stephan told everyone. "But we have dress rehearsal Friday night so come early and be prepared to stay a bit late."

In contrast to how he'd been before rehearsal, Ben simply said good-bye to Ryan—not in an unfriendly way but not in his normal cheerful tone—and hurried upstairs. Anne bit her lip as she watched him disappear, but then Alex was by her side.

"Think you're ready for opening night?"

"I think so. Thanks for kiss... you know what I mean."

He looked thoughtful for a moment. "Eric died only a few years ago, and I didn't want you to feel awkward."

"It wasn't anything to do with Eric that made me feel awkward. It was strange to me because it reminded me of..."

"High school?" Alex finished for her. "I understand, a little."

"It reminded me of how relationships change."

He hesitated. "Do you think our relationship would ever change again?"

Anne didn't know how to answer him. She missed Eric, but her feelings were fading. She liked her friendship with Alex the way it was, but how would it be if it changed to something else? "I'm not sure."

His brows wrinkled as he thought a minute. Then he looked in her eyes. "I want you to know that I value my friendship with you."

He smiled, and it made Anne's spine and shoulders relax. "I do too."

"I'll see you Friday." He grabbed Ryan, who was chatting with one of Wendy's kids, and headed out the front door.

After all the theater club members had left, Anne took Liddie upstairs with her. Ben had already gotten ready for bed and was in his room, reading.

Anne went through Liddie's evening rituals and said her prayers with her, then went to Ben's room and sat on his bed. "How are you doing, honey?"

His brown eyes were confused. "I'm okay, I guess."

"Did rehearsal tonight make you a little uncomfortable?"

He nodded, not looking at her.

"I know it's hard to remember, but just tell yourself that it's only pretend."

He stared at his bed covers. "Do you like Mr. Ochs?"

"He and I are friends, just like you and Ryan are friends."

Ben thought about that for a long moment, and Anne patiently waited for him to respond. She didn't want this play to affect Ben's affection for Ryan or for Alex.

Ben finally snuggled down in his covers. "Okay." His expression was still uncertain, but his eyes on hers were completely trusting.

Anne was warmed by his faith in her words, especially since he was obviously still a little confused in what he thought about hers and Alex's roles in the play. She kissed Ben and wished him a good night. "I'll always love you, honey."

He grimaced. "I know, Mom." Apparently her show of affection was a little too icky for him. "I love you too," he added.

Anne hid her smile and left his bedroom. As she got ready for bed, she remembered her conversation with Alex just tonight. Did Alex want a change in their relationship? His words and body language made her suspect that he was wondering about it.

Did Anne want a change in their relationship? She wasn't sure.

But as she began to worry about it, she remembered to stop and pray.

Lord, thank You for my friendship with Alex. You know what's best for me. I trust You.

The short prayer made her feel better. Soon the play would be over and everything would be back to exactly the way it was before. Wasn't that what she wanted?

CHAPTER NINETEEN

R emi and Bella had asked Anne if they could switch their normal Friday shift at the library to Thursday so that they could help set up the backdrop and props for the dinner play on Friday. Anne agreed, but the library was strangely quiet on Thursday.

After finishing all the paperwork she had to do, Anne sat at the checkout desk with Remi and Bella, twiddling her thumbs.

She checked her e-mail and was surprised by a new message. It was from Dr. Harry Glendenning, the author of the Bettridge biography.

Hi Anne, I got your message about getting you a sample of Bettridge's handwriting. I'm attaching a scanned picture file of a letter Bettridge wrote to the producer for one of his later plays. I hope this helps you find the missing play!

Best, Harry

Anne opened the file and printed it out. It was almost as if she held the original letter in her hands. Bettridge's handwriting had a strange backward slant, the letters narrow and long. He signed his name simply "B" with a wavy line after it.

"Could you two hold down the fort for me?" Anne asked.

"Sure," Remi replied.

Anne headed upstairs to the attic. She dragged out the box where she'd been throwing all of Aunt Edie's letters and, sitting in a chair, began to sort through them. However, she got through almost the entire box without seeing a single note that had Bettridge's distinctive backward slant to his writing. Anne was hoping for letters he might have written to her aunt. Had he never corresponded with her?

At the bottom of the box was an old hatbox filled with more of Aunt Edie's letters, which Anne had originally found in an old wooden chest. At the time, she'd noticed that the hatbox had some mold damage to one side, although the wooden chest didn't. Many of the letters in the hatbox also had mold damage or water stains.

Anne remembered that some of the papers in the safe deposit box also had some mold damage. Perhaps this hatbox had been in the same place as those papers and they'd all been damaged together. Aunt Edie must have moved some of the papers to the safe deposit box and the hatbox to the chest.

Inside, Anne found a note card so water damaged that she couldn't make out the picture that was originally on the front. However, she clearly recognized Bettridge's backward slanting handwriting.

Edie, thank you for helping me with Nanette, *for sharing your heart and helping to heal mine. Please accept my gift. Read it, smile, and then put it away. Have it produced when you feel you are ready—I leave it up to you. It is as precious to me as your words of wisdom, and I hope it will bring you joy, my lovely Ninion.*

The bottom had a *B* and a wavy line after it.

Anne's breath caught. This had to be the note from Bettridge. He had given Aunt Edie a gift that was to be produced — it must be the missing script! At least here was proof that Aunt Edie had not stolen the script, as unlikely as that was.

Anne read the note again, and her breath caught a second time, but for a different reason. Could it be — ? The only way she could be sure was to speak to Lynne Bettridge Sallman.

She hurried downstairs to find the checkout desk empty. She could hear Remi's voice in the History Room, apparently speaking to a library patron, and Bella was probably helping someone else in another area of the library.

Anne found Lynne Sallman's phone number again and called to leave a message.

"Hi, this is Anne Gibson from the Blue Hill Library. I left a message for you several days ago. My aunt was Edie Summers, and I recently discovered that she was good friends with your father, Billy. I think that you might have known her when you were a child. Could you please call me back? I'd love to chat about how my aunt Edie got to know your family." She gave the number for the library and hung up.

She hoped Lynne returned her call soon. Anne thought she knew why Bettridge had given Aunt Edie his missing script, but only Lynne could confirm if she was right.

* * *

Before the library opened on Friday morning, Alex arrived with the set and props for the dinner play. Anne woke extra early and let him in.

"Do you want a breakfast burrito?" she asked. "I'm making some right now."

"I already ate, but coffee would be welcome."

"Coming right up."

Anne started a pot in the kitchen on the first floor, and when she returned to the History Room with Alex's mug of coffee, Ben and Liddie wandered in. Alex had already unrolled the large painted backdrop, a Victorian city street with shops and gas lamps.

Liddie stared with round eyes. "The shops look funny."

"Look at that shoe shop." Ben pointed to a cobbler's storefront. "You won't find your pink princess sneakers there, Liddie."

She giggled.

"Did you need help?" Anne asked.

"Nope. Some of the community theater club members should be arriving soon," Alex said.

As he spoke, Bella's voice called out, "We're here."

"In the History Room," Anne said.

Remi and Bella walked in, followed by Tami and Aiden. Soon Alex had them setting up the stands that would hold the backdrop, and Anne hustled her children upstairs to eat breakfast.

When Anne had returned from walking the kids to school, Wendy was just entering the library with her arms full of bags. "These are the last of the silent auction items."

Anne helped set up several items on the table in the Nonfiction Room, including a tennis bracelet and a cruise vacation package. "I'm amazed at what the local businesses donated."

"Some were donated by individuals through local businesses," Wendy said. "Isn't it great? I'm thinking of bidding on that cruise!"

Anne, through the library, had donated a set of brand-new children's books, which she fanned out on the table. She'd picked the books personally, hoping they'd bring enjoyment to the lucky child who received them.

"Now that that's done, I can head home to work on tomorrow night's dinner," Wendy said when they had set out all the auction items.

"You must have a ton to do."

"Actually, it's not too bad. The members of the high school cooking club have been helping me all week to prepare as much as we could in advance, and there are a troop of them coming to my house today. Tomorrow, we'll arrive here about two hours before the dinner."

"You'll be using my kitchen, right?" The first-floor kitchen appliances were old, but Anne's kitchen on the second floor had been remodeled when she moved into the library. "Will the cooking club members help you serve tomorrow night too?"

"Of course. They want a chance to eat any leftovers." Wendy grinned.

After Wendy left, Anne officially opened the library, then peeked in the History Room. The stage was being set up at a slow, steady pace.

Throughout the day, community theater club members stopped in at the library to see the stage progress and also to bring chairs and small tables that would be used for the dinner play guests. Anne stored them in the Resource Room. All the tickets sold out, so they'd have a full house tomorrow night.

Mildred arrived at noon for a volunteer shift. "Hello, Anne."

"Am I glad you're here."

"Busy today?" Mildred put her purse behind the checkout desk.

"People have been coming in droves to see the silent auction items, most of which were set up only this morning. After they bid, people browse around the library shelves. I just helped a woman who read *A Room with a View* by E. M. Forster, and she wanted more novels set specifically in Edwardian England."

At that moment, the phone rang at the same time that a man approached the desk saying, "I heard about your Victorian mystery novels display."

"You take the phone," Mildred told Anne, and turned to the gentleman. "It's upstairs in the Fiction Room. I'll show you what books we have." She and the man left to go upstairs.

Anne answered the phone. "Hello, Blue Hill Library, Anne Gibson speaking."

"Hi, this is Lynne Sallman."

Bettridge's daughter! Anne hadn't been sure Lynne would return the call, much less this quickly. "Thanks for calling me back. I know you must be terribly busy."

"I was so surprised and pleased to hear Edie's name in your message." There was a warmth in Lynne's voice that made Anne hope her suspicions were right about Aunt Edie's relationship with the Bettridge family. "I wanted to call you back right away, although I'm afraid I only have a few minutes before I have a phone meeting."

"I didn't realize until recently that my aunt Edie might have been your nanny when you were a child." It had been Bettridge's note that clued her in. He'd called Edie "Ninion," after the character in his play, *Nanette*. Ninion had been the hero's nanny after the death of his wife, and the phrase "sharing your heart and helping to heal mine," had been in Bettridge's note to Aunt Edie and also the words the hero used to refer to Ninion.

"Yes," Lynne said. "A few months after my mother died, my father met Edie through my godfather, Quentin Chandler. Edie was working as his assistant, but after the job ended, she'd often babysit me and my brother while my father was writing. When we moved to Derbyshire for the summer, he hired her as our full-time nanny for a few months. We loved her."

"Aunt Edie was wonderful with children. Was she close to your father too?"

"Oh yes, they were good friends, but they didn't have a romantic relationship. Edie helped him to recover from my mother's death."

"It must have been so hard for you to lose your mother at such a young age."

"Edie helped all of us so much that summer. She didn't just babysit. She listened to us and encouraged us to talk about my mother, and it made the grief a little more bearable. We were so sad when she had to leave England that fall, but Edie kept in touch with us. When I became a literary agent, she sent me a note of congratulations and a gift, and whenever my father had a new play that opened, she'd send him a congratulations note."

"It's just like Aunt Edie, to never tell anyone she was friends with a famous playwright."

Lynne chuckled. "Yes, that's another reason why we all loved her so much. So many people were friendly with me and my brother in order to get close to my father, but Edie genuinely cared about us and my father too. In fact, when she worked as our nanny, she'd do her best to appear like just one of the servants so people wouldn't notice her."

Perhaps that was why none of Bettridge's friends had mentioned her friendship with the playwright. Aunt Edie would have been invisible to them, and so none of them knew about her friendship with Bettridge. "Aunt Edie never liked being in the spotlight when she was helping others."

"I was so sad to hear she died. I sent a condolence note. I didn't expect you to know who I was, but I wanted you to know that Edie touched our lives in such a deep way, even though it was only for a few months."

"Thank you for sharing your memories of my aunt." Anne didn't want to take up too much of Lynne's time, so she asked in a low voice that no one could overhear, "I did have a question for you. I recently found a note from your father that makes me think he might have given an unproduced script to Aunt Edie." Anne read the note to Lynne. "Unfortunately, I haven't found any script among my aunt's things. Do you know what script this might be?"

"There were rumors about a 'missing' script, but we never found any unproduced plays in my father's effects."

"Do you think it exists?"

"I didn't before hearing that note, but now I can believe my father would have given Edie an unproduced play. He was so grateful for her friendship, and Edie would have appreciated something special like a play written just for her."

"I never considered that your father might have written a play just for Aunt Edie." But now that Lynne had confirmed Aunt

Edie's close relationship with Bettridge and his children, it made sense.

"Edie didn't even accept payment for her job as a nanny to us that summer. The script must have been my father's only way to show her how much she meant to us."

"Aunt Edie would have treasured it dearly."

"You can't find it?"

"I'll keep looking." Anne hesitated. Flores Sanchez had mentioned to Anne about how Lynne had told a reporter that the missing script rightfully belonged to her family. "Did your family want the script back?"

"Oh, goodness no. My father gave it to Edie as a gift. It doesn't belong to us."

The tension in Anne's shoulders eased.

"I'm afraid I need to go," said Lynne.

"Thanks again for calling and telling me about Aunt Edie." They said good-bye and hung up.

How like Aunt Edie to give so selflessly of her time and love to Bettridge and his children. At least now Anne knew how Aunt Edie had gotten the script. But it still didn't answer the vital question: Where could it be?

CHAPTER TWENTY

O n Saturday morning, Liddie and Ben woke extra early, excited about the play that night. Anne went with them on a long walk with Hershey to help burn off nervous energy, both theirs and hers. She breathed in the crisp morning air, fragrant with roses, and tried not to think about things like forgetting her lines.

"Mommy, can I wear my pink dress tonight?" Liddie skipped along beside Hershey.

"You can't wear your dress," Ben said. "You have to wear your costume."

A pout began to form on Liddie's mouth.

Anne said, "Didn't you enjoy wearing Aunt Edie's black lace hat and that big puffy skirt?" The dress rehearsal had been last night. The pauper children weren't supposed to be very finely dressed, but none of the girls wanted to be in rags, so Wendy and Anne had rigged some black and brown Victorian style dresses with crinolines, and then added mismatched hats and shoes to give them a poorer appearance. The boys, on the other hand, were delighted they were required to wear stained, wrinkled clothes.

"But I want to wear pink," Liddie said.

"How about you wear one pink sock and one purple sock?" Anne said. The socks wouldn't show very much under the dress and the mismatched appearance would be in line with her costume. "And you get to have makeup put on tonight too."

Liddie's eyes shone. "Like you, Mommy?"

"Lipstick and all."

Delighted, Liddie began to twirl around, laughing. Anne couldn't help but smile at her enthusiasm, and even Ben grinned at his sister.

After a hearty breakfast of eggs, bacon, toast, and muffins, Anne sent Ben and Liddie outside to play since the day was fine. If they were cooped up indoors, they might get too rowdy because of their excitement.

Wendy arrived right after breakfast with two high school girls from the cooking club. "Are we too early?" She entered Anne's kitchen with her arms full of plastic tubs of food.

"Not at all. We just finished breakfast. Did you need help?"

Wendy and the two teenagers deposited their boxes and bags on the kitchen table. "No, we only have one more trip to make from the car, then we'll start prepping. My husband's coming later with more food and more helpers."

Anne opened the library at ten o'clock to find a line of people already waiting to be let in. The majority of them headed to the Nonfiction Room to look at the silent auction items. However, after looking at the auction, many stuck around to look through the shelves for books, so Anne was busy helping patrons.

Anne was grateful for the work, because it kept her from thinking about the play that night. However, every so often the thought would pop into her head and she'd feel butterflies in her stomach. She firmly closed her mind to her anxiety and sent a fervent prayer to God for help. The play was still hours away, and she didn't want to be feeling anxious all day.

When she finally closed the library at one o'clock, Anne peeked at the bidding sheets and was delighted to see so many bids. The theater club fund-raising was going quite well.

Anne returned to her kitchen to find Ben and Liddie helping out, under the supervision of one of the high school students. They had an assembly line going where each person put a few different types of berries into glass sundae goblets.

"Later, I'll be topping them with zabaglione," Wendy told Anne.

"What's that?"

"It's a light, frothy custard."

"*Mmm.*"

Wendy winked at her. "Don't worry, I'm already planning to make some extra for the theater club."

"How about I pick up lunch for everyone?" Anne said to the room in general. "Pizza sound good?"

After returning with a few pizzas she set them out in the living room with napkins and plates, since the kitchens—both hers and the one on the first floor—were bustling with dinner preparations. People trooped into the living room in pairs to wolf down pizza and then return to their work.

A few minutes later, Alex and some of the theater club members arrived at the library.

"You're early," Anne said as she let them in.

"We need to put the finishing touches to the set," Alex said. "We're adding a few props and also setting up the curtain."

"I'd forgotten about the curtain. The set already looks wonderful, like a gas-lighted London street."

"With the lights turned down low in the History Room, it'll be great."

Anne and a couple other theater club members went to work to clear away the center of the History Room and set up the small tables and chairs that had been stored in the Resource Room that week. It didn't take long, and the room looked like an elegant bistro with round tables surrounded by bookshelves. Wendy came in to supervise the table settings, which included candles in heavy glasses, the utensils, and napkins folded into fans.

All too soon, it came time to dress. They had arranged for all the children to come to the library early so Anne could help them get ready. She managed to fix a torn sleeve and a broken shoe string with minimal fuss. Then she sent the children to Remi and Bella, who had also arrived early to help with makeup.

Anne got into her Victorian dress. The bustle was still strange to her, feeling like a flopping appendage off her lower back, but with the dress on, it all looked very elegant. She slipped on her low-heeled button-up boots and put her hair in a simple bun so it would fit under her Victorian bonnet trimmed with lace. Remi did her makeup for her.

The high school cooking club had changed into black skirts and white button-down shirts in their roles as waiters and hostesses. Guests had been instructed to arrive at five o'clock, so the teens trooped downstairs to welcome people and seat them.

Anne wanted to do something to calm her nerves as she waited for the play to start, but the second-story library rooms were packed with other people getting ready, so she made do with pacing the short stretch of hallway in front of her living quarters. The door was locked, but Wendy had the key so she could still use the second-story kitchen and lock up after she was done.

"All right, everyone, it's time," Stephan called out.

Anne gripped her shaking hands together, then took a deep breath before heading downstairs with everyone else. They entered the History Room from the door behind the stage; it was hidden from the audience by the curtain that had been erected and now hung closed. Anne could hear gentle murmurs from the guests.

Then Stephan stepped in front of the curtain and the noise subsided. "Ladies and gentlemen, welcome to our dinner play for this evening." His voice rolled rich and full in the packed room. "We thank you for joining us and supporting the Blue Hill Community Theater Club. We hope you will enjoy the play and your dinner. *Bon appetit!*"

Amid applause, the curtain rose, the stage lights were turned on, and the play began.

It went great. Everyone remembered their lines, and there was an excitement in the air that was almost tangible. In the play, there were written places where the actors occasionally went out to rope in a surprised audience member, and there were smiles and laughter at people's spontaneous reactions. Wendy and the waitresses served the appetizers during the first act, creamy carrot soup with homemade croutons and a swirl of *creme fraiche*, along with bread and various dipping sauces.

When the curtain went down after the first act, all the actors helped transform the stage into a library. A cloth, painted to look like a papered wall, was dropped in front of the London street scene, and chairs and other props were set up.

The second act went even better than the first. There were even some gasps from the audience as new clues to the mystery came to light, and Anne heard some giggles at the gypsy's flirtations with the librarian. She'd seen Alex in costume at the dress rehearsal, but tonight he seemed to have even more flamboyant dash in his colorful loose shirt and black trousers. Dinner was served during the second act, roast chicken in orange sauce, little tournedos in a rosemary gravy, and phyllo-wrapped baked garlic mashed potatoes with sautéed asparagus on the side.

For the third act, the stage was again turned back into the London street, and as the curtain opened, Anne saw that dessert was being served.

She felt her stomach flip-flop as the kiss approached, and she delivered her lines a little stiffly. *Lord, please help me,* she prayed, and immediately felt a flood of peace and the assurance of God's presence with her.

"My darling, my love for you has grown to encompass every thought," the gypsy said, clasping the librarian's hand.

Alex's touch was warm against Anne's clammy palms. When she hesitated, he gave her a soft squeeze. She took a deep breath. "I have loved you since the moment you first kissed my hand." Anne heard a few sighs from the audience.

Alex looked into her eyes as he raised her hand to his lips. His gaze held Anne's, and she began to hear the throb of her heartbeat in her ears.

He pulled her into a dip to kiss her, but he missed the side of her mouth and instead kissed her lips.

It was a nice kiss, but she suddenly missed Eric with a pang. And her feelings and thoughts came into full clarity.

When Alex put her on her feet, the audience was applauding. Anne couldn't help smiling at their reaction to the gypsy and the librarian's stage romance.

The play ended to enthusiastic applause, and the actors took a second bow before the lights went back on in the History Room. It was all over.

Tami and Aiden were the first to come up to Anne behind the closed curtain. "You did really great," Tami said.

"Thanks to Aiden's coaching."

"I knew you could do it," Aiden said. "You just needed more confidence in yourself."

"Now what happens?" Anne asked.

"You go out and greet your fans!" Tami said.

Coffee and tea were being served in the Nonfiction Room, and many of the guests headed there to look at the silent auction items. However, several people remained in the History Room to greet the actors as they emerged from behind the curtain.

Anne was engulfed by her friends, Jennifer and Michael Banks and Heather and Mark Stafford.

"You were great!" Jennifer squealed.

"You and Alex looked just like high school again," Heather said.

Rather than answer that, Anne said, "It was fun to pretend to be someone else for a while."

"Good job, Anne." Donna Slade and her husband came up to them.

"Thanks, Donna."

Wendy swept by, pausing only to tell them all, "There are cookies in the Nonfiction Room in addition to coffee."

"Oreo truffles?" Jennifer asked her.

"You betcha," Wendy said.

"Oh." Michael perked up. "Let's get some before they're all gone."

After they all drifted away, Reverend Tom and his wife Maggie approached Anne, followed by Mildred.

"Anne and Alex, great job," Reverend Tom said.

Anne turned to see that Alex had come up behind her. "Thanks," she said to Reverend Tom.

"It was fun." Alex grinned.

"You both look marvelous in your costumes," Maggie said.

"I recognize yours," Mildred said. "It was Edie's, wasn't it? It fits you like a glove. It reminded me of when Edie wore it for a few Victorian plays."

"There's Stephan," Maggie said. "I wanted to congratulate him. I think this was the best performance he's ever done." She, Reverend Tom, and Mildred headed toward him.

Alex turned to Anne. "How are you feeling?"

She heaved a huge breath. "Relieved it's over."

His brow wrinkled. "I hope it wasn't awful."

"Oh, nothing like that. I was just so nervous."

"You didn't seem like it. You did a great job."

"Thanks. You did too."

"I'm, uh…" He colored and said in a low voice, "I'm sorry about the kiss. It was an accident."

"It's all right." Anne sighed softly. "It made me miss Eric, though."

Alex looked guilt-stricken. "I understand how hard it is when you lose a loved one. I still miss my sister."

"Remembering Eric doesn't hurt, like it used to. But I realized I haven't quite let go of my grief yet."

He nodded and touched her shoulder. "I'll always be here as your friend."

"Thanks." Anne felt at peace, knowing God would take care of her now as He had when she'd first lost Eric. She also was thankful at how her friendship with Alex had weathered the dinner play—it was maybe even a little stronger than it had been before.

Wendy came up to them. "I didn't get to see much of the play, but everyone's been saying it was terrific."

"How did people like the dinner?" Anne asked.

"I was asked to do some catering jobs, can you believe it?" Wendy chortled. "I said no."

"Are there leftovers for hardworking actors?" Alex said.

"Extra dessert is in the first-floor kitchen, and extra appetizers and entrees are in the second-floor kitchen. Ryan already headed upstairs."

Alex went to find his nephew, and Anne continued circulating with guests. Many admired her costume and a few ribbed her about the onstage kiss, which she was able to laugh off with more ease than she'd have expected.

The guests eventually left, and the theater club members changed out of their costumes and began cleaning up. Most of the cleanup would happen tomorrow, after church, since the library wasn't open, but the foodstuffs had to be packed away and dirty dishes washed. It was accomplished quickly, and then everyone said cheerful good nights to each other as they headed home or out to celebrate with friends.

Ryan was hanging out with Ben and Liddie upstairs in the living room while Anne, Alex, Stephan, and Wendy finished up downstairs.

When Stephan saw Alex start to break down the set, he said, "Leave that for tomorrow. I don't know about you, but I'm beat!"

"I am too, but it was fun." Anne looked at Wendy. "For us, at least."

"Oh, I had fun too, even if it was hectic," Wendy said. "People were even asking if we'd do it again next year."

"I don't want to think about next year just yet," Stephan said with a groan. "I'll see you all tomorrow." He left with a wave.

"Before I forget, here's the key to the living area. Thanks for letting us use your kitchen." Wendy passed it to Anne. "Did you get some food?"

Anne shook her head and was surprised when Alex did too. "I wanted some dessert but didn't have time to snag one," Anne said.

"I had a feeling you would be too busy. I left two for you in the second-floor kitchen."

"You're a true friend." Anne grinned.

"I'll help you carry this stuff to your car," Alex said to Wendy, then winked at Anne. "But I'll be back, so don't even think about eating my dessert."

"Now, would I do that?" Anne asked innocently.

Alex stacked several tubs of leftover vegetables into his arms and followed Wendy, who carried bags of extra food, out the front door. Anne went around the first floor making sure everything was locked up, although she left the front door unlocked for Alex to return. She turned off all the lights and headed upstairs.

However, as she passed the Resource Room, she suddenly heard a soft footfall, then the creak of the door opening. She turned, expecting to see a theater club member who had perhaps forgotten something, but instead came face to face with a short, dark-haired man with menace in his eyes.

CHAPTER TWENTY-ONE

It was the stranger she'd seen around town, who Tami thought might be following her, and who had been asking about Edie and a manuscript.

And he was here, in her house.

"Who are you? What are you doing here?" Anne tried to keep her voice from shaking.

"Where's the script?" He had a gravelly voice that sounded almost like a growl.

"What script are you talking about?"

He took a step toward her, and she noticed his stocky, powerful build. "I know Edie had the missing Bettridge script."

"I don't have it."

"I *know* you have it."

Anne took a step backward. "Why would you think that?"

"Don't play dumb." As he spoke, his British accent became clearer. "Roy called Edie because she had the script. I heard the entire phone conversation."

"How could you possibly overhear a private phone call?" Anne tried not to look toward the stairs. Where was Alex?

"I was Roy's personal assistant."

"If you're really his assistant, you could have gotten Edie's address and visited her yourself."

His mouth pinched. "I didn't get a chance to. Look, I don't want to have to hurt you, but you and your kids are all alone."

He didn't know Alex was returning. She had to keep him talking until then. "How do you know my aunt is the same Edie who has the script? It could be anyone."

"Do you think I'm stupid? Tami O'Brien made inquiries about the Bettridge script back in London, then as soon as she came here, she visited you, living in your aunt *Edie's* house."

Was that a shadow on the stairs? Anne tried not to look, for fear it would alert the man to Alex's presence. "You followed Tami all the way here just because you heard she made inquiries about the Bettridge script?"

"No, I followed her here because she had also made inquiries asking if a woman named Edie Summers had known Roy Underwood," the man said with a sneer. "Now where's the script?"

There was the sound of rapid footsteps coming up the stairs. The man turned but not in time to stop Alex from tackling him to the ground. They both hit the wooden floor hard, making it shudder.

Anne ran to the door to the living quarters, thankful it was locked. She was fumbling for her keys when it opened. Ben and Ryan stood there with eyes wide. "Mom, what—?"

"Inside," Anne told him, and grabbed the phone. She dialed 911 and told the dispatcher about the stranger.

The sounds of struggling in the hallway ceased, and Alex called out, "Anne, could you get me some rope to tie his hands?"

Anne hurried out with some strong nylon cord. Alex knelt on top of the man, who scowled as he lay stomach down on the floor.

"I called the police. Are you all right?"

"I'm fine." Alex tied the man's hands. "Are you and the kids okay?"

"That's cool, Uncle Alex!" Ryan's excited voice came from the open doorway. "Can you teach me how to do that?"

"Me too," Ben added.

"Mommy, who's that?" Liddie peeked behind Ben and Ryan, who seemed to be trying to keep her safely in the living quarters.

The police arrived within a few minutes, and Anne was surprised to see Michael Banks. "Anne, I heard the call and had to come right over. Are you all right?"

"I'm fine, thanks to Alex."

Michael grinned and gave his friend a mock punch to the shoulder. "Way to go. Maybe you should be coaching the football team."

Alex flushed but smiled. "I'm just glad everyone's okay."

Anne told Michael about her conversation with the man. "I need to call Tami. She'll be relieved to know she doesn't have to keep looking over her shoulder anymore."

"She should have told the police about it," Michael said.

"She thought she was being paranoid and that it was her imagination. And he had stopped following her this past week or so."

"And you don't know where the script is?"

Anne shook her head. "I've looked everywhere. I'm starting to think that maybe Aunt Edie didn't want it to be found."

But in her heart, Anne couldn't quite believe that to be true. *Lord, please help me to find Aunt Edie's script. It was so precious to her...*

And suddenly Anne had an idea why.

* * *

"Quite a bit of excitement last night!" Tami came up to Anne after church service the next day. "Are you all right?"

"I'm fine, thanks to Alex."

"Yes, all the boys are looking up to him as their latest superhero." Tami nodded toward the corner of the fellowship hall where several young boys were with Alex. It looked like he was demonstrating with Ryan the proper way to do a football tackle.

"But he didn't play football in high school."

"I taught him those takedown moves," Michael said as he joined them. The former high school football player had a rueful look. "And Alex gets all the glory."

"I'm just glad you're all fine," Tami said to Anne.

"Did you find out anything more from him?" Anne asked Michael.

"His name's Joe Mulcahy, and he really was Roy Underwood's personal assistant, or secretary. Until Roy fired him a few weeks before he died."

"So he could have overheard Roy's phone conversation with Aunt Edie?"

"He didn't know Edie's last name until he happened to hear about some inquiries Tami made about Edie and Roy on a few online forum boards."

Tami groaned and buried her face in her hands. "I can't believe it. I'm so sorry, Anne."

"You couldn't have known." Anne patted her shoulder. "At least now we know why he was following you."

"I wish he'd known more about the script. It seems like you had to endure all that for nothing."

At that moment, Alex called, "Michael, come here and show these boys some football moves."

Michael eagerly trotted over.

Mildred then approached with Mr. Willet. "Anne, what happened last night? Are you all right?"

Tami excused herself since she'd heard the story already, and Anne told Mildred and Mr. Willet an abridged version. "I'm fine, really."

"Thank the Lord for that," Mr. Willet said.

"Anne, I know you're not working today, but Mr. Willet and I were talking about that Wilkie Collins book he borrowed from the library."

"Did you enjoy it, Mr. Willet?"

He smiled. "It brought back wonderful memories of reading those mysteries as a boy. In fact, I also remembered an old mystery novel my father used to read to us, and I wanted to find a copy. I'll come to the library tomorrow."

"What was the title? If I have time today, I'll look it up for you."

"The book was called *Tales of the Jewelled Men,* but I'm afraid I can't remember the author."

"I've never even heard of it. The title sounds unusual enough that I think it won't be hard to find."

"It's probably a very old book. I remember my father's hardcover copy was coming apart at the seams."

"Anne, are you all right?" Wendy hurried up to them. "I just heard…"

Anne was touched by the number of people who came up to her to ask how she was doing. She was so blessed by the new friendships God had given to her since she moved her family to Blue Hill.

Wendy invited Anne's family and others of the community theater club to her home since she had cooked up a storm, using up the rest of the food staples that had been donated. Anne was able to eat some of Wendy's delectable carrot soup, rich and creamy, which Ben tried but didn't care for. Liddie ate an entire plate of carrot sticks and then hopped around the house like a bunny.

After lunch, the community theater club headed to the library. Alex supervised the dismantling of the stage, while Anne helped to store in the Resource Room the tables and chairs that had been donated for the dinner play until their owners could pick them up on Monday. The silent auction items would remain in the Nonfiction Room until Monday night, when the auction ended.

"I've been outbid on that cruise," Wendy bemoaned.

"Maybe you and Chad should save up for a cruise for your next big wedding anniversary," Anne said.

"That would be fun. Did you bid on anything?"

"I got outbid for the gaming console, but I'm still in the running for that hand-knitted lace shawl."

"That was gorgeous! I would have bid, but I can't see it surviving in my household. With my luck, one of the twins would decide to use it as a Superman cape or something like that."

With everyone's help, the library was clean in no time, and the History Room was restored to the way it had been before. Everyone said thanks and good-bye to Anne as they headed out.

"Next year?" Stephan said to Anne with a broad grin just before walking out the front door.

Anne gave a mock groan. "Maybe you shouldn't ask that right after this year's performance just ended."

"Good point. I'll come bother you in a few months." He winked at Anne, then departed.

"*Shh*. The library is quiet," Liddie said as she exaggeratedly tiptoed up the stairs.

"It almost seems too quiet," Ben said.

"Are you going to miss not having the play?" Anne asked.

He tilted his head to think about that for a minute. "Yeah, even though it was a lot of work it was fun to be with everybody."

"I got to wear my lacy hat!" Liddie giggled as she ran up the last few steps.

"The costumes were kinda neat," Ben said.

"That reminds me, I need to put Aunt Edie's dress back in the trunk upstairs."

"Can we watch a movie?" Liddie asked. "With popcorn?"

The day had turned cool, and the sky hinted at rain tonight. "Sure."

Liddie picked a fairy tale movie, but Ben opted to read in his room. Anne put the movie in, made popcorn, and then left Liddie on the living room couch while she went up to the attic with Aunt Edie's Victorian costume.

She didn't stay long because the attic had become dim and moody with the darkening skies. She carefully folded Aunt Edie's dress and laid it in a trunk with tissue paper.

On her way out of the attic, she accidentally bumped into the box with Aunt Edie's letters. It tilted, then fell on its side. Anne replaced the letters that had fallen out, several of which had stains from mold damage. It wouldn't be good to leave them for too long in the box with other letters that weren't contaminated. She put all the letters together for now, and made a mental note to figure out later what to do.

Since Ben and Liddie were occupied, Anne went downstairs to the computer to look up Mr. Willet's book. If the library had it, she could have it ready for him, but she had a feeling that she would have to order it through interlibrary loan.

She was astonished to find that the book had a publication date of 1851. One library had an original copy of the book in its archive room, not for public circulation. Then Anne found a company that said it could print and bind the book for any library, for a rather hefty fee.

How could they print the book if it was obviously out of print? Anne dug further and realized that the original book had been scanned by a nonprofit organization that specialized in digitizing historical collections to make them available to the public. The novel Mr. Willet wanted was available for free online as a pdf file.

Anne downloaded the file. The original book that had been scanned had been very old, with age spots and mold stains over the pages, but the text was legible. She was amazed that this story, with so few copies printed and still existing, might have been lost if this organization hadn't scanned the book so that others could read it.

As she stared at the images of the stained pages of the book, suddenly a light went on in her head.

All the documents in Aunt Edie's safe deposit box had been mold stained. The letters had been mold stained. And when Anne had first looked through the attic with Wendy, she'd found office equipment including a scanner.

Was it possible the script had been damaged by mold? Would Aunt Edie have used the scanner to digitize a copy of the script? But then where would the digital copy be? Anne had gone through all the files on Aunt Edie's computer and hadn't seen a script.

If the script was precious to Aunt Edie, wouldn't she put it somewhere safe? Like the safe deposit box? But how could she put a digital file in a safe deposit box?

The keychain.

Anne went upstairs to her bedroom and rummaged in her nightstand drawer for the keychain she'd taken from Aunt Edie's safe deposit box. The circular key fob was thick and solid with the logo of the Blue Hill bank printed on one side.

At Anne's old library in New York, the computer repair company the library used gave out promotional key fobs that held hidden USB flash drives. She never thought of it when seeing the bank fob since she associated the USB flash drives with the computer repair company, but now she grasped the two ends and pulled.

It came apart to reveal a USB flash drive.

Anne hurried back downstairs. With shaking hands, she plugged the flash drive into the computer.

There were a few files on the drive, including digital scans of the mold-stained documents that had been in the safe deposit box. And then there was a file named *Had We Never Loved*. Anne caught her breath as she opened the file.

It was a file of scanned typed pages, heavily stained by mold, with many pages showing extensive crinkling from water damage. The first page was a title page that said *Had We Never Loved*, a play by Hugh Bettridge. Beneath that were the words *For Edie, my dear Ninion*.

Anne felt as if a weight had been lifted from her shoulders. She'd found the script! And if she was right, she knew why Edie never showed it to anyone, even though it was the famous missing Bettridge script. Anne began reading.

The play was set in 1940 in the fictional town of Green Lake, Pennsylvania, about two lovers, Ruth and Harry. It unfolded exactly like Aunt Edie's manuscript that Anne had found when she first moved into the library, the fictionalized account of Aunt Edie's true, tragic love story. The names of the town and the characters were all the same as Aunt Edie's book.

Anne's breath caught. She'd been right. Aunt Edie wouldn't have shown this script to anyone because it was her own story, told by a masterful storyteller. As Anne read the script, tears sprang to her eyes at the beautiful lines of dialogue, the heart-wrenching emotion of the scenes. Aunt Edie must have told Bettridge about her youthful relationship with Joe Riley in detail, and Bettridge had woven a glorious tapestry of love and loss. It was obvious to Anne that Bettridge's writing held genuine tenderness for the main female character, Ruth. She was sure Bettridge wrote this for Edie out of his close friendship with her.

Anne finished reading the play and sat back, sniffling into her tissue. The ending had a thread of hope and joy at the wonderful way Ruth touched other people's lives despite the sadness of her own. It was a beautiful play and Aunt Edie had probably been deeply touched by the gift.

Having so recently learned about her aunt's tragic love story, Anne couldn't imagine letting anyone see this play. It would be like letting people see the manuscript Aunt Edie had written, or the wedding photos of the marriage that had never taken place.

Anne closed the file and removed the flash drive from her computer. She'd go to the bank tomorrow and put it back in the safe deposit box. One day she might know what to do with it. Perhaps she'd talk it over with Ben and Liddie when they had grown to adults but not now.

She looked up at the portrait of her aunt on the wall over the checkout area. "Aunt Edie, you helped so many people. You helped Bettridge and his family heal from the death of his wife. You helped me by leaving me your house for a library. I pray my life is filled with your generosity and compassion for others."

Aunt Edie's smiling face looked back at Anne from the field of daisies, and she seemed to be filled with confidence in Anne's decision.

* * *

There was a crowd gathered in the Nonfiction Room on Monday evening just before the library closed. They seemed to be holding their breath as they looked to Wendy, who was staring at her watch.

"Three… two… one! The silent auction is officially over."

There was a smattering of applause and lots of smiles.

People lined up to collect their prizes. Wendy and Stephan sat at a table to collect the checks.

Anne lifted the lace shawl she'd won. It floated in her hands, made of a fine, lofty wool yarn that had been knitted into an intricate lace pattern of vines and ladders. The soft green color would go perfectly with her wardrobe.

"That's pretty, Mommy." Liddie reached out a hand to touch the soft yarn.

"You could've worn that with your costume," Ben said.

"I think I'll wear it to church next Sunday." If the day was fine, she could wear it with her green flowered dress. The shawl would be perfect to keep off any slight chill in the air.

Donna was grinning from ear to ear. "I won the cruise! My husband and I are already planning for it."

Anne moved around the room, chatting with people who had won items. Remi had won a tennis racquet, and Bella had won a dainty gold bracelet. But Anne was most surprised by Mildred.

"You won drum lessons?" Anne could only stare at her friend.

Mildred looked abashed. "I didn't think I'd win. I only bid on it because there weren't any other bids and I felt sorry for whoever donated it."

Anne could understand that many parents would definitely not want their children to have drum lessons. She couldn't help the grin on her face. "So when do you start lessons?"

"Ha-ha, Miss Smarty-pants." Mildred looked at the business card of the teacher. "Maybe I can trade it for some other type of lesson. Like the ukulele." That thought brightened her up considerably.

Tami came by to give Anne a hug. "Aiden and I are leaving tomorrow for London. Can you believe it's already been four weeks?"

"You must miss the excitement of the theater."

"But I'll miss Blue Hill too. And I'm so sorry for bringing danger to your family."

"Don't worry about it. Everything turned out okay."

Tami sighed. "I wish you could have found Edie's play, though."

"Maybe it'll resurface in a few years," Anne said.

"What a stir that would cause!"

Eventually, people started leaving with their auction items. Ryan was upstairs playing a computer game with Ben and Liddie, so Alex remained with Wendy and Stephan after Anne locked the front door.

Wendy gave a hundred-watt smile. "We've raised more than enough to repair the theater roof!"

There were cheers and high fives all around.

Stephan's eyes were misty. "I'm floored at how the Blue Hill community supported us for this. What a town."

Alex nodded. "What good neighbors."

Anne smiled at them all. "What good friends."

ABOUT THE AUTHOR

Camy grew up in Hawaii and now lives in San Jose, California, with her engineer husband and rambunctious dog, Snickers. She graduated from Stanford University and worked as a biologist researcher for nine years, but she now writes full-time. She is a staff worker for her church youth group, and she leads one of the worship teams for Sunday services. On her blog, she ponders knitting, spinning wool, dogs, running, the Never Ending Diet, and other frivolous things. Visit Camy's blog at http://blog.camytang.com.

A CONVERSATION WITH THE AUTHOR

Q. *Aunt Edie has had a lot of adventures in her life. Can you tell us about the most exciting adventure you've experienced?*

A. One thing on my bucket list was to travel to England because I love British history and I even enjoy British television and movies! So for my fortieth birthday, instead of throwing a party for other people, I threw a party for me — I went to England for two weeks. I turned forty in London! It was an amazing trip and I'm so glad I was able to go.

Q. *Aunt Edie loved to travel. What's your favorite vacation or tourist destination?*

A. My favorite city when I went to England was Bath. The architecture is so beautiful and so old, and the city is incredibly elegant. Lunch in the Pump Room was fantastic, eating great local food and being surrounded by the Regency-era decor.

Q. *Anne moves back to her hometown after years in New York City. What do/would you miss about your hometown?*

A. I grew up in Hawaii, and I miss lots of things from home. The Hawaiian culture is very easygoing and friendly, and people who live in Hawaii always seem to be courteous and nice to one another. I also really miss the food — there's a lot of different ethnic influences in Hawaii. Every time I go back to Hawaii to visit my family, I make sure to eat Loco Moco (homemade hamburger patty over rice with brown gravy and a fried egg), saimin (noodles in broth), and a burger and fries from Kua'aina, a famous local hamburger joint.

Q. *What is the most memorable photograph you have on your wall?*

A. There used to be a cross on a hilltop in Hawaii, and I could see it as we drove past on the freeway. It was torn down many years ago, but I found a black-and-white photograph of the cross that a photographer had taken many decades ago. I had it framed in a black bamboo frame and it hangs in my living room. The sight of that cross on the hilltop, with Diamond Head crater in the background, is so peaceful and reminds me of God's beauty and loving sacrifice.

Q. *What advice would you give an aspiring novelist?*

A. Just write! The hardest part about writing is finishing your first book. It doesn't matter if you do it "right," just finish it first because you can always fix things later. Typing "The End" is still a huge sense of accomplishment for me, each time I do it.

Q. *What characteristics of Anne's personality do you see in yourself? In what ways are you a total opposite of Anne?*

A. I am most like Anne in that I love reading and libraries! However, Anne is much more patient and kind than I am, although I am a work in progress. God is still working to make me more like Him.

RECIPES FROM THE LIBRARY GUILD

Anne's Raspberry Spoon Bread

1 cup cornmeal, medium or
finely ground
1 cup buttermilk
²⁄₃ cup maple syrup
2 tablespoons butter
½ teaspoon salt
4 large eggs

¼ cup flour
2 teaspoons vanilla extract
¼ cup sugar
3 cups raspberries
8 tablespoons Greek yogurt

Preheat oven to 375 degrees. Spray an eight-inch square baking pan with nonstick cooking spray.

Combine the cornmeal, buttermilk, maple syrup, butter, and salt in a large saucepan. Cook over medium-high heat, stirring constantly with a wire whisk, until the mixture bubbles and thickens. Remove from the heat. Separate egg whites from egg yolks. Whisk egg yolks in a large bowl. Whisking constantly, add half a cup of the hot cornmeal mixture until completely combined. Scrape in the remaining cornmeal mixture and whisk until smooth. Whisk in flour and vanilla until smooth.

Beat egg whites in another large bowl with an electric mixer on high speed until soft peaks form. Gradually mix in sugar, continuing to beat until soft glossy peaks form. Fold the whites into the cornmeal mixture. Fold in two cups of the raspberries. Spoon the batter into the prepared dish.

Bake thirty-five to forty minutes, until golden brown and puffy. Let cool for twenty minutes, serving slightly warm. Top each serving with a dollop of the Greek yogurt and remaining raspberries just before serving.

FROM THE GUIDEPOSTS ARCHIVES

This article by Rick Hamlin originally appeared in
Guideposts magazine.

I have a confession to make. I didn't come to New York to be a
writer and editor. I came here to be a professional singer. I'd
sung a lot in college, in the chapel choir, in glee club, in an a capella
men's group, and in musicals. I figured I was ready to take on the
Big Apple. I was accepted at the Manhattan School of Music,
snagged a paid gig in a church choir and found a couch to sleep on
in a rambling Upper West Side apartment.

Two of my roommates were actor/singers. They were
actually in Broadway shows at the time. They would come home
from the theater and start singing arias at midnight. "Rick, check
out my high C." "How do you think my French accent is on this
song?" "Do you think this piece will work for my audition
tomorrow?"

I loved all of it, even if I found it intimidating. Would I be
able to perform in a Broadway show or sing opera and concerts
the way they did? The city was full of talented up-and-comers.
There was good singing everywhere . . . clubs, Broadway, Lincoln
Center, even in the parks and on the subway. But we all knew the
very best place to be heard, the venue that signaled you had
really made it: Carnegie Hall.

I remember taking a girl to a sold-out recital there, when the only seats left were tucked onstage behind the singer. For most of the concert we could only see his back—occasionally he'd turn and bow to us—but we could see the hall as he saw it: seemingly limitless rows of seats rising all the way to the upper balconies, where the people looked like peapods.

"Can you imagine singing here?" my date whispered.

Funny thing was, I could. I mean, it would be scary, but wouldn't it be amazing? Just to feel your voice disappear into the vastness of that celebrated hall, the famous acoustics of the place amplifying your singing so you could be heard by the peapods all the way in the back of the upper balconies.

Maybe, I said to myself, *someday*.

"How do you get to Carnegie Hall?" the old joke goes. Answer: "Practice, practice, practice." Well, I practiced hard. I took dance lessons and acting lessons along with my voice lessons so I could market myself as an actor/singer who could "move well." I had professional photos taken and mass-mailed my eight-by-ten glossies and résumé to casting directors and agents.

I auditioned all over town, waiting at cattle calls to sing "a few measures" before being told "Thank you," which usually meant "No thanks." I did musicals in church basements, sang *South Pacific* and *West Side Story* in summer stock, was a spear carrier in Shakespeare, got tenor gigs in various choruses and did so many performances of children's theater that I could recite lines in my sleep.

And yet my dream did not come without doubt. I asked myself and God, *Is this really what I'm meant to do?* Not that I wasn't grateful to be employed in such an incredibly competitive business, but was it really me? If God gave me this gift—and singing felt like a God-given gift—was this how I was supposed to use it?

I liked the people I worked with, but to tell the truth, I didn't really like the work. I didn't like traveling all the time. Didn't like bonding with a group of singers and actors for several intense weeks only to go our separate ways after the show was done. Didn't like not knowing where the next job was coming from. Didn't like getting nervous before a show. More important, I had fallen in love with the woman I'd taken on that date to Carnegie Hall, and if we were to be married and have children someday, was that the life I wanted as a husband and a father? The life of a vagabond tenor?

We got married and had so many of our musical friends perform during the ceremony, hitting their high C's, that it sounded like a concert. By then I had relaunched myself as a writer/editor, almost as precarious an existence as that of an actor/singer, but not quite.

"Practice, practice, practice" is good advice for writers too, and gradually I made a career for myself, landing on staff at *Guideposts* magazine, where I have been very happy, happier than I would ever have been as a professional tenor. Besides, I still found places to sing for the sheer amateur joy of it. Sundays with our church choir, concerts here and there, and an excellent Gilbert and Sullivan group, the Blue Hill Troupe, where I often was cast as the lead. Performing a few nights a year for friends and family was better than a life on the stage. Broadway didn't miss me.

Then, a dozen years ago, the Blue Hill Troupe was asked to give a concert with the New York Pops orchestra. Guess where? Carnegie Hall. It would be a night to remember, singing in the chorus, looking out over that famous hall. Then the director called. "We want a couple of our soloists to perform. I want you and Joanne to do the love duet from *Pinafore*. Okay?"

"Sure," I blithely said. I hung up and pulled out the score. My friend Joanne Lessner and I would have to stand up in front of the orchestra next to the conductor and sing forty-two measures all by ourselves onstage at Carnegie Hall. How thrilling! How absolutely terrifying!

We practiced, practiced, practiced. On our own, together, with a pianist, and on the afternoon of the actual performance with the full orchestra. The red seats were empty, but I did steal a glance up and could picture someone looking down and seeing how very small I was on the vast, fabled stage where the greatest singers on earth had performed. "God," I muttered, "this might have been a dream of mine long ago, but I feel completely inadequate now. Why on earth did you let me say yes?"

"You sounded great up there," my fellow tenors said. They had to be lying. Couldn't they see me balling my hands into fists to keep them from shaking? Couldn't they tell that that vibrato was coming from sheer nerves? That I was squeezing out every note? If I could only back out of the whole thing now . . . but my name was in the program. People were depending on me. I couldn't disappoint them.

My long-lost dream of performing at Carnegie Hall was coming true, whether I liked it or not.

I prayed on the subway train that evening, wearing my tux, heading to Fifty-Seventh Street. *Please, God, just don't let me mess up. That's all I ask.* I kept picturing the conductor waving his baton at me and nothing coming out of my mouth.

Backstage the conductor gave the troupe a pep talk: "Have fun out there." We patted each other on the back and then filed out onstage. Joanne's and my duet wouldn't come until halfway through the program. That meant I had to sing a half dozen other pieces with the chorus, marking the minutes to my doom.

Finally it was our turn. Our cue came and Joanne and I walked forward. The conductor lowered his baton. The orchestra began. And we sang, the music rising to the back of the hall. I don't know how it happened. I didn't flub a lyric, didn't miss a note, didn't run out of breath, didn't trip over my feet. Didn't mess up. The nerves gave way to calm and then the calm gave way to joy, the joy of using a God-given gift. God wouldn't have put me there if I couldn't do it.

We finished and bowed. The audience applauded. The forty-two measures were over. We walked back to join the group for the rest of the concert. "Flawless . . . awesome," my friends in the tenor section congratulated me under their breath. *You did it,* I thought with glee. *You really did it. You've sung in Carnegie Hall!* I was in awe. But at the same time I told myself, *You don't ever have to do this again.* Once for a lark, once for the challenge, once to say that you've done a thing you dreamed about. Once to know that you have made the right choices in life and have used your gifts to the best of your ability.

Once in a lifetime was enough. More than enough.

Read on for a sneak peek of another exciting book in
Secrets of the Blue Hill Library!

All That Glitters

A gust of wind shook the old house and rattled the kitchen window. Anne Gibson looked up from her preparations of supper for herself and her two children. Outside the window, tree branches tossed wildly in the wind. The sky had darkened too early, obscured by brooding clouds.

She wiped her hands on a dish towel. Time to bring the children in. As she turned toward the door, her phone rang. When she answered it, a recorded voice said, "A tornado warning has been issued for your area until 6:45 PM. Take shelter immediately."

Anne caught her breath. She switched on her battery-operated weather radio, ran down the stairs to the rear entrance of her house, which also served as the town's public library, and shoved open the door. The backyard stood eerily empty, the only movement coming from the wind-tossed trees and plants in the flower beds. An empty plastic bag gusted across the lawn.

Anne's chest tightened. Not ten minutes ago, she had seen Ben and Liddie from the kitchen window, playing fetch with Ben's dog, Hershey. She walked out on the back deck and scanned the scene once more before yelling, "Ben! Liddie! Where are you?"

The wind snatched her words, and a fat raindrop smacked her forehead.

"Ben!"

Thunder rumbled as the rain cascaded down. The roiling clouds above her took on a greenish cast. Anne's heart pounded. Over the rush of the wind, she heard the tornado siren from the fire station.

"Liddie!" she screamed, but her five-year-old's mop of curls was nowhere to be seen.

Anne dashed down the steps and around the corner of the house, scanning the library parking lot, the front yard, and down Bluebell Lane.

Another rumble of thunder, louder than before, made her jump. Lightning cracked. It was too close. A wave of adrenaline washed through her as she considered what to do. She ran back the way she came, to the last place she'd seen the children, but nothing had changed in the backyard, except that the rain fell faster.

Her longtime friend Alex Ochs would come immediately if she called him. Anne reached in her pocket for her phone but realized she'd left it in the kitchen. As she turned to run up and get it, a sharp yip reached her over the howling of the wind, and she jerked back around. Hershey bounded toward her from the creek path, out of the trees that bordered the far edge of the back lawn.

Anne hurried toward the steps, with the rain beating down her hair and soaking through the shoulders of her sweater.

The chocolate Lab leaped onto the deck and skidded to a stop by the door.

"Hershey! Where's Ben?" She whirled and looked again toward the creek path. The wind whipped the branches of the trees, and a branch tumbled down from the large maple near the garage. She wanted to yell again, but she couldn't pull in a full breath of air.

And then she saw him—her son, running in slow motion from the woods. Ben was leaning forward, pushing against the wind. *Thank God!* But—where was his sister? Anne sent up a quick prayer as she ran toward Ben.

"Where's Liddie?" she yelled.

Ben turned and waved vaguely toward the path. Anne lifted her gaze, and a wave of shock hit her. A man she'd never seen before emerged from the trees carrying her precious daughter. Liddie was upright in his arms, clinging with her arms around the stranger's neck. He lifted a hand in a brief wave and then lowered his head against the wind as he trudged toward her, stepping around a large tree limb that had fallen on the edge of the lawn.

Thunder rolled so loud Anne's ears hurt. She bent close to Ben's ear and yelled, "Come on!" She grabbed his hand and pulled him up onto the deck. She opened the door, and the wind tore the knob from her hands, thrusting the door back against the wall inside with a thump. She hauled Ben through the opening, and the dog pushed past them. They stood inside, staring out at the man who carried Liddie ever closer.

He was nearly to the steps. Anne plunged out into the rain again and met him on the deck. She held out her arms for Liddie, but he lumbered past her and through the doorway. She hurried in behind him and managed to shut the door against the raging storm.

In the quiet of the entry, they all stared at each other for a moment. Outside, the wind and rain raged, and the thunder kept up a near-constant growling. From upstairs in the kitchen, the radio continued to broadcast the warning, and she heard the calm female announcer say, "The storm will reach Blue Hill within the next ten minutes. If you're in its path, go immediately to your shelter or the strongest part of your house."

"Mommy!" Liddie wriggled in the man's grasp and leaned toward Anne, her arms outstretched.

"Baby!" Anne took her and held her close. "I was so scared. Where were you?"

Ben, his eyes wide, stared at her. "We were playing down by the creek. I heard the thunder and knew we should come home, but Liddie started crying. I couldn't make her walk. The wind came up so fast!"

The man cleared his throat. "That was the situation when I saw them. I hope you don't mind. The lad seemed to need a little help."

"I—no. Of course not." Anne shifted her gaze to him. He was older than she had realized—past seventy, anyway. She was surprised he had carried Liddie so far. His wrinkled, weather-beaten face looked none too clean, and raindrops streak his cheeks below his keen blue eyes. "Thank you," Anne said.

"I tried to carry her." Ben's voice cracked, and tears mingled with the raindrops on his face.

"You did fine," Anne told him. Wind buffeted the old house, and the door shook in its frame. "Right now we need to go down in the basement." She glanced at the stranger. She didn't really want him in their house, but did she have a choice? If he had a car, it was probably some distance away. She couldn't send him out into the path of a tornado. "Come along, sir. You too."

"Thank you, ma'am." He took a pair of glasses from his jacket pocket and slid them on.

"And Hershey," Ben said quickly.

"Yes, of course. Hershey too."

"Come on, boy," Ben called, and the dog hopped to his side.

Anne opened the basement door and shifted Liddie to her hip. As she put her foot out toward the top step, the lights flickered and went out.

Liddie let out a little scream, and Anne steadied herself and patted Liddie's back.

"*Shh*. It's all right, honey. Ben, there are two flashlights right here beside the stairs. Can you get past me and find them? Careful, now. Don't fall down the steps."

Ben brushed past her, and she could hear his labored breathing and soft taps as he felt along the ledge next to the stairway. Hershey whined and pressed against her leg.

"Got one!" A moment later, a beam of light shone on the stairway.

"Good job," the man behind her said. He stood very close to Anne, and hearing his voice so suddenly and so near made the hair on the back of her neck stand up.

"Give me the other one," Anne said, and Ben shoved a plastic flashlight into her hands. "Okay, go on down now, slowly. When you get to the bottom, shine it on the steps behind me for Mr. –uh, for this gentleman."

Slowly she descended the twelve steps, hugging Liddie against her and holding the flashlight. She should have given one to the stranger. That thought raised a flock of confusing impressions. What "should" she have done? What "ought" she to do now? She had carefully instilled in the children the rule that they mustn't talk to strangers or let people they didn't know into the private part of their house. But this situation was different. It went beyond the "library rooms versus Gibson family rooms" distinctions, and it scrambled all the rules the way the wind tossed the tree limbs about.

She reached the concrete floor, and something nudged her leg. She flinched. Hershey rushed past her and joined Ben with a muffled bark, and she almost laughed.

Near the washer and dryer was a reinforced area of the basement. Anne felt it was the most secure place in the house, and she had stocked the shelter corner with a case of bottled water and a canister containing granola bars and dried fruit.

"Over there, Ben," she called. "There's an old blanket on the box. Can you spread it out for us to sit on?"

They all sat down by the wall. The old man settled on the extreme edge of the blanket. Anne sat between him and Ben, cuddling Liddie on her lap. Dampness from the little girl's wet clothes soaked through Anne's jeans and sweater. She shivered and held Liddie closer.

Ben played the beam of his flashlight around the cellar. "Why did the lights go out?"

"Probably a tree fell on a power line somewhere," Anne said.

The roar of the storm was muffled now but still constant. Above them, the old Victorian house creaked and shuddered.

Liddie clutched the front of Anne's shirt. "Mommy, I'm scared! Will the house fall down?"

"No, sweetie. It's going to be okay." She kissed the top of Liddie's head and stroked the little girl's shoulders. "A few more minutes, and the storm will go away." Even as she spoke, Anne couldn't help imagining the worst. She probably should have taken more precautions against nature, but usually the small Pennsylvania town stayed calm. They were far enough west to miss most of the hurricanes that swept the coast, and far enough east that tornado watches or warnings came only once or twice a year.

An enormous peal of thunder was followed by a loud *crack!*

Ben jumped closer to her, and Liddie squeaked. Hershey whined and burrowed his nose under Ben's elbow.

"Well, now," the old man said. "That was a close one."

Anne tried to suppress the chill that seized her as the thunder rolled again. The last thing she wanted was for Liddie to realize she was frightened too. But what if the house *did* fall down? Would the cellar walls and joists support the debris and keep it off them? Best to think about something else.

In the dimness, she turned to the man. "I'm Anne, by the way. I want to thank you again for helping my children. This is Liddie and Ben."

"How do you do," he said, with a gentlemanly tone. "I do apologize for the abruptness of our meeting."

Anne hesitated, expecting him to come forth with more information. After a few seconds, she said, trying to keep her tone light, "Well, this isn't the way I expected to spend my Sunday evening. And who are you, sir? I don't believe I've seen you around Blue Hill before."

He chuckled. "No, you wouldn't have. I'm a wanderer, you see, and I haven't roved in this direction for a long time. You might say I let the wind take me wherever it wills. Today it brought me to Blue Hill. But I'm a bit of a vagabond, a teller of tales, and a weaver of dreams."

His answer did nothing to take away Anne's uneasiness, and once more she regretted inviting him into their home. A man who was not forthcoming with his identity usually had more things to hide. Nobody else knew they were down here in the basement with this interloper. Still, she couldn't very well have left him outside. In all the confusion, she never retrieved her cell phone from the kitchen. She wished she had called Alex before coming down the stairs to let him know she was taking shelter with the children and a visitor, at the very least.

"Do you have a name?" Ben asked, leaning forward to peer around her at the man.

He chuckled. "Most folks just call me Jack."

Ben seemed satisfied with that, but Anne was far from it. For once, she wished she had Ben's forthrightness. It went against her nature to confront people, though. She leaned back against the wall and kept quiet, though plenty of thoughts cycled through her mind. The sooner Jack left her home, the better.

Liddie stirred, and Anne shifted her position.

"Liddie, did you know I put treats down here? They're in that can over there." She pointed to the round canister decorated with daisies and topped by a smooth green lid.

"What kind of treats?" Liddie asked.

"Chocolate dipped granola bars," Anne replied, knowing those were a favorite of Liddie's. "Want to help me get some out for everybody?"

"I'll help," Ben said.

"Thank you. You may get the water bottles."

The distraction lasted a few minutes as the children helped her distribute water and snacks by the dancing illumination of the flashlights.

"I don't usually give treats at suppertime," Anne said to Jack, "but it may be a little while before they get to eat their meal."

"Probably a wise plan," Jack said, uncapping his water bottle.

Anne tried to remember if she had turned off the burner she had used to heat chili before going outside to call Ben and Liddie in. She was almost sure she had, and it wouldn't matter now, anyway, since the power was out.

Ben settled down beside Hershey and took a bite of his granola bar. After he had swallowed it, he said, "What kind of tales do you tell?"

Jack laughed. "All sorts, lad. I tell tales of the far places I've been to, the people I've met on my journeys, and the strange sights I've seen."

In the semidarkness, the pupils of Ben's eyes were huge. "Will you tell us a story?"

Anne checked the time on her watch. They still had another twenty minutes before the tornado watch would be lifted. Maybe a story would help pass the time and tell them more about their uninvited guest.

Jack set down his water bottle and pulled up his knees. He rested his arms on them and gazed over at Ben. "Well, now, have you ever heard of the Great Wall of China?"

"Of course," Ben said. "It's like the longest man-made structure on earth, and you can see it from space."

"Ah, that's true. Have you ever seen it?"

"In real life?" Ben shook his head. "I've seen pictures. It looks really cool, like a castle wall."

"That it does," Jack said. "I was there a few years back."

"Really?" Liddie asked, turning and nestling against Anne's side, so she could watch the storyteller and still be comfortable.

"Indeed." Jack smiled at them. "I walked a good many miles along the top of it, and impressive it was."

"You can walk on it?" Liddie was deeply interested now.

"Oh yes," Jack said. "It's as wide as the street in front of your house. The emperor had it built that way so that his soldiers could march along it to get where he wanted them quickly. But alas, after about a week of hiking along that magnificent thoroughfare, I had used up all my provisions."

"What's that?" Liddie asked.

"He ran out of food," Ben said. Hershey whimpered, and Ben slipped him a morsel of his granola bar.

"You're right." Jack chuckled. "I went on, thinking that soon I'd find a village near the wall, where I could buy some rice. But all day, I saw no place to buy food. Oh, how I would have loved to find your mother's canister of snacks. But, alas, such was not to be. I was far out into the countryside, not on the part of the wall near the city, where lots of tourists go. I'd wanted to see the countryside, and now I surely was seeing it. The vistas were gorgeous. But I was hungry."

"What did you do?" Ben asked.

"I happen to speak a little Chinese," Jack said.

"Cool." Ben slipped another piece of his granola bar into Hershey's mouth, but he kept his eyes on Jack. Anne almost scolded him for feeding the dog human treats but decided not to break the mood.

"I told myself that I could communicate enough with some of the residents that I could ask them how to find a place to eat. So the next time I met someone—two Chinese men, it was—I asked them."

"What did they say?" Ben asked.

"They laughed at my accent. And they kept going."

"That was mean of them," Liddie said.

"I expect they didn't understand a word I'd said," Jack replied. "There are many dialects in China, and I knew only one. Perhaps these men, out in a rural province, didn't understand me at all. At any rate, I kept on walking until sunset. Then I spied an old man below the wall, down on the ground gathering sticks. I called out to him, and he answered me."

"Was he mean too?" Liddie asked.

"On the contrary, he was very kind. He spoke slowly so that I could understand, and he invited me to come down at the next set of steps and join him for dinner."

"He fed you?" Ben asked.

Jack nodded. "Not only that, he showed me how to make a delicious soup that is found only in the Orient."

"What's the Orient?" Liddie asked.

"Far eastern Asia. We used to call it the Orient in the old days. I don't suppose young folks say it much now."

"What kind of soup was it?" Ben asked.

"Was it chicken noodle?" Liddie asked. "I like chicken noodle."

Jack grinned. "No, it was bird's nest soup. If you ordered it in a restaurant, you'd have to pay hundreds of dollars for a bowl. That's if they had it on their menu at all. It's a very rare delicacy."

Liddie sat up and frowned at him. "You mean you ate a bird's nest?"

"Yes, sort of," Jack said. "The man showed me how it's made. You soak the nest in water and cook it gently until the stuff it's made of—sort of a dried, glue-like substance—softens and melts into the water. Then you drink the broth or mix it with rice and other foods. It's very high in calcium and other nutrients."

"What kind of glue was it?" Ben asked.

"Yeah, where did the bird get the glue?" Liddie demanded.

"Why, he made it. For it's the male that makes the nest, you see."

"I never heard of birds making glue," Ben said doubtfully.

Anne smothered a smile.

"Well, it's made from his saliva."

"Ick," Ben said.

"What's that?" Liddie scowled at Jack.

"It's bird spit," Ben said.

"Gross." Liddie buried her head in Anne's shoulder.

"It's very good for you," Jack said.

"I'll bet it's not good for the bird, when you steal his nest," Liddie said.

"You have a point," Jack replied gravely. Anne tried hard to keep a straight face. Like the children, she didn't think she wanted to taste the delicacy Jack described.

"So, how does that work exactly?" Ben leaned forward, eyeing the old man with fascination.

Anne decided they'd had about as much detail as she and Liddie could take, and she shifted to set Liddie down on the blanket.

"It sounds as though the wind has let up." She checked her watch again. They were past the deadline she had heard broadcast earlier for the tornado warning. "Why don't I go upstairs and see if it's safe for us to come out of hiding?"

"Okay," Ben said.

She hesitated. She hated to leave them down here alone with Jack, even for a minute. But that was silly. He'd saved their lives, or something close to it. Still, she wasn't ready to trust him. Where did he come from, this "weaver of dreams"? And why did he show up in her backyard today?

As she stood, she said, "Oh, Jack, you never did tell us what brings you to Blue Hill."

"Didn't I?" He turned his ready smile on Anne. "That's an easy question to answer. I came in search of an old friend. Perhaps you know her — Edie Summers."

A NOTE FROM THE EDITORS

We hope you enjoy Secrets of the Blue Hill Library, created by the Books and Inspirational Media Division of Guideposts, a nonprofit organization that touches millions of lives every day through products and services that inspire, encourage, help you grow in your faith, and celebrate God's love in every aspect of your daily life.

Thank you for making a difference with your purchase of this book, which helps fund our many outreach programs to military personnel, prisons, hospitals, nursing homes, and educational institutions. To learn more, visit GuidepostsFoundation.org.

We also maintain many useful and uplifting online resources. Visit Guideposts.org to read true stories of hope and inspiration, access OurPrayer network, sign up for free newsletters, download free e-books, join our Facebook community, and follow our stimulating blogs.

To learn about other Guideposts publications, including the best-selling devotional *Daily Guideposts*, go to ShopGuideposts.org, call (800) 932-2145, or write to Guideposts, PO Box 5815, Harlan, Iowa 51593.